THE QUILT

and Other Stories by Tayama Katai

Tayama, Katai

THE QUILT

and Other Stories by Tayama Katai

Translated and with an Introduction by
Kenneth G. Henshall

UNIVERSITY OF TOKYO PRESS

UNESCO COLLECTION OF REPRESENTATIVE WORKS:
JAPANESE SERIES

This book has been accepted in the Japanese Series of the Translations Collection of the United Nations Educational, Scientific and Cultural Organization (UNESCO).

Publication aided by a grant from The Japan Foundation.
Translated from the Japanese originals: FUTON, JŪEMON NO SAIGO, IPPEISOTSU, SHŌJOBYŌ, SENRO, SHASHIN, KURUMA NO OTO, and SAMUI ASA
English Translation © 1981 UNIVERSITY OF TOKYO PRESS
UTP Number 3093-87393-5149
ISBN 0-86008-279-2

Contents

Introduction

IN terms of the development of Japan's modern literature, Tayama Katai (1872–1930) was one of that country's most significant writers. In the course of a prolific literary career spanning some forty years, he was initially to make a substantial contribution to the romantic movement, then subsequently to create a new literary genre and to become widely accepted as the chief representative of the naturalist movement. Yet despite the significance of his literary role he has barely been introduced to Western readers, for of his twenty or more full-length novels and many hundreds of novelettes, short stories, and critical articles, to date only one short story appears to have been published in English translation. In fact the very movement with which he is by his own words commonly associated—naturalism —has itself been only barely introduced to Westerners, for only a very few naturalist works by any Japanese author have been translated into English (notably *The Broken Commandment* and *The Family* by Shimazaki Tōson [1872–1943]).

Of course, the classification of literature into "isms" is something of a two-edged sword: it is, usually, convenient for generalizations and overviews, but is often misleading and restrictive if adhered to too closely. Similarly Katai's writing, taken as a body, transcends the relatively narrow confines of any particular ism, and is a developing continuum reflecting an individual's unique but changeable attitude towards life. The common theme is his life-long concern with nature, and the changes in his work are largely reflections of the changes in his conceptual model of nature and their effect on his attitude towards life.

As I will try to illustrate in the course of this introduction, Katai's naturalism is just one phase of this continuum. At the same time it is, in the eyes of the literary world at least, his main phase, and is therefore worthy of particular focus. It is the focal link between the various works assembled in this collection, each of which illustrates a slightly different characteristic of Katai's naturalist phase.

At the mention of the term "naturalism" most Western readers probably call to mind the pseudo-scientific, deterministic theories of the French novelist Emile Zola (1840–1902)—undoubtedly the most widely known of all naturalist writers—and may imagine that Katai's naturalist literature is similarly concerned with the analysis of often rather unpleasant hereditary and environmental influences on the human being. This is not generally the case, although the reader will certainly find occasional examples of it. Katai was to an extent impressed with Zola, but more with his bluntness in attempting to show life "in the raw" than with the esoteric aspects of his doctrine; moreover, as for "bluntness," he was actually far more impressed with Zola's less scientifically pretentious colleague Guy de Maupassant (1850–1893).

While de Maupassant will be seen to have been the immediate literary catalyst in Katai's change from romanticism to naturalism in 1901, there were soon to be other literary influences that were to prove equally significant, influences of a lesser known variety of Western naturalism practiced mainly in Germany and represented by certain works of Gerhart Hauptmann (1862–1946), Hermann Sudermann (1857–1928), and others. This naturalism was more concerned than was that of Zola or de Maupassant with quintessential nature, especially in relation to man's inner being, and tended to view man as essentially natural, but society and its conventions—including the morality and set behavioral patterns necessary for communal living—as restrictive of the freedom of the instinctive individual, as artificial and, in that sense, unnatural. That is, whereas Zola's conceptual model of nature was, under the influence of such early sociologists as Auguste Comte (1798–1857), widely embracing and inclusive (albeit at times grudgingly) of society, the German model in question tended to be deeper but narrower, and exclusive of society. As a result, some of its more forcefully expressed works, particularly of Sudermann, can be seen as a *de facto* literature of protest championing the natural individual over unnatural society. This anti-societal, pro-individual model was strengthened by the similar philosophies of Friedrich Nietzsche (1844–1900) and Leo Tolstoy (1828–1910), and the whole was received most enthusiastically in a Japan that was, in the early years of the twentieth century, just awakening to the concept of the individual after centuries of convention-bound Confucianism.

This was the ground in which Japanese naturalism was nurtured, and Katai was to play his leading part in producing a similar literature of protest, championing the individual in the name of nature and attacking the restrictiveness of socio-moral convention. But, while this stance can rightly be seen as a major characteristic of Japanese naturalism, and while Katai can rightly be seen as, in real terms, the leading writer of Japanese naturalism, it would be wrong to assume the apparently obvious and conclude that Katai's naturalism amounted to such a simple principle as "revere the natural individual, condemn unnatural society and convention." Some naturalist writers did indeed go no further than that, but Katai's concept of nature was too large-scale for him to hold very long to a belief that society was categorically unnatural. He soon became convinced that society had in fact a bona fide place in the workings of nature, which he came to see as a metaphysical force controlling all aspects of life, and he was eventually to turn to religion in seeking an answer to the paradoxes implicit in this theory. His religious writings are generally placed after his naturalist period, but what is significant is that, even while writing his naturalist works of protest, Katai had doubts that weakened the force of his protests. He could protest on a human level against the restrictiveness of life in society, but he could not, except perhaps in the very early stages of his naturalism, bring himself wholeheartedly to reject society as unnatural, despite the fact that he felt the individual was somehow closer to the core essence of nature. This confusion and doubt may well be one of the reasons that Japanese naturalism is commonly seen by critics as a half-hearted literature of protest. As a movement this is probably true, but it does not detract from the value and authority of Katai's work as a whole, for this was greater than naturalism itself.

Thus to appreciate properly Katai's attraction to naturalist literature (and his subsequent writing), it is necessary to appreciate it in relation to the continuum of his work and the continuum of his concept of nature. And, just as Katai's writing is inseparably connected with his view of nature, so too is his view of nature inseparably connected with his personal life—the three elements are in fact one largely cohesive whole. Therefore I believe the best way to treat Katai's complex literature in this brief introduction is to give a chronological account of the development of his life-nature-literature continuum, with a special focus on the naturalist middle period for which he is most generally known.

Katai was born Tayama Rokuya on January 22, 1872 (texts that ignore the calendrical change in 1872 give December 13, 1871), in Tatebayashi in what is now Gumma Prefecture. His father, like his own father before him, had been a samurai retainer to the Akimoto Clan but had lost that rather aristocratic position as a result of the abolition of feudal status in 1871. The Meiji era (1868-1912), which followed the Imperial Restoration of 1868, was a time when sweeping Westernization heralded the end of much of Japan's traditional life style and gave to many people a mixed sense of dynamic enthusiasm and modernity on the one hand, yet insecure confusion and loss of cultural identity on the other (as is in fact clearly reflected in much of the literature of the day, including Katai's). Like many former samurai in those days of particular turbulence in the early years of the era, Katai's father had tried, unsuccessfully, to make a new career as a farmer and then as a policeman, before volunteering for action in the Seinan Civil War in February 1877. He was killed in action two months later, when Katai was five years old.

Katai's later memoirs reveal that this early loss of his father contributed greatly to a sense of insecurity and a sense of being a victim of fate, feelings that were developing within him and were in fact to stay with him throughout his life.[1] The insecurity had a practical as well as emotional basis, for his mother now had to support Katai himself, one of his two elder sisters, one elder and younger brother, and her own aged parents-in-law, relying almost entirely on an insubstantial war widow's pension. Life was now a bitter struggle for the once proud and semi-noble Tayamas. Necessity obliged Katai to be apprenticed at an early age to a bookstore in Tokyo, but he hated the work and was eventually allowed to return to Tatebayashi—or, more exactly, he appears to have deliberately got himself sent back in disgrace after a series of petty thefts—where he resumed his schooling, proving to be an enthusiastic and excellent student of literature. As his memoirs and many autobiographical works also tell us, life was hard, but he could find considerable comfort in books and in the renowned natural beauty of the Tatebayashi area. He could claim to have read all of Japan's literary classics by his mid to late teens, and he had poetry published regularly from the age of thirteen, though unfortunately only on an amateur basis. His poetry was essentially lyric and pastoral, a reflection of his self-confessed emotional personality and love of nature.

In July 1886 the Tayama family moved to Tokyo to be supported by Katai's elder brother Miyato, for whom work had been found, through family connections, in the Department of Historical Documents. For many years subsequent to this, Katai tended to drift through life, attending private poetry and English lessons and publishing innumerable lyric poems and an increasing number of similarly lyric short stories in various amateur magazines. At one stage he attempted to join the army but failed the medical because of poor eyesight; he was also forced to abandon his alternative career plan of becoming a lawyer, as a result of insufficient funds for law school. He became increasingly troubled by feelings of guilt about his negative involvement in life and his consequent tendency to live off his brother—"the sacrifice of the family," as Katai refers to him later, while he refers to himself in those years as "a useless daydreamer."[2] His mother, too, was concerned by his lack of contribution to their daily struggle for survival, and constantly criticized him as a good-for-nothing.

Eventually, after a particularly bad period in which he and his brother contracted typhoid, he decided to take positive steps to earn money from his one definite skill, writing, and in May 1891 he approached Ozaki Kōyō (1867–1903), the leading literary figure of the day, and requested patronage. (This seeking of literary patronage was by no means uncommon in the Meiji literary world. Many an aspiring writer would seek to become a protégé of some well-known literary figure, who would then offer advice and use his good name and contacts to launch their literary careers. Katai himself had, at various stages of his life, at least four protégés, including the heroine of *Futon*.) By sheer good fortune (fate was not always against Katai, though he tended to overlook such moments) the somewhat aloof Kōyō was at that precise moment making plans for a magazine *Senshibankō* (A Thousand Purples, Ten Thousand Crimsons), specifically to launch new young writers, and he accepted Katai. He himself paid little further attention to the newcomer, but the magazine's editor, Emi Suiin (1869–1934), had had a very similar set of experiences to Katai, was greatly sympathetic, and proved to be an enormous aid and mentor, arranging publication of his stories in other well-known professional magazines and newspapers and establishing Katai as a professional writer.

Katai was, in Suiin's own words, "a despairing young man sensitive to the beauty of nature,"[3] and in fact this comment neatly captures the essence of Katai's early life and literature. Katai himself was very much prone to despair and self-pity, partly because of his family's decline from relative nobility to wretchedness, partly because of his own inability to involve himself, through his own efforts and his own efforts alone, in life as positively as he would really have liked, and partly because of his inability to overcome his timidity sufficiently to strike up a successful relationship with women (his attitude towards sex is a complex matter discussed in greater detail below).

As a result of these factors, plus circumstantial blows, such as his illness, his poor eyesight, and the deaths of his father, his eldest sister (1883), and his sister-in-law (1891), he came to feel a virtually awe-struck respect for the disaster potential of what he saw as essentially cruel fate. At the same time his sensitive side appreciated life's beauty, which he attributed to nature. Thus he saw fate and nature as basically separate, cruel and comforting respectively, and this attitude is reflected clearly in his writing of the time. The typical early Katai prose work was a short story in which a young male protagonist suffers some terrible blow from fate, invariably involving the break-up of a budding love affair, and is left to seek solace and companionship from the beauty of nature and to ask himself, "Why is fate so unfair, so cruel, so unfeeling?" (from "Wakare" [Parting], 1897).[4] Fate would strike in a variety of ways—death, duty involving separation, irreconcilable social differences—but in most cases the protagonist is frustrated further by his own inability to act sufficiently positively and decisively even to attempt to overcome these circumstances. And even if he does manage the attempt, invariably he is unable to sustain his positiveness to a degree sufficient to achieve victory, and in fact ends up all the worse for daring to oppose fate.

While autobiography proper is held to be a characteristic of Katai's middle and later periods, it is significant that even in his very early works there was a close link between protagonist and author. Similarly the other characters in these works are closely modeled on real persons from Katai's immediate circle of friends and acquaintances, and the settings and major circumstantial developments are likewise identifiable from the author's personal life. It is as though Katai had, for his stories, a limited number of basic ingredients essentially consisting of more or less factual elements from his own life, and that while he would change the order and combinations of these ingredients, even producing the most fanciful of combinations, he would rarely introduce anything new or constructively revise the basic composition of the ingredients themselves. This technique has been criticized by a number of Japanese literary critics as lacking artistic merit, and as "fiction of altered fact" rather than "unified, creative fiction." This may or may not be an accurate assessment of Katai's artistic potential. Personally, I am not pretentious enough to attempt a demarcation between what is artistic and what is not, but my aim in raising the matter is to illustrate that the autobiographical aspect of Katai's literature is demonstrable in his earliest prose, and that this prose, too, is part of the continuum.

During the 1890s, then, Katai was on the one hand gradually establishing himself as a professional writer of lyrical stories full of pathos and natural beauty, and drawing heavily upon autobiographical material. Many of his works in this vein were published in the *Bungakukai* (Literary World) magazine, the organ of the romantic movement, and in this respect Katai's contribution to the movement was by no means insubstantial. But on the other hand Katai was, throughout the 1890s but particularly towards the end of the decade, acquainting himself with a wide range of Western literature (mostly read in English translation). In those days he was particularly fond of such lyric romantics as Heine and Wordsworth, but by no means confined his enthusiastic reading to this type of literature. He read, for example, a number of works by Zola, and though he was not greatly impressed by the objective, analytical style, he did admire the impact which Zola's works made on the reader through the bluntness and frankness of his depictive approach. He was not unmindful of the deterministic doctrine propounded in Zola's writings, and in fact as early as 1896 wrote an experimental work in exactly this vein, but he felt that a deterministic approach necessitated an objective and analytical style which he simply did not relish. It was, as stated earlier, the frankness of Zola's works which he admired, and in this respect he also developed an admiration for Tolstoy, translating the English version of *The Cossacks* into Japanese as early as 1893. He also read Chekhov, Daudet, Flaubert, Dostoevsky, and a whole host of other Western writers, and if he did not actually read the authors themselves, then he would often read about them in critical works. He read de Maupassant as early as 1897, but the work which he read, *The Odd Number*, was a collection of thirteen stories that were not really representative of de Maupassant as a whole. They tended to be rather mild and dealt mostly, and in an untypically non-cynical way, with love, and as a result Katai formed rather a misleading impression of the writer (as he was later the first to admit). In May 1901, however, he obtained the complete works of de Maupassant from Maruzen Bookstore, and this was to rectify that mistaken impression, to make Katai fully aware of the merciless scalpel with which de Maupassant exposed so many of man's less praiseworthy features, and to provide an immediate and very considerable influence on Katai's whole approach to life, nature, and literature.

He records in his main memoirs, *Tōkyō no Sanjūnen* (Thirty Years in Tokyo, 1917), how he was at first shocked by the frequent and unrelentingly blunt depiction of such matters as selfishness, crime, rape, masturbation, deceit, hatred, and sexual perversion, but how he very quickly came to realize that this was merely life as it really was, "raw," and unveiled for the reader by a writer who was very much a man of the world. He felt disturbed and embarrassed, not by the contents themselves, but by the lesson he had been taught about his own previously "blinkered" naiveté:

> How deeply my thoughts, my vision, my whole being was
> struck by these dozen wonderful volumes of short stories.
> I had been strongly moved by Zola's *Thérèse Raquin* some

time before, but the effect of these stories went far beyond that. I felt as though I'd been struck a sharp blow on the head with a stick, as though my whole way of thinking had been sent topsy-turvy. . . . Until then I had only looked longingly at the heavens—I didn't know a thing about the earth, I knew nothing at all. I'd been a feeble idealist.[5]

He immediately expressed these thoughts publicly as well, in a series of critical articles he was engaged upon during 1901:

Now I have realized the truth of things, and I find it increasingly regrettable. . . . But these feelings of regret do not relate to the works themselves, rather to the fact that I have encountered new reflections of life of which I myself was ignorant. . . . The works are true to nature, . . . nature as it is, raw.[6]

Clearly Katai had come to see nature in a rather different light. If this was attributable to de Maupassant alone, then it would certainly be open to criticism as something of an over-reaction. However, de Maupassant was really only a catalyst, a final straw as it were, for Katai's view of life was, through recent personal experiences, already starting to change, and with it his view of nature.

In February 1899 he had married, with poor preparation, nineteen-year-old Risako, the sister of a literary colleague, Ōta Gyokumei (1871-1927). He had liked the girl—merely an infatuation, as it was unfortunately to turn out—and for once, she being the sister of a friend, he was actually in a position to form a relationship. On the other hand, since a friend was involved, it had to be an honorable one. Before Katai really knew what was happening, he found himself married to the girl, ironically largely due to the somewhat excessive decisiveness of his dynamic (and much admired by Katai for that reason) friend Yanagita Kunio (1875-1962), a well-known ethnologist whom Katai had met at private poetry classes a decade earlier and who was responsible for arranging the marriage. Almost as soon as he was married he began to regret it, and his feelings for his wife soon cooled, especially as he found her to be old-fashioned, submissive, and unstimulating. In August that year his mother died, and the following month, through a friend's intercession, he began his first full-time employment, as a staff writer for the Hakubunkan publishing house.

Katai soon came to consider the work, mostly editing and proofreading, as beneath his talents and burdensome in the extreme. It also meant that he could only get on with his writing proper in the evenings and his spare time, which added to the stress. In February 1901 his first child, a daughter, was born, and added parental responsibility to the realities of life with which he was now beset. In other words, he could no longer drift rather naively through life with cruel fate on one hand and benign nature on the other. He was now very much in the thick of life, "real" life. This necessarily involved a more mature outlook, and he came to see that it was not simply a black and white question of life being composed of good and bad forces, such as nature and fate. He came to feel that there were many apparent shades of grey; most notably, he now came to suspect certain social obligations, which he had previously tended to regard as, if anything, unpleasant weapons in the armory of fate, as being part of a not quite so benign nature. His feelings just after the birth of his daughter are revealed in the later autobiographical work *Tsuma* (Wife, 1909):

> Sometimes he would even think, " Now I've fallen into the trap of life. A wife is encumbrance enough to me, and yet now there's a child too. Things are hopeless now—now I'll never be able to get out from this trap, this frightening, horrifying trap of life."
>
> Sometimes he would get angry. "A wife and child! What exactly does that mean? . . . For what reason exactly am I living? For what reason am I suffering? To raise children?! There's probably some significance in that. But why is it that I should have to make myself a sacrifice for the sake of the child? The child is the child, the wife is the wife, and I am myself."
>
> He put down Rousseau's *Confessions*, which he had just started to read, and clasped his hands to his head in thought.
>
> "Reproduction? Does one marry simply in order to reproduce? If that's the case, and one does marry to reproduce, then that means that the blossoming of the beautiful flower of love is simply something to bring two physical bodies together, just a means of nature to bring about reproduction."[7]

He also realizes that he must come to terms with life:

" . . . Up till now I've been concerned with too many irrelevant things. I'd always talk about fighting, but I hadn't really tackled anything. I didn't understand anything. I feared contact with real life. Real life—that's the real fight!" he cried within himself.[8]

Although the intensity with which these doubts and feelings are expressed may owe more to the time in which they were written (1909) than to the time about which they were written (1901), it is nonetheless clear that Katai's new responsibilities in life had brought on a new outlook and a new, somewhat suspicious view of nature. He simply encountered de Maupassant at a point when he was particularly receptive to a view of life and nature such as that held by de Maupassant. Similarly, as the above reference to Rousseau (and his pro-individual, antisocietal writings) reveals, Katai was receptive to other influences as well. His encounter with de Maupassant was to inspire him to an even more enthusiastic reading of Western writers. He felt that they had something to say which Japanese writers, including himself up till that point, had lacked. He writes how he and his colleagues had already started to think "There's nothing for it but to turn to Western literature,"[9] and how now "We all buried our heads in the study of foreign literature, to learn how not to be tossed around by the waves of real life."[10] (Exactly what he and his colleagues found there will be discussed shortly.)

His new view of nature and his new realistic approach to life were soon reflected in his writing, and especially in his critical articles. He now felt that nature, which was certainly something which should be treated with respect, even if a little caution and suspicion were included in that respect, had in fact been abused by Japanese writers, who instead of showing nature as it really was, distorted it by their own petty interpretations and embellishments. As early as May 27, 1901 (he had bought de Maupassant's complete works on May 10) he wrote:

In our present-day literary world [in Japan] nature is sacrificed to the petty subjectivity of the author, and mighty, omnipotent nature . . . is reduced, sadly, to a much belittled object. . . . I would like to see this fanciful interference disappear and writers to depict things without reservation and without personal coloration, even if it be the whisperings of the Devil.[11]

He went on to cite de Maupassant (with Flaubert) as one example of a writer who did not distort nature through petty subjectivity.

Within a year or so Katai had developed his views on subjectivity into a somewhat esoteric theory. He came to feel that there were two types of subjectivity, approximately corresponding to the id and the ego, which he termed "natural subjectivity" (*daishizen no shukan*) and "petty subjectivity" (*sasai na shukan* or *shōshukan*) respectively. By the former he intended man's intrinsic uniqueness as an individual human being, and he felt that this could not be left out of a work since to do so resulted in a superficial and forced objectivity (this was, in fact, one of the criticisms he applied to Zola's style). By "petty subjectivity" he intended opinionated interference by the author, deliberate falsification of observed material, petty value judgments, embellishment, etc., and he felt this to be most undesirable since it effectively distorted nature. He also referred to it as "plating" (*mekki*), since he felt the author who gave rein to his petty subjectivity was disguising real nature.

In practice, however, the subtle balance of correct subjectivity proved difficult to achieve, and in fact Katai could not really effectively demonstrate his theory until a subsequent refinement in 1908 (as will be discussed later). *Jūemon no Saigo* (The End of Jūemon), for example, though written early in 1902 while Katai was vigorously condemning petty subjectivity, is certainly not without personal intrusion by Katai. Nevertheless, the fact that Katai's new, cautiously respectful approach to nature could lead him to develop almost immediately the core of a depictive theory intended to be faithful to nature, is indication of the extent to which his life and literature were connected.

Having turned to Western literature to seek a philosophy suited to real life, Katai found the North European writers to be particularly attractive. Within a very short space of time he learned of the German writers' concern with man's quintessential nature, and read the often defiant, "pro-individual, anti-social convention" works of Ibsen, Hauptmann, Sudermann, in some cases Turgenev, and again Tolstoy. Certain of their works were, as will be seen, to influence him very directly. He also read of the concept of the "superfluous man" as developed by Turgenev and Goncharov, and felt a great personal sympathy with this tragic figure, apparently imbued by fate with an innate lack of positiveness and with an inability to tackle the problems of life with which that same fate confronted him. The superfluous man was the loser in the battle with real life, the man whom no one wanted to be but the man in whom, in fact, everyone recognized aspects of himself. Katai was often to write of himself as a superfluous man, but of course he much preferred to be the victor in the battle with real life, and in this respect he was enormously impressed by Nietzsche.

Nietzsche's fiery philosophy had been introduced into Japan in 1897 by Katai's friend and associate, the critic Hasegawa Tenkei (1876–1940), and had been propounded particularly enthusiastically by another friend, the critic Takayama Chogyū (1871–1902), especially during the years 1901 and 1902. As stated earlier, Japan was at the time just starting to come to an awareness of the concept of the individual, and Nietzsche's "superman" was an ideal that became so popular so rapidly, at least among the young people of the age, that the term "Nietzsche fever" arose. Katai wrote of the "enormously influential concept of the individual which arrived like a great crashing wave on this Oriental literary world,"[12] as a result of such writers as Tolstoy and Nietzsche (and a reinterpreted Rousseau), and wrote of Nietzsche in particular:

> The upheaval in the standards of good and bad, the transcendence of morals, the world of the strongman, the superman—the man who advocated this, Friedrich Nietzsche, was truly great. His is an ideology that belongs not to good or evil but makes itself a part of the strength of nature.[13]

The association made between Nietzsche and nature is particularly significant, for Katai and others soon to be associated with the naturalist movement in Japan, especially the influential critic Shimamura Hōgetsu (1871–1918), interpreted Nietzsche in very much the same light as Ibsen, Tolstoy, de Maupassant, and other such blunt, "raw" writers: that is, because of his bluntness of approach and his defiance of petty moral and social standards where these obstructed his attempt to seek and reveal raw nature, Nietzsche was seen as a *de facto* naturalist. In the West Nietzsche is not generally associated with the movement, despite a detectable influence on certain German writers who are accepted as naturalists, and in fact his forceful call for a return to basic nature

—*Naturschwärmerei*—generally results in his being classified, along with Rousseau and Wordsworth in this same respect, as a romantic. While illustrating the danger in following ism classifications too rigidly, it is clearly a problem that is bound up with semantics and one's interpretation of the various terms involved. This was exactly the point which Hōgetsu was to make in a series of articles on naturalism a few years later, in 1908.[14] Hōgetsu had recently returned from a visit to Europe, during which he had acquainted himself with various forms of naturalism, and he spoke for Katai when he wrote that the common chief aim of naturalism was to seek and demonstrate the truths of nature; that *Naturschwärmerei* was necessary for this; and that if such a spirit happened to be generally classified as romantic, then naturalism must necessarily overlap with romanticism, notwithstanding the fact that most critics might traditionally have treated the two movements as literary opposites.

At more or less the same time as he encountered de Maupassant's complete works, Katai also encountered the English translation of a work which clearly embodied the spirit of Nietzsche, and which impressed him greatly. This was Sudermann's *Der Katzensteg* (The Cats' Bridge, also translated as *Regina*, 1890), depicting a young woman, Regina, a coarse and wild-living child of nature despised and ostracized by her village, who becomes the mistress of an equally wild and despised baron living a Byronesque existence in a ruined castle. Though Regina is eventually killed by the villagers, it is unmistakably clear that Sudermann holds her primitively natural ways in far greater esteem than he does the petty, convention-bound ways of the villagers (who represent society). He refers to her as "one of those perfect, fully developed individuals such as Nature created before a herding social system, with its paralysing ordinances, bungled Her handiwork,"[15] and he makes it clear that he includes among these "paralysing ordinances" such things as moral codes, stereotyped behavioral patterns, and petty |standards of good and bad.

Katai was so impressed with the forcefulness of the work that he considered translating it into Japanese, but instead, in May 1902, he produced his own equivalent, *Jūemon no Saigo*. The work is based on an incident which he had in part witnessed in Nagano some nine years before, and depicts the life and eventual murder by villagers of a coarse and wild-living man unable to fit into the society represented by his village. He also has an equally coarse, wild-natured mistress, who similarly finds the ways of society unacceptable. Apart from several changes of detail and a certain exaggeration, such as of Jūemon's deformity and of the arson committed by Jūemon's mistress, the events are recorded reasonably accurately, a testimony to Katai's belief that truth was more interesting than anything man could dream up. The interpretation of the facts in a Nietzschean light by the author-narrator, which comprises a virtual postscript to the work, is, however, inaccurate in that it did not take place at the time depicted (summer 1893), but at the time of writing (early 1902). Katai may well have been moved to contemplation of nature at the time of witnessing the incident, but the Nietzschean slant is categorically attributable to his ideas at the time he wrote the story. Katai himself acknowledged this in a critical article several years later, when he wrote that "the only fiction in *Jūemon no Saigo* is the part at the end where I put forth the argument about the child of nature."[16]

The final section of *Jūemon no Saigo*, that is to say chiefly the interpretative postscript, reveals a concept of nature as something raw and elemental, a powerful entity that is both beautiful yet horrific. It is shown as an entity that has been, as it were, "plated" by man's society, but which manifests itself with great impact in figures such as Jūemon, who, having abandoned the ways of society for one reason or another, "display the unbridled workings of nature." It is man the "innate individual," not man the principled member of society, who is closer to this raw nature. The author appears to come very close to believing that society is not a part of this nature, and he goes so far as to term it "a second nature" and to write of the misfortune of "children of nature born into the world of man," but at the same time such expressions are qualified by doubt, and it is doubt and confusion about the relationship between man and nature and society which come across as the real attitude of the author. Deep down, Katai could not bring himself to dismiss absolutely the possibility that the workings of society were in fact part of the grander-scale workings of nature, although he could see that society was often repressive of the individual. *Jūemon no Saigo* is arguably the closest he ever comes to a full rejection of society. Certainly its Nietzschean mood held considerable appeal for the readers of the day, and it was his most successful work to date.

Another significant aspect of *Jūemon no Saigo* is the open parallel drawn at the very beginning with Western literature (though it is difficult to explain why Katai should refer to Turgenev's *Sportsman's Diary* and not to Sudermann's *Der Katzensteg*, when it is clear from his memoirs that the latter work was the more significant influence). After having decided to turn to Western literature, Katai was from this point on to seem obsessed with making reference to it and drawing parallels with it. Often the references are so esoteric that they would not have been understood by many of his readers without a wealth of footnotes, such as for example the references the reader will find in *Futon* (The Quilt) to various free-thinking heroines such as Nora from Ibsen's *Doll's House*, Magda from Sudermann's *Heimat* (Home), and Elena from Turgenev's *On The Eve*. The casual way in which these references are often made will probably seem pretentious and irritating to the reader, but it is something which it is impossible to escape in much of Katai's subsequent literature. While on the one hand it may be partly just a reflection of the inferiority complex which many Japanese writers felt towards Western literature, the fact that Katai does not always acknowledge his parallels, and that they so frequently involve himself (in *Futon*, for example, he openly parallels himself both with the protagonist of a work by Hauptmann and with the figure of the superfluous man), suggests that it may have been a more personalized and poignant search for security by borrowing the identity and authority of a figure from Western literature. However, too many critics end up playing the amateur psychoanalyst, and it is a trap that I would not like to fall into here. I will simply say that it is a major characteristic of Katai's post-1901 literature, especially of his longer works, and that I have generally tried to avoid disrupting the flow of the text by numerous explanatory notes (such as, for example, pointing out various unacknowledged parallels between the characters in "Shashin" [Photograph] and a certain work by Chekhov).

Apart from *Jūemon no Saigo*, Katai was unable to produce a satisfying work for some six years after his change of direction in 1901, and this is no doubt a reflection of the confusion in his mind as he tried to reorientate his attitudes towards life and nature and literature. He mostly, during this period, produced translations and adaptations of various works by de Maupassant and became increasingly frustrated at his failure to produce a substantial work of his own. The frustrations and stresses of his personal life continued to mount, particularly with the regular increase in his number of children, and his view of life, and of nature that he felt to be somehow involved in his unhappiness, became increasingly gloomy. He began to long for freedom from his marital and parental obligations, especially to pursue relationships with what he saw as more interesting women than his wife, and he even began, from about the end of 1902 on, to wish her dead. On the other hand, this thought immediately filled him with remorse, and the resultant guilt added further to his unhappiness. To add even further to his frustrations in this respect, from the summer of 1903 on he started receiving letters from a young girl, Okada Michiyo, who was a great admirer of his works and wished to become his pupil. She seemed to be just the sort of girl he himself admired—modern in her outlook, assertive, vivacious, interested in literature—and he eventually felt obliged to accept her as his private pupil. She came to his house in Tokyo in late February 1904, and the events that followed are described with almost complete veracity in *Futon*, which is basically an honest account of his unrequited desire to possess her and the concomitant guilt which this desire entailed.

A further factor involved in the situation was that he had, at this stage, recently read a work by Hauptmann that was, like Sudermann's *Katzensteg*, to prove enormously influential on his life and literature. Hauptmann was a complex writer who went through several distinct, often esoteric, phases of naturalism, but the work in question, *Einsame Menschen* (Lonely People, 1891), was unmistakably the sort of thing that Katai was interested in at the time, demonstrating as it did how socio-moral convention —regardless of whether or not convention was ultimately part of the design of some metaphysical nature—in real terms restricted the ability of the individual to follow what appeared to be the primally natural dictates of his instincts. The work shows a young intellectual, Johannes Vockerat, who is misunderstood by, and frustrated by, his old-fashioned wife Kitty, and subsequently attracted to a vivacious, modern-thinking girl student,

Anna Mahr, who comes to stay at his house. He is instinctively drawn to this kindred spirit, but his morally upright parents disapprove of his attraction to her, and thus prevented by marital, filial, and in a wider sense reputational obligations from acting as he personally wishes and from developing his relationship with Anna, Johannes kills himself, unable to live in a world so restrictive of the personal freedom of the individual.

On a personal level Katai felt that there was much in common between his own marriage and that of Johannes, and it may even have been a not-untypical desire to extend this parallel that partly led him to accept Okada Michiyo as his house-pupil; certainly, as will be seen, he was later to refer to her as his "own Anna Mahr." On a philosophical level, Katai saw the work as having great relevance to Japan, where the family system was felt by many contemporary intellectuals to be the greatest of all socio-moral restrictions upon the individual. It was certainly one of the main works to figure in discussions between himself and naturalist colleagues, such as Shimazaki Tōson (who was similarly impressed), and was one of the major external influences on the basic ideology of Japanese naturalism.

Michiyo returned home early in 1906, and Katai very much wanted to write about his feelings for her just as Hauptmann had depicted Johannes's feelings. On the other hand, he was afraid that to do so would cause such embarrassment to her and her family that it would, in his own words, "mean the complete end of any future love affair with her."[17] As a further obstacle he still lacked the assertiveness necessary for such a bold undertaking. However, the frustrations building up within Katai were so strong that this situation could not continue for long: some catharsis was inevitable. "Shōjobyō" (The Girl Watcher) of May 1907 was the beginning of that catharsis, and is a poignant but often overlooked indication of what was soon to follow in *Futon*. "Shōjobyō" depicts a highly sexed but basically conscientious and morally decent writer unhappy with his banal editing work, his wife, his lack of literary success, and his present life in general with its various burdens and obligations, and pathetically frustrated by the conflict between his strong sexual drives and his deeply inculcated morality, a frustration aggravated by his basic inability to tackle his critical situation positively. The protagonist is a tragi-comic figure who longs to strike up a relationship with one of the "exciting" women he sees around him when, for example, he commutes to work, but he is trapped by his inability to overcome the restraining hand of his own moral conscience, and contents himself with ogling and fantasizing. This eventually leads to his death when, absorbed in his girl-watching, he gets pushed out of a crowded train.

While it was patently obvious, from the minutiae as well as the overall character, that the protagonist was a representation of Katai himself, the work was not at the time appreciated as the poignant cry from the heart that it actually was, and the mock-heroic caricaturing of the protagonist led to its reception as a simple and not very significant humorous work. (A number of recent works by the extremely popular novelist Natsume Sōseki had established mock-heroicism and humor, previously quite rare in Japanese literature, as bona fide literary elements, and this may have affected the reception of "Shōjobyō.") But with the benefit of hindsight and Katai's memoirs it is clear that the ridiculing of the protagonist is linked to his pathetic end, and that the story was an attempt by the author to "kill off" his old self and to clear the way for a fresh start in life, when he could openly be his real and unashamedly frank self.

One personal matter which Katai particularly wanted to set publicly straight was that his reputation as something of a sentimentalist was not fully justified, and that his apparent (from his romantic works to date) sweet and wishy-washy attitude towards women was not a true reflection of his real, primal self. In this respect he was to write, in an article in 1909, that his apparent sentimentalism was actually largely due to the excessive suppression of his physical desires as a result of being raised in a puritanical family,[18] and later he was to write of this period that "my need for women was greater than that of most men,"[19] that "I fought long and hard against sexual pressures,"[20] and that "it was endless suppression of sexual desire that led to my sentimentalism, and I was not really as effeminate as my early works suggest: in fact, I was rather a wolf wearing a mask of gentle timidity."[21] "Shōjobyō" began the process of revealing the "real" Katai and dispensing with the "artificial" one—Katai's first real step towards becoming the bold, frank, and positive individual he had tried to be since encountering de Maupassant —but the story had not had the desired impact on the public.

It was thus even more important to him that he write *Futon*, in which he was, in his own words, "simply to cast off that mask."[22] (It is, however, important to appreciate that the unmasking in *Futon* is not entirely a simple affair, for whereas the author was the "new," bold Katai of 1907, the protagonist was necessarily the old, indecisive Katai of 1904–5, and this "distance" results in a similar but less obvious type of contempt and ridiculing to that in "Shōjobyō." This is especially true of the end passages.)

The need to reveal himself as a "masculine" man was of course only one aspect of the build-up to *Futon*, and Katai explains the situation further in his memoirs:

> In the literary world, Tōson's *Hakai* [The Broken Commandment] had appeared and had received a great deal of praise, and Doppo's *Doppo-shū* [Doppo Collection] had also been popular for some time and looked like it would be reprinted. "It looks like our time has arrived," Doppo had laughed.
>
> I alone felt left behind. . . . I couldn't stand it. I had to write something. . . . This time I had to put everything I had into the work, I realized.
>
> Just at that time I was deeply moved, mind and body, by Gerhart Hauptmann's *Einsame Menschen*. I felt that Vockerat's loneliness was my own. And again, with regard to my domestic situation and my work, I had to break my previous pattern and open up some new road. Fortunately I had profited from the many works I had read of foreign literature, especially from the new ideological trend in Europe. Tolstoy, Ibsen, Strindberg, Nietzsche—in the ideology of such writers I felt that the *fin-de-siècle* distress appeared clearly. I felt I too would like to suffer this in my turn. I felt I too would like to try revealing things that I had hidden, that I had covered up, things that might even break me if I were to reveal them.
>
> I decided to write about my own Anna Mahr, who had tormented me for some years dating from the spring of the 1904 war with Russia.[23]

He wrote *Futon* in the space of ten days during July 1907, and it caused a sensation when it appeared in *Shinshōsetsu* (New Novel) magazine in September. It was greeted variously as "epoch-making" and "the flesh and blood of naturalism,"[24] and was seen as constituting the real emergence of the naturalist movement that had been fermenting for some years. Shimazaki Tōson's *Hakai* (Broken Commandment) of the previous year, which dealt with the suffering of individuals of the pariah class as a result of traditional social prejudice, had been welcomed as a bold work, but Katai was now seen as the first writer to respect truthfulness and frankness to the point where he could ruthlessly portray aspects of his own character which society would traditionally consider as vices; and do so, moreover, in a meaningful way which illustrated how the instinctive and apparently primally natural desires of the individual were repressed by social and moral conventions, such as the obligations of marriage and of a teacher towards his pupil.

Futon brought Katai enduring success and a considerable amount of confidence and relief, both with regard to his literary and personal frustrations. It is from this point on that both he himself and the literary world in general started using the term "naturalism" with some conviction, although it had been in use since the beginning of the century. (The term "neo-naturalism" was, in fact, sometimes used after *Futon*, to differentiate the style from a form of Zola-ism which had briefly appeared some seven years before, largely in the works of the former social satirist Kosugi Tengai [1865–1952], but which had been criticized as shallow by Katai and others and had simply not proved popular.) Katai had, in fact, started a new autobiographical genre, later to be known as the "I novel." Naturalist writers, such as Tōson and Tokuda Shūsei (1871–1943), were to take up the genre, and works started to appear which took readers on a detailed tour of the author's home and introduced members of his own intimate circle of family and friends. Tōson's *Ie* (Family) of 1911 is one well-known example, while Katai himself went on to write "I novels," such as *Sei* (Life) in 1908, focusing on his mother, and *Tsuma*, focusing on his wife and sisters-in-law. He also wrote works on his brothers and sisters, their spouses and offspring, his aunts and uncles, and in fact just about every member of his circle of family and friends.

Somewhat ironically perhaps, in view of Katai's labored theorizing about the optimum depictive technique, the genre had emerged naturally and spontaneously from within him, simply as a catharsis of his personal frustration. But at the same time it was in many ways a very suitable means of achieving many of the things which were, at the time, considered desirable in literature, especially bluntness, frankness, and truthfulness. One can be frank about anything, but the effect is much greater if one is frank about oneself. Similarly, provided the author is sincere, he can be much more truthful and accurate about autobiographical material, for it is usually the material about which he is most factually sure. It was, as it were, testimony to Katai's view that what comes naturally is best.

The way in which *Futon* highlighted the clash between the freedom of the individual and the obligations of life as a member of society was also to be a major characteristic of Japanese naturalism. The theoretical ideal was that man the individual was natural, society was unnatural and should therefore be attacked. However, while we can and do use the word "unnatural," the word cannot have an absolute value in philosophical terms, for if man is a part of nature, and man creates society, then society is, even if relatively less directly, also a part of nature's creation. Although a number of writers and critics attached to Japanese naturalism simply seem to have ignored this point, Katai himself was always aware that his support of the individual against the corporate could only ever be relative. However, while he could not say that socio-moral convention was absolutely unnatural, he could say that it was *relatively* unnatural, and that to all intents and purposes the individual seemed closer to nature. The confusion and paradoxes inherent in this position were quite soon to bring him to grave philosophical misgivings about nature and to lead him to turn to religion for a possible answer, but for the moment he contented himself with showing how the individual was truly a part of nature. In this sense it is possible to interpret his writings as *de facto* anti-societal individualism propounded in the name of "nature." At the same time, it should always be borne in mind that the individual never seems to triumph in Katai's works, and that while he often exposes the factors responsible for man's social unhappiness, he never seems to point to a positive way to achieve victory over those factors.

Katai's concern with the individual, unhappy and cramped in the social fabric, led him, in an article in March 1908 entitled "Shizenshugi no Zento" (The Future of Naturalism), to describe one main characteristic of Japanese naturalism as "a strong sense of self-awareness which tries to establish individuality and to touch upon truths of human life, destroying old morality and conventions,"[25] and to focus, in his immediately subsequent autobiographical novels, upon the co-functions of man as an individual on the one hand and a member of various social groups on the other. Of the members of his family depicted in *Sei*, for example, he was to write that "When in a group they are a family joined by flesh and blood, but when looked at separately, each is an individual with the aims of his or her own individual existence."[26]

At the same time, beneath this immediate level of individualism, Katai was still trying to come to terms with nature. As Chapter 4 of *Futon* reveals in the description of his thoughts on his way to Yoshiko's (Michiyo's) house, Katai had by this stage come to see man as a helpless pawn in the unfathomable workings of an all-powerful nature, a nature which controlled life and death, man's destiny. Clearly, he had now come to see nature and fate as, to all intents and purposes, the same indifferent force. The time of *Futon*'s action is 1905, whereas it was written in 1907, and it is always possible that the intensity of Katai's ideas belongs more to the later date (temporal dislocation is always a potential problem in any chronological appraisal), but to judge from other writings it does seem likely that Katai had arrived, in essence, at this view of nature by the earlier date. One causative factor in his increasingly harsh view of nature is not mentioned in *Futon*: from April to September 1904 Katai had been in Manchuria, covering the Russo-Japanese War as a correspondent for Hakubunkan. He had been sent home earlier than expected following contraction of typhoid (for which, incidentally, he was treated by the great literary figure, Surgeon-General Mori Ōgai), and the suffering he experienced during his illness (it was not the first time he had contracted typhoid), and the suffering he encountered in general, almost inevitably obliged him to take a gloomier view of life and whatever forces controlled it.

His experiences in Manchuria, as well as his now gloomy view of life, were to appear clearly in a number of war stories which he wrote shortly after *Futon*. "Ippeisotsu" (One Soldier) and "Kuruma no Oto" (The Sound of Wheels), both written in 1908, are two examples in this collection, and both deal with the suffering and death of sick and/or wounded soldiers. Both stories are in one sense protests against the degradation of the individual caught up in the conventions of patriotism, honor, military duty, and so forth, but in another sense are poignant illustrations of how man is helpless in the forces that control life and death. The real protest is against something much greater than society; it is a protest against a cruelly indifferent nature.

Futon, then, was Katai's real attempt to be bold and positive, to cast off his "mask of gentle timidity," and, as his true self, to fight "the real fight—real life." And in real life his new decisiveness also achieved success of sorts, for in the summer of 1907 (it is not known precisely when) he formed an extra-marital relationship with a geisha named Iida Yone. (Katai had started to frequent the demimonde following Okada Michiyo's departure in January 1906, and it is my personal belief that he met Iida Yone prior to writing *Futon*, and that it was she who gave him the necessary confidence to "write off" his future chances of a relationship with Okada Michiyo.) She was to remain his mistress, on and off, for the rest of his life, and was actually, through her frequent affairs with other men, to cause him far more distress than his unfortunate wife Risako had ever done. He seemed fatally captivated by her, unhappy as this made him, and as a result he came to hold an even harsher view of the workings of nature, which he considered responsible for his misery.

Despite his increasing suspicions of nature, Katai still felt that it was the writer's job to represent it accurately, and stylistically he did not feel that *Futon* was an optimum, even though it had great merits as a genre piece. He felt, in fact, that it was rather analytical and somewhat prone to petty subjectivity, and within a matter of months he had, perhaps benefiting from his new confidence as a writer, succeeded in refining his earlier stylistic ideas into a workable theory. The theory, known as *heimen byōsha* (single-plane depiction), advocated passivity and impressionism, and did not differ greatly from the *Kleinmahlerei* (miniature painting) style of German naturalists, such as Arno Holz (1863–1929), with whose work Katai was now familiar. Both theories held that the author should permit himself to be willful and assertive only sufficiently to focus upon his chosen material; that he should

next put himself into as receptive and passive a mood as possible
(known as *Stimmung*), and receive data rather like a gramophone
record being pressed, and should then simply reproduce those
impressions without further interference. An author should not,
for example, try to interject his own petty opinions, or to analyze
his material and attempt to sort the important from the unim-
portant, for he could never hope to know nature's real values
and could only distort nature by such selectivity. Just as German
naturalism is famous for its view that, as far as nature is concerned, the birth of a cow is probably as important as the death
of a hero, so too did Katai feel that the author should, as far as
humanly possible, reproduce all his impressions, however trivial
they might seem. This was known as *zattafunpun* (odds and ends).
By this method the author would be able to represent nature
through the medium of his intrinsic individuality (his "natural
subjectivity"), and also be largely able to avoid intruding his
petty subjectivity.

"Ippeisotsu" is a prototype of *heimen byōsha*, in that it is largely
an impersonal account of something the author had no doubt
experienced, but it falls short in that the thoughts of the soldier
seem very likely to be the thoughts of the author himself, at least
in the parts relating to nature's power. *Heimen byōsha* proper held
that the author should not attempt to probe the thoughts of others
(possibly a reflection of de Maupassant's "illusionism," which
held that one person could never properly know the thoughts
of anyone but himself), and in this respect "Kuruma no Oto,"
which appeared in November ten months after "Ippeisotsu," is
a much better illustration of this theory of style. The structure of
the story is relatively fragmented, and the elements it contains
are presented rather like a series of photographs, with no attempt
to explain or to analyze beyond the absolute minimum necessary
for meaningful comprehension (even so, the reader may find
the vagueness in relation to certain aspects of the scene, such
as which hill is which, etc., somewhat confusing). The focus is
on the dying soldier, but he by no means dominates the story,
and is just one of the elements of the overall picture. The final
impression is vague yet vivid and clear at the same time.

Theoretically, the ideal naturalistic work might therefore seem
to Katai to be the "I novel" treated in the *heimen byōsha* style,
and in fact Katai attempted this in *Sei* and *Tsuma*. He was not

terribly successful, however, and soon came to consider that, by its very episodic and largely external focus, the style was not very well suited to the normal full-length work. He did persist in trying, however, and achieved some success in his well-known full-length work *Inaka Kyōshi* (Country Teacher, October 1909), which was not an "I novel," but generally, until his abandonment of the style around 1915, he used it only in short works.

In Katai's works, style is generally subordinate to theme, and while his various stylistic developments were of course an attempt to pay homage to nature, it is his thematic treatment of nature that is usually felt to be more significant. In this respect, his works were becoming ever gloomier as his view of nature became less and less benign. To add to matters, his much beloved brother Miyato died in November 1907, and Katai was led to remark that "life and death were nature's real concern,"[27] and that in this harsh reality it was the strong and ruthless whom nature seemed to favor, not the meek and innocent as popular morality led one to believe. The unhappiness he felt over the burden of his marriage was raised openly again as a result of his encounter with Iida Yone, and as mentioned earlier, the intensity with which he wrote in *Tsuma* of his unhappiness in the early years of his marriage no doubt owes much to his unhappiness at the time of writing, as also does the particularly distrustful view of nature with regard to the institution of marriage itself. He soon became convinced that what he had suspected ever since those days was in fact true: marriage was a device ultimately part of nature. He went so far as to write, in 1909, "Wana" (Trap), a story specifically advancing this view and concluding that marriage was an institution actually resulting from man's natural instincts, which drove man blindly on to carry out nature's ultimate design without regard to the happiness of the individual. A few months later, in *En* (Relations, March-August 1910), he expanded this view to one which saw society in general—the interrelationship of human beings—as part of nature's workings, and saw its prime aim as to bring man and woman together in order to perpetuate the species and perpetuate the cycle of life and death. The unhappiness which the individual felt in society, with its necessary limitations on individual freedom, was therefore only superficially attributable to man and society, and was more accurately attributable to the force that controlled life, whether that was called fate, destiny, nature, or whatever. The protagonist (openly Katai himself) remarks, "We exist from start to finish amid some great entity, under the control of a certain power. . . . Whatever we might call it, it's a fact that something is there, working indirectly on us."[28]

Katai was prompted to write *En* by what he saw as the strangeness of the workings of this power with regard to the destinies of himself and Okada Michiyo, for their two lives seemed to be mysteriously interwoven. She had in fact returned to Tokyo after the events depicted in *Futon*, but had continued associating with Nagashiro Shizuo (Tanaka Hideo in *Futon*), becoming pregnant by him, and had been disinherited by her family. Katai had then taken the significant step of adopting her as his daughter, in January 1909. The child, a girl, was adopted by Katai's brother-in-law Ōta Gyokumei, who since 1899 had renounced literature to take up residency as officiating priest at a country temple. Michiyo continued her love-hate relationship with Nagashiro, eventually marrying him, having another child by him, and leaving Tokyo. These are the events depicted in *En*, which in many respects is an epilogue to *Futon*. (As a matter of interest, the marriage eventually broke down due to Nagashiro's excessive drinking, and Michiyo went off to America and remarried.)

From this point on Katai came to look upon nature as a terrifying force, terrifying because of its omnipotence, its omnipresence, and its apparent indifference when it came to using man as a pawn in its ultimate designs. In *En*, for example, he blames the forces of nature for the unhappy situation depicted in *Futon*, and in works from this period on he focuses in particular on the way in which nature controls man's life, especially where unhappiness and suffering—even, sometimes, death—are wreaked on apparently decent and innocent individuals. "Senro" (The Railway Track, 1912), included here, is a typical example of such works, telling of the gruesome death of a young child who is chopped to pieces by a train while picking flowers by the track. The contrast between the beautiful and the ugly, both aspects of a nature that Katai was seeing as increasingly paradoxical, is made obvious to the point of melodrama: "[The passengers saw] green grass, a scattered bunch of flowers, crimson blood, a small crimson lump with dismembered hands and feet. . . ."

Also very noticeable in the work is the sense of fearful yet at the same time reverential awe which Katai had now come to harbor towards mysterious and all-powerful nature. All the mothers present on the train are gripped with this same primal fear, and all are motivated by primal instincts of motherhood to protect their own young children. One can sense the nervous fear filling the train. And yet, with the passage of time, the fear subsides, and life goes on, for man must necessarily learn to accept and to live with the ever-present threat of attack from this cruelly indifferent master of his life.

In an attempt to resolve the paradoxes he now saw in a hostile nature that had once been his friend, Katai resigned from the Hakubunkan in December 1912 and undertook two periods of intense meditation (May-October 1913 and July-October 1916). The fact that, apart from a certain calmness, he gained little from the former is illustrated by the short story "Samui Asa" (One Cold Morning), which appeared in January 1914. While its message is more subtly and calmly expressed than was the case with "Senro," the message is still the same: man is helplessly carried along in the ebb and flow of nature's workings, and somewhere cruelty and suffering will inevitably be involved. The work is autobiographical, even to the extent of using real names, and shows Katai's two young sons killing a mouse they had caught. Though there is arguably no need for them to kill the mouse, events just seem to roll on beyond the conscious control of the humans involved. They seem compelled by instinct to kill the poor creature—which is deliberately described by Katai in human terms—and, significantly, there seems almost a sadism inherent in these instincts. The children kill the mouse with indifference, but having done so, "the two boys marched triumphantly off. . . ." It is not a conscious delight in suffering, but an instinctive delight in asserting one's natural superiority over a lesser being. If there were really any value system built into nature, then this, Katai felt, was what it amounted to: the ruthless survival of the fittest, the domination of the weak by the strong. It was at the same time a demonstration of the "satisfaction of instinct" with which Nietzsche was so concerned, but it is portrayed in "Samui Asa" in a much different way from the "Nietzsche fever" days. There is also present in the work, as in "Senro," the same primal fear that is generated in the presence of "raw" nature, and this is captured at the end by the feelings of the little girls who had witnessed the scene—bewilderment, and a strange sort of fear that prompts the younger one instinctively to cling to her mother for protection. The work finishes, as it were, with a shudder.

"Samui Asa" is written in the *heimen byōsha* style, and it is testimony to the author's skill that he can so effectively convey his intended impression without breaking the somewhat restricting principles of the technique. It is just a simple but meaningful real-life episode, presented like a picture scroll being unfurled without further explanation. In my personal opinion it is in many respects, such as stylistic accomplishment, effective communication of the author's viewpoint, readability, impact, and provocation of thought, Katai's finest work.

Katai's first period of meditation had caused him to feel with certainty that the individual was greater than society, for individuals could exist and procreate without the need for a permanent social relationship, whereas society was nothing without the individuals who gathered to form it. However, he could still not understand why man should be caused such unhappiness in life, especially when most of that unhappiness seemed to stem from clashes between instincts revolving around the need to procreate and perpetuate the species. That is, he saw the relationship between the male and the female as the key factor in life, yet at the same time as the major source of unhappiness in life. This theme was in fact to be the major concern of his work for the next few years, and is undoubtedly a reflection of the suffering he was still enduring at the hands of the capricious Iida Yone. She was a very different woman from his meek wife, and had once even attacked a rival geisha with a razor and had thrown herself into a river, to be rescued half-dead, when the attack was thwarted. One can imagine how Katai, fatally drawn to this woman, suffered when he was on the receiving end of her obviously intense feelings. One can also imagine the suffering of his wife, who had to bear the humiliation of Katai's conducting a *mariage à trois* and openly describing it in works from about 1912 on. Katai was aware of the distress he was causing his wife and family (his eldest daughter, for example, eventually left home in apparent disgust at his behavior), but he attributed the whole situation to the inescapable workings of nature. In this sense, it is possible to argue that Katai had gone full circle and had returned to the indecisiveness of his earlier days, but this time with a philosophy to support his "drifting through life" attitude.

His second period of meditation saw him becoming increasingly concerned with man's inner being, and during this period he was much influenced by the later writings of Joris-Karl Huysmans (1848–1907), who had renounced Zola's group in favor of religious meditation, and had become convinced that religion and spiritualism held the answer to man's lot in life. Katai similarly adopted a theological approach and benefited greatly in this respect from advice on Buddhism from his brother-in-law. The results are recorded in faithful detail in various writings, some published as memoirs and others as extremely introspective novels, full of obscure and esoteric Buddhist philosophy and seemingly written for the benefit of the author himself rather than his readers. Certainly his works lost popularity from this point on, and it is similarly seen as the renunciation of naturalism on his part. Despite their general obscurity, his writings do however make it clear that he had come to see nature as the ultimate force in life, the ultimate power worshiped by all religions. In Buddhist terms, for example, it equated to the Ultimate Void that was both the sum of all things and the negation of all things, just as eternity was both timeless yet the sum of all time. Opposition to this power was hopeless, and could only bring suffering. Man simply had to accept nature. He could accept that he was basically, intrinsically, a unique individual, but he could not attempt to assert this individuality for he would soon clash with the greater designs of nature. It was as if Katai had renounced the assertive individualism of his earlier years and had brought his philosophy of life into line with his depictive technique, which maintained that the assertion of willful subjectivity went against nature. Perhaps, indeed, much of his recent unhappiness had stemmed from this dislocation between his approach to life and his approach to literature: while in so many respects his life and literature were inseparable, he had tried for a time to be assertive in life, but passive in literature.

His second period of meditation afforded him some measure of relief, in that he now maintained he should derive happiness merely from loving Iida Yone and should not concern himself with whether or not she really loved him in return. On the other hand, he still had basic misgivings about the role of the individual, for while he could see non-assertiveness and resignation as one factor in happiness, at the same time he knew full well—as indeed "Samui Asa" had earlier demonstrated—that it seemed to be an equally basic law of nature that the strong dominate the weak, and there very much seemed to be a link between strength and assertiveness. It is true to say that Katai never really overcame these philosophical doubts: all he could content himself with was the ideal that, if no one were assertive, there would be no suffering, although he still saw obvious paradoxes in this. On a literary level, he henceforth produced "pantheistic" religious works that revered this nature-spirit, especially in terms of how it was manifested in the inexorable power of time, and eventually, in his final years, produced a number of works on historical figures. On a personal level, he did eventually succeed in achieving security in his relationship with Iida Yone, though this was not attributable to his philosophizing so much as to the fact that her house was destroyed in the Great Tokyo Earthquake of 1923 and, while she was seeking refuge in a nearby river, Katai sought for her amid the smoking ruins and eventually rescued her. This display of no little heroicism on his part finally seems to have won her heart, and he could relax fully for the first time since meeting her sixteen years previously. These events are largely recorded in his last major work, *Momoyo* (One Hundred Nights) of 1927.

Katai's health failed badly in 1928 and, following brain haemorrhage and cancer of the throat, he eventually died in hospital on May 13, 1930. In his final days he had refused intravenous food, preferring to give in to nature's workings and resign himself to death. Tōson was among those who visited him in those final days, and he records how, as befits men in search of the truths of nature, they discussed Katai's feelings as a man on the verge of death. Katai remarked that, since he was entering the unknown, his feelings were necessarily "mixed."[29]

Katai's literature is the record of a simple man's concern with nature, a concern that brought him into contact with the nature views of such diverse figures as Wordsworth, de Maupassant, Nietzsche, and various Buddhist philosophers. We have seen how at the peak of his literary career the view of nature which he then held largely coincided with the spirit of the day—an individualism that opposed the conventions of society in the name of nature—and how he became the leading writer of the naturalist movement. We have, however, also seen how his view of nature transcended that held by the movement as a whole.

The works in this collection, then, are illustrations of his view of nature during the period in question. *Jūemon no Saigo* is the closest he came to a total rejection of society as unnatural. "Shōjobyō" and *Futon* are both intensely personal works that, while continuing to show how the individual appears repressed by life in society, contain a deeper message that man is a pawn under nature's control. "Ippeisotsu" and "Kuruma no Oto" are war stories that develop this idea further, and show that much suffering results from the individual's helplessness before the indifferent forces that control him. "Senro" is a gloomy picture of a terrifying and cruel nature, and "Samui Asa" is a somewhat subtler portrayal of the indifference with which nature carries out its workings. "Shashin," of 1909, is included in this collection largely to bring in something of a lighter, balancing note. It is possible to interpret the work as a cynical comment on the vacuousness entailed in much of human life, but Katai himself wrote the work as something of a "light break" from his more serious literature, and it is included here as such.

My thanks are due, for their encouragement of my interest in Katai, to Mr. Kenneth Strong of the School of Oriental and African Studies, London, the late Dr. Geoffrey Sargent of Sydney University, and Professor Bertie Davis, also of Sydney University. For their assistance on points of linguistic detail my thanks are due to Mr. Akima Toshio of Auckland University, and to Messrs. Okamoto Yoshio and Yagi Masamitsu, private individuals of Kobe. I am also indebted to Nina Raj of University of Tokyo Press for her interest, her helpful advice, and her enthusiastic efforts on my behalf.

The mistakes that are inevitably contained in these pages are sometimes Katai's, mostly mine.

1. See, e.g., "Dakkyaku no Kufū" [A Means of Escape], 1918; or Yanagida Izumi, *Tayama Katai no Bungaku* [The Literature of Tayama Katai], Tokyo, Shunjūsha, 1957, Vol. I, p. 184.

2. *Tayama Katai Zenshū* [The Complete Works of Tayama Katai], Tokyo, Bunsendō, 1974, Vol. I, pp. 17 and 9 respectively.

3. Quoted in Fukuda Kiyoto and Ishibashi Tokue, *Tayama Katai: Hito to Sakuhin* [Tayama Katai: The Man and His Works], Tokyo, Kiyomizu, 1968, p. 63.

4. *Bungakukai*, No. 54 (June 1897), p. 2.

5. *Zenshū*, Vol. XV, p. 565.

6. Quoted in Ōnishi Tadao, "Mōpassan to sono Nihon e no Eikyō" [De Maupassant and His Influence on Japan], in *Shizenshugi Bungaku*, ed. Kawauchi Kiyoshi, Tokyo, Keisō, 1962, p. 323.

7. *Zenshū*, Vol. I, pp. 358–59.

8. *Ibid.*, p. 359.

9. *Zenshū*, Vol. XV, p. 531.

10. *Ibid.*, p. 577.

11. *Tayama Katai Shū*, Meiji Bungaku Zenshū 67, Tokyo, Chikuma, 1968, p. 14.

12. *Zenshū*, Bekkan (supplementary volume), p. 263.

13. *Zenshū*, Vol. I, p. 418.

14. See especially "Bungei-jō no Shizenshugi" [Naturalism in Literary Art], in *Waseda Bungaku*, January 1908 issue.

15. Sudermann, *The Cats' Bridge* (trans. anon., New York, Collier, date unclear), p. 376.

16. Quoted Fukuda and Ishibashi, *op. cit.*, p. 118.

17. *Zenshū*, Vol. XV, p. 602.

18. Quoted in Hata Minoru, "Tayama Katai Nōto" [Notes on Tayama Katai], in *Komazawa Kokubun*, No. 10, Komazawa University, June 1973, p. 10.

19. "Watashi no Yatte Kita Koto" [Things I Have Done], in Yoshida Seiichi, Ishimaru Hisashi, and Iwanaga Yutaka (eds.), *Tōson: Katai*, Tokyo, Sanseidō, 1960, p. 293.

20. *Zenshū*, Bekkan, p. 676.

21. "Watashi no Yatte Kita Koto," *loc. cit.*, p. 292.

22. *Ibid.*

23. *Zenshū*, Vol. XV, pp. 600–601.

24. Maeda Akira, "Futon," appendix to *Futon, Ippeisotsu*, Tokyo, Kadokawa, 1969, pp. 229–30.

25. *Shinchō*, March 1908 issue, p. 14.

26. Quoted in Yoshida Seiichi, *Shizenshugi no Kenkyū* [A Study of Naturalism], Tokyo, Tōkyōdō, 1955–58, Vol. II, p. 173.

27. *Zenshū*, Vol. I, p. 659.

28. *Zenshū*, Vol. II, pp. 280–81.

29. See *Nihon Bungaku Arubamu 24: Tayama Katai* [Album of Japanese Literature] No. 24, Tokyo, Chikuma, 1964, p. 59.

The Quilt

1

AS he started down the gentle slope of that road in Koishikawa that leads from Kirishitanzaka to Gokurakusui, he thought things over. "Well, this is the end of the first stage of my relationship with her. It's ridiculous to think I could ever have considered such a thing, what with me being thirty-six and with three children as well. And yet . . . I wonder—can it really be true? All that affection she showed me—was it really just affection, and not love?"

All those emotional letters—their relationship was certainly something out of the ordinary. He had a wife, he had children, he had a reputation to consider, and, moreover, he was her teacher, so they hadn't gone as far as falling madly in love. And yet, the beating of their hearts when they talked together, the sparkle in their eyes when they looked at each other—there was definitely something tremendously powerful deep beneath it all. He felt that, if only there was an opportunity, this hidden force would suddenly gain strength and destroy at a stroke that teacher-pupil relationship, that morality, that reputation, that family of his. At least, that was what he believed. But then the events of the last few days would mean that her feelings had just been put on. The thought that she had deceived him went time and again through his mind. However, while he could, being a literary man, consider his own state of mind objectively, the mind of a young woman was not something that could easily be fathomed. Perhaps her warm, cheerful affection was just part of a woman's nature, and perhaps that beautiful look in her eyes, that tenderness, were all subconscious, all meaningless, just like a flower in nature giving a sort of comfort to those who look upon it. Even assuming for argument's sake that she did love him, he was the teacher and she was his pupil, he had a wife and children and she was a beautiful young flower just coming into bloom, so perhaps it was inevitable that they should both come to realize this. Then again, he had failed to clear the question up when she had sent him that one really intense letter, complaining of her anguish both openly and implicitly, and, as if to oppress him with the force of nature, conveying her feelings to him for a final time. With her female modesty, how could he now expect her to make things any clearer than that? Perhaps, with her mind in such a state, she had acted as she had now through despair.

"Anyway, the chance has now gone. She already belongs to someone else!" he exclaimed aloud as he walked along, and pulled at his hair.

He went slowly on down the slope, his figure, in suit of striped serge and straw hat, bent slightly forward as he thrust out his wisteria-vine walking-stick. It was the middle of September and still insufferably hot, but the sky was already filled with a re-freshing air of autumn, and its deep, rich blue vividly stirred the emotions. Round about were fish shops and saké shops and grocery shops, beyond them rows of backstreet tenements and temple gates, and in the low-lying ground of Hisakatamachi numerous factory chimneys poured out their thick black smoke.

It was in one of those many factories that he went to work every afternoon, in a large Western-style room upstairs with a single large table standing in the middle and a Western-style bookcase, full of all sorts of geographical works, at its side. He was helping, on a part-time basis, with the editing of some geographical works for a certain publishing house. A man of letters editing geographical works! He had taken on the work pretending that he had an interest in geography, but of course, deep down, he wasn't happy with it. What with his rather tardy literary career, his despair at only having produced odds and ends without an opportunity for putting all he had into a work, the painful abuse he received every month from the young men's magazines, his own awareness of what he ought to do some day —it was inevitable he should feel upset. Society was advancing with each new day. Suburban trains had revolutionized Tokyo's transport system. Girl students had become something of a force, and nowadays, even if he'd wanted to, he wouldn't have been able to find the old-fashioned sort of girl he'd known in his courting days. And the young men, like young men in any age, had a completely different attitude towards everything, whether love, literature, or politics, and he felt an unbridgeable gap between them and his own generation.

Every day, then, he would go mechanically along the same route, in through the same big gate, along the same narrow passage with its mixture of vibrating noise from the rotary press and smelly sweat from the factory-hands. He would casually greet the employees in the office, climb laboriously up the long and narrow steps, and finally enter that room. The east and south sides were open to the sun, and in the afternoon, when the sun was at its strongest, it grew unbearably hot in there. To add to it all the office-boy was lazy and didn't do the cleaning, so the table was covered with an unpleasant layer of white dust.

He sat down at his desk, smoked a cigarette, then got up again to take down from the bookcase some bulky statistical works, maps, guides, and geography books. Eventually he quietly took up his pen to continue from where he had left off the previous day. However, for the last few days his mind had been troubled, and he found it hard to write. He would finish one line, then stop to think things over, then write another line only to stop again. The thoughts that filled his mind were all fragmentary, intense, hasty, and often desperate. Then suddenly, by some chain of thought or other, he called to mind Hauptmann's *Lonely People*. Before things had turned out as they had, he had thought about teaching her this drama as part of her curriculum. He had wanted to teach her about the hero's—Johannes Vockerat's—mind, about his grief and the wife who misunderstood him. He had read the work some three years before, before he had even known of her very existence, and since then he too had been a lonely man. He didn't go so far as to try to compare himself to Johannes, but he did feel, with great sympathetic understanding, that if such a woman as Anna, Johannes's student, appeared, then it was only natural if things ended in such a tragedy. "And now I can't even become a Johannes," he thought, letting out a long, deep sigh.

Not surprisingly, he didn't teach her *Lonely People*, but instead Turgenev's short work *Faust*. There in the tiny little study,

bright with the light of the lamp, her heart had been filled with
longing by that colorful love story, and her expressive eyes had
sparkled with a still deeper significance. The lamplight shone
on the upper part of her body, on her chic and fashionable
hairstyle, her comb, her ribbons, and when she had drawn her
face close to the book that indescribable perfumed smell, that
fleshy, female smell. . . . As he explained to her the part in which
the protagonist reads Goethe's *Faust* to his former lover, his own
voice too had trembled with passion.

"But it's no good now!" he exclaimed to himself, and pulled
at his hair again.

2

He was called Takenaka Tokio.

Three years before, when his wife was expecting their third child,
he had already been completely disillusioned of the pleasures of
newly wedded life. The busy affairs of the world had no meaning
for him, he lacked even the enthusiasm to work on his life's
masterpiece, and as for his everyday life—getting up in the morning, going off to work, coming home at four in the afternoon
and seeing, as ever, his wife's face, eating his dinner and going
off to bed—as for this monotonous existence, he was thoroughly
and absolutely bored with it. Moving house all the time wasn't
interesting, talking to friends wasn't interesting, and he failed
to find satisfaction in searching out foreign novels to read. In
fact, he even felt that the various forms of nature—the thickly
growing trees in the garden, the raindrops, the blooming and
withering of the flowers—were making his banal life even more
banal. He was desperately lonely. As he walked along the streets
he would invariably see beautiful young women, and feel an
acute desire for a new love, if only such were possible.

His was the anguish which in reality every man feels in his
mid-thirties. Many men of this age flirt with low-class women
for the sake, in the final analysis, of curing this loneliness. And
many of those who divorce their wives are of this age.

Every morning, on the way to work, he would encounter a
beautiful woman, a teacher. In those days he saw this encounter

as his only pleasure in life, and would dream all sorts of dreams about her. What if they were to fall in love, if he were to take her to an assignation house in Kagurazaka, if they enjoyed themselves away from the eyes of others . . .? What if they went for a walk through the suburbs, without his wife knowing . . .? Indeed, at the time his wife was pregnant and so, if she suddenly died of complications in the birth, and then if afterwards he were to make the other woman his new wife . . .? Would he then so calmly be able to make her his second wife . . .? Such were his thoughts as he walked along.

It was at that time that he had received an absolutely idolizing letter from a girl named Yokoyama Yoshiko, a great admirer of his works from Niimimachi in Bitchū, and a pupil at the Kobe Girls' Academy. Under the name of Takenaka Kojō he wrote novels of elegant style, and was not unknown in the world, so he quite frequently received letters from various devotees and admirers in the provinces. He didn't concern himself overmuch even with letters asking him to correct the sender's texts, or asking permission for the sender to become his pupil. And so, even when he received this girl's letter, his curiosity hadn't especially prompted him to reply. But after receiving three such enthusiastic letters from this same person, even Tokio had to take notice. She said she was nineteen but, judging from the phrases in her letters, her powers of expression were surprisingly skilled. Her one great hope, she said, was to become his pupil and devote her whole life to literature. Her characters flowed smoothly and easily, and she seemed to be quite a sophisticated girl.

He had written a reply from that upstairs room at the factory. That day he had stopped his daily geographical work after just two pages, and the scroll letter which he then sent her was a long one, several feet in length. He explained in detail in the letter the imprudence of a woman getting involved in literature, the need for a woman to fulfill her biological role of motherhood, the risk involved in a girl becoming a writer, and then added a few insulting phrases. He had smiled to himself at the thought that this would surely make her lose heart and give up her ideas. Then, taking a map of Okayama Prefecture from the bookcase, he had looked up Niimimachi in the district of Atetsu. He was surprised that such a sophisticated girl could come from such a place, in the middle of all those hills some thirty miles or more inland up the Takahashi river valley from the San'yō Line. And yet, somehow Tokio felt familiarly attracted to the place, and looked carefully at the hills, rivers, and other features of the area.

He had thought she would be unable to reply, but far from it. Four days later an even thicker letter arrived—three pages of small characters written laterally in violet ink across blue-ruled Western-style paper—in which she repeated over and over again how she hoped he would not abandon her but make her his pupil, and how, if she could get her parents' permission, she hoped to come to Tokyo, enter a suitable school, and faithfully and whole-heartedly study literature. Tokio had to admire her resolve. Even in Tokyo the graduates from the girls' schools didn't under-stand the value of literature, and yet, to judge from the remarks in her letters, this girl did seem to know about everything. He promptly sent off a reply and formed a teacher-pupil relation-ship.

Many letters and texts were to follow. There were still points of immaturity in her writing, but Tokio felt that she wrote smoothly and without affectation, and that there were sufficient prospects for future development. And then, as they gradually got to know each other a little better, Tokio started to look forward to her letters. Once he had thought about asking her to send a photograph, and had written a request in a corner of his letter, but then had blacked it out. Looks were essential for a woman. If a woman were unattractive, then no matter how much talent she might have men wouldn't take to her. Deep down, Tokio felt that since Yoshiko was a woman who wanted to write literature she was sure to be physically plain. Yet he hoped she would be as presentable as possible.

It was in February the following year that, having obtained her parents' permission, Yoshiko had come to Tokio's house, accompanied by her father. It was exactly seven days after the birth of Tokio's third child, a son. His wife was still in confine-ment in the room next to the parlor, and was much disturbed when she heard from her elder sister, who had come to help out, how beautiful this young girl pupil was. Her sister was also worried about Tokio's intentions in making such a young and beautiful girl his pupil.

Tokio talked in detail to Yoshiko and her father about the circumstances and aims of a writer, and sounded out beforehand her father's views on the question of marriage. He learned that Yoshiko's family was wealthy and one of the leading families in Niimimachi, that her father and mother were both strict Christians, and that her mother in particular was a devout believer, having once studied at the Dōshisha Girls' College. The eldest son of the family had been to England, and after returning to Japan had become a professor at a government school. Yoshiko had, after leaving the local primary school, gone straight to Kobe and entered the Kobe Girls' Academy, where she had led the life of a sophisticated girl student. Compared with other girls' schools, the Christian schools were all open-minded when it came to literature. At that particular time there was a stipulation forbidding the reading of works such as *The Wind of the Devil, the Wind of Love*, and *The Golden Demon*,* but before the Ministry of Education had interfered there had been no problem about such books, provided they weren't read in the classroom. In the school church Yoshiko had learned the preciousness of prayer, the pleasure of Christmas night, the cultivation of ideals, and she had become one of a group that ignored mankind's base aspects while celebrating its attractive ones.

At first she had missed her home and mother and had been greatly upset, but eventually she had forgotten all that and had come to appreciate above all else the life of a girl student at boarding school. No pampering with tasty pumpkin there, and no side-dishes for your soy sauce either. So you simply learnt to put your sauce on your rice instead and to ease your feelings by grumbling about the cook, just as you moaned about the crotchety old dormitory mistress behind her back. When you've been involved in student life like that, how can you be expected to view things simplistically, like a girl raised in the home? Beauty, ideals, and vanity—these Yoshiko had now acquired, and thus she had all the good traits, and the bad, of a Meiji-era girl student.

At least her presence broke the loneliness of Tokio's life. Yesteryear's lover—today's wife. That his wife had once been

---

* *Makaze Koikaze* by Kosugi Tengai (1903) and *Konjiki Yasha* by Ozaki Kōyō (1897) respectively. The former deals with student life, the latter with a love affair.

his lover was a certain fact, but times had changed. With the sudden rise of women's education over the past four or five years, the establishing of women's universities, and the fashion for low-pompadour hairstyles and maroon pleated skirts, women no longer felt self-conscious about walking with a man. To Tokio nothing was more regrettable than his having contented himself with his wife, who had nothing more to offer than her old-fashioned round-chignon hairstyle, waddling walk, and chastity and submissiveness. When he compared the young, modern wife —beautiful and radiant as she strolled the streets with her husband, talking readily and eloquently at his side when they visited friends—with his own wife—who not only didn't read the novels he took such pains to write but was completely pig-ignorant about her husband's torment and anguish, and was happy as long as she could raise the children satisfactorily—then he felt like screaming his loneliness out loud. Just like Johannes in *Lonely People*, he could only feel how insignificant his own domestically minded wife was. All this, all this loneliness, was shattered by Yoshiko. For who could remain unmoved when a beautiful, modern, sophisticated girl pupil respectfully calls him Sensei as though he were a man of great standing in the world?

For the first month she had stayed at Tokio's house. What a contrast her gay voice and charming figure made with his previous sad and lonely life! She would busy herself helping his wife, just up from the childbirth, and would knit socks and mufflers, sew clothes, play with the children. Tokio felt as if he'd returned to his life as a newly-wed. He would feel a sense of excitement when he approached the door of his house. When he opened that door, there in the porch was her smiling face, her colorful figure. In the evenings before, his wife and children used to fall fast asleep, and the lamp, burning brightly but in vain in that little living room, would actually be if anything a source of misery. But now, however late he came home, beneath that same lamp Yoshiko's white hands would be nimbly plying knitting needles, and on her lap would be colorful balls of wool. Now, it was cheerful laughter that filled the brushwood-hedge confines of his home in the heart of Ushigome.

But before a month was out Tokio had realized the impossibility of having that lovable girl pupil stay on in his house. His docile wife didn't go so far as to complain about things, nor did she show any signs of so doing, but nevertheless her mood got gradually worse. Amid the endless laughter spread an endless unease. He knew for a fact that his wife's relatives had started to treat it as a major problem.

After much worry Tokio had arranged for Yoshiko to stay at the house of his wife's elder sister, a military widow who lived off a pension and needlework, and that from there she should attend a private girls' school in Kōjimachi.

3

Since then until the present incident one and a half years had passed.

During that time Yoshiko had returned home twice. She had written five short novels, one long one, and several dozen passages of elegant prose and new-style poetry. At her school her English marks were first-class, and she had bought the complete works of Turgenev in English, which Tokio chose for her, from Maruzen Bookshop. The first time she had gone home was during the summer holidays, and the second was in compliance with the doctor's advice that she should relax in the quiet countryside of her home, following occasional hysteria-like convulsions due to nervous debility.

The house where Yoshiko was staying was in Kōjimachi Dote Sanbanchō, next to the embankment where the Kōbu Line trains passed. Her study was the guest room, a fairly large room fronting on a busy road that was a noisy place what with the din of children and passers-by. Next to her lacquered paper-ply desk was a bookcase rather like a smaller version of the Western-style bookcase in Tokio's study, and on top of it stood a mirror, a lipstick tray, a jar of face powder, and a large bottle of potassium bromide, which she said was for her nervous headaches. Prominent in the bookcase were the complete works of Kōyō,* Chikamatsu's realistic *jōruri* ballad-dramas,** English textbooks,

* Ozaki Kōyō, 1867–1903, was popular for his combined modernism and Japanese spirit.
** Chikamatsu Monzaemon, 1653–1724, was a famous classical dramatist, considered essential reading for any student of literature.

and in particular her newly purchased complete works of Turgenev. However, upon returning from school, rather than sitting at her desk writing fiction or poetry this aspiring authoress of the future preferred writing numerous letters. She had a considerable number of male friends, and a considerable number of letters in male handwriting would arrive for her. These friends included a student from the Tokyo Teachers' College and a student from Waseda University, who apparently came to see her from time to time.

There were not many such modern-minded girl students in that corner of Kōjimachi Dote Sanbanchō. Tokio's wife's folks lived there, beyond the Ichigaya Approach, and there were as well many girls from conservative merchant families. Thus Yoshiko's Kobe-bred sophistication drew the attention of the locals. Tokio was forever being told by his wife what her sister had said:

"She's having trouble with Yoshiko-san, she was saying only today. It's one thing for her boyfriends to come calling, but in the evening they go off together round the neighborhood and don't get back till late, she says. Yoshiko-san always tells her there's nothing to worry about, but rumors are rumors, my sister was saying."

When he heard such things Tokio would always side with Yoshiko and tell his wife, "You old-fashioned people will never understand what Yoshiko does. You only have to see a man and woman walking together and you think there's something strange going on, but you only think that way because you're old-fashioned. Nowadays women too are aware of themselves, and do what they want to do!"

Tokio would also proudly preach this ideal to Yoshiko. "Nowadays women have to be self-aware. It's no good having the same sort of attitude of depending on others as the women in the past. As Sudermann's Magda says, it's hopeless if you go straight from your father's hands into your husband's, with no pride in yourself. The modern woman in Japan must think for herself and then act for herself." He would go on to tell her about Ibsen's Nora and Turgenev's Elena, about how rich in both feeling and willpower were the women in Russia and Germany, and would then add, "But self-awareness also involves self-reflection, so you mustn't simply go throwing your willpower and ego about recklessly. You must realize that you have full responsibility for your own actions."

Yoshiko would listen to Tokio's sermonizing as though it were of the utmost importance, and her feelings of admiration grew ever stronger. She felt it was more liberal than Christian teaching, and more authoritative.

Even for a girl student, Yoshiko's personal appearance was excessively showy. Her gold ring, her very fashionable pretty waist-sash, and her carefree posture were more than enough to draw the attention of people along the road. Her face was, rather than beautiful, extremely expressive, and while there were times when it did seem beautiful in the extreme, there were also times when it was somehow ugly. There was a sparkle in her eyes, and this was very often used to effect. Until four or five years before, women had been extremely simplistic when it came to expressing feelings, and were able to express only three or four different sorts of feeling, with basic looks such as of anger or joy. Now, however, there were quite a lot of women who could very cleverly express their feelings facially, and Tokio always felt that Yoshiko was one such woman.

The relationship between Yoshiko and Tokio was just too intimate merely for that of pupil and teacher. One female third-party, having observed the state of affairs between the two, had remarked to Tokio's wife, "Ever since Yoshiko-san came Tokio-san seems to have changed completely. When you see the two of them talking together it's as if their souls were reaching out for one another. Really, you should watch out, you know!" To other people, of course, it certainly looked that way, but as for the two people themselves, were they really that intimate? . . .

The feelings of a young woman, prone to high spirits. But then, just when you think she's in high spirits, suddenly she's dejected. Feelings aroused by trivial things, similarly often upset by trivial things. A tender attitude neither of love nor yet devoid of love. Tokio was always confused. The strength of morality, the strength of convention—if only there were once an opportunity, destroying these would be easier than tearing silk. However, such opportunities did not come readily.

And yet, Tokio himself believed that there had been two occasions in the last year when such an opportunity had at least come close. One had been when Yoshiko had sent him a lengthy letter tearfully stating her belief that she was incompetent and unable to repay his kindness as her teacher, and that therefore it would be better for her to go back home, become a farmer's wife, and lose herself in the oblivion of the countryside. The other time had been when Tokio had chanced to visit her one evening and had found her alone in the house. As for the letter, Tokio clearly understood its meaning. He had spent a sleepless night worrying about how he should reply. Giving searching glances at the face of his peacefully sleeping wife, he had censured himself for his lack of conscience. And so, the letter which he sent in reply the following morning was that of the stern teacher. The second instance was a spring night some two months later, when he had chanced to call on Yoshiko and found her sitting alone by the *hibachi*,* her face powdered and beautiful.

"What's going on?" he had asked.

"I'm looking after the house."

"Where's my sister-in-law gone, then?"

"Shopping, over in Yotsuya."

She had looked him straight in the face as she replied. She was so very seductive. His heart had raced shamelessly at the overpowering look she gave him. Then they exchanged a few banal words, but both seemed to feel that those banalities were not quite so insignificant. What might have happened had they gone on talking for another quarter of an hour or so? Her eyes had sparkled expressively, her words were coquettish, her attitude was most definitely something out of the ordinary.

"You're very pretty tonight," he had said in a deliberately light-hearted tone.

"I've just been in the bath."

"Your make-up's very attractive, that's why you're so pretty!"

"Now Sensei, what a thing to say!"

She had laughed and moved her body coquettishly.

Tokio had returned home straight away. She had tried to get him to stay, but he had insisted on returning home, and so, looking reluctant, she had seen him off through the moonlit night. There was certainly something very mysterious contained in that powdered face of hers.

In April Yoshiko had come to look really off-color following

---

* A charcoal-burning brazier, the traditional Japanese domestic heater.

numerous bouts of illness, and her nerves had developed into a highly strung state. She took vast quantities of the potassium bromide, but apparently still couldn't sleep. Constant desires and reproductive forces never hesitate to take possession of a woman when she is of suitable age. Yoshiko grew familiar with a great number of medicines.

She had returned home at the end of April, had returned to Tokyo in September, and it was then that the present incident had occurred.

The present incident? Yoshiko had a lover! On the way back to Tokyo she had gone off with him to Saga, in Kyoto. As a result of those two days spent in merrymaking the timetable failed to tally between her departure from home and her arrival in Tokyo. Letters had therefore been exchanged between Tokyo and Bitchū, and after questioning Yoshiko it turned out to be a case of "love, pure love—the two of them most definitely hadn't done anything wrong, and wished desperately, at all costs, to continue their love in the future." As her teacher, Tokio found himself obliged to act as a sort of go-between, a witness to this love.

Yoshiko's lover was a Dōshisha student, a prodigy from the Kobe Church by the name of Tanaka Hideo, aged twenty-one.

Yoshiko swore to her teacher, in the name of God, that their love was pure. Her parents back home felt that to have gone secretly flirting in Saga with some man, while still only a student, already meant her spiritual degeneracy. She however maintained, amid a flood of tears, that there had definitely been no dirty act, and that the mutual awareness of their love had come only after she had left Kyoto. On arrival back in Tokyo she had found awaiting her a passionate letter from him, and it was then that they had first made their promises for the future. They had definitely done nothing wrong, she maintained. Tokio, while feeling a sense of martyrdom, was obliged to act in the interests of their so-called pure love.

He was in torment, greatly depressed at having been deprived of someone he cherished so very much. From the first he had had no thought of making his pupil his lover. If he had had any such fixed and clear-cut thought in mind he would not have hesitated to seize those two earlier potential opportunities. However, his beloved pupil added beautiful color to his bleak existence and gave him a sort of limitless strength, so how could he be expected to endure her being snatched suddenly away by someone else? He had let two opportunities go by, but the vague hope at the bottom of his heart was to wait for the arrival of a third and a fourth opportunity, and then to build a new destiny, a new life. He was in torment, his thoughts in confusion. Feelings of jealousy, regret, and vexation merged together and spun round in his mind like a whirlwind. To add to his confusion, a sense of his moral obligation as her teacher was also mixed in, as was too a feeling of martyrdom that it was all for the sake of his loved one's happiness. He drank a great deal of saké with his evening meal and went off to sleep as drunk as a lord.

The next day was Sunday and it had rained, the steady downpour in the woods behind his house seeming twice as miserable as usual, and all for Tokio's benefit. His thoughts dwelled upon how long the streams of rain were that fell onto the zelkova trees, falling endlessly from an endless sky. He had no enthusiasm for reading or writing. He just lounged in his wisteria chair—cold to the back now that it was coming into autumn—and gazed at the streaming rain, thinking, in the light of this incident, how his life had been till now. He had already suffered similar experiences. He invariably tasted the bitterness of lonely torment, the torment of forever being made to stand on the outside of things and, because of some wrong step, never being able to enter into the heart of destiny. It was the same with literature, the same with society. Love, love, love . . . Was he still being tossed, even now, by the waves of a negative fate? The thought left him overcome by his wretchedness and by the ineptitude of fate. "I am Turgenev's 'superfluous man,'" he thought, and went over in his mind the transient life of that protagonist.

Unable to endure the loneliness, that afternoon he said he wanted to drink saké. He moaned because his wife was slow preparing things, and then the food he was given was tasteless, so he ended up getting angry and drinking out of desperation. One bottle, two bottles . . . the number grew, and soon Tokio was hopelessly drunk. He even stopped moaning at his wife. He would simply yell "Saké! Saké!" whenever he emptied the bottle. He gulped it down. The timid maid looked on in surprise and disgust. First he hugged and kissed his five-year-old son with a great show of fondness, but then got angry when the child started to cry and slapped his behind furiously. The three children grew frightened and backed away from him to a respectful distance, gazing in bewilderment at the red, drunken face of their extraordinarily behaved father. He drank close on three pints and then simply collapsed on the spot in a drunken heap, not minding that he sent the table flying as he did so. Then presently, in strange, disjointed stanzas, he started to chant an infantile verse of new-style poetry that had been popular some ten years before:

I haunt your doorway
Like the dust of the street
Blown about by the storm.
More than that storm,
More than that dust,
It's the remnants of our love,
That lie scattered in the dawn . . .

Halfway through the verse he suddenly stood up, still wearing the quilt with which his wife had covered him, and, looking just like a little mountain, moved towards the parlor. His wife, very worried, followed and asked where he was going. He paid no attention and tried to enter the toilet, still clad in the quilt. His wife was flustered:

"What *are* you doing? You shouldn't get drunk like this! It's horrible! That's the toilet!"

Suddenly she pulled at the quilt from behind, and was left holding it there in the entrance to the toilet. Tokio was relieving himself in a dangerously erratic manner, and on finishing he promptly flopped straight down on his side, still in the toilet. His disgusted wife tried her best to move him, but he would neither move nor stand. Yet neither did he fall asleep, but rather, with wide piercing eyes in a face like red clay, he just stared at the rain pouring down outside.

4

Tokio came plodding back at the usual hour to his home in Ushigome Yaraichō.

For three days he had been struggling with that torment. Part of him had a sort of strength that made it impossible for him to abandon himself to indulgence. He always regretted being controlled by this strength, but sooner or later he was always beaten and forced into submission by it. For this reason he was obliged always to taste the bitterness of standing on the outside of destiny, and was considered by society to be a correct and trustworthy man. After three days of anguish he could at least now see how things stood before him. The curtain had come down on the first act of his relationship with Yoshiko. From now on he would just have to do his duty as a teacher and think of the happiness of the woman he loved. It was hard, but life was hard. Such were his thoughts as he went home.

His wife came up to greet him as soon as he opened the door. The day was still hot, a late fling of summer, and his underwear was soaked in sweat. He changed into a simple unlined starched white kimono and sat in front of the *hibachi* in the living room. His wife took a letter from the sideboard, as though she had just remembered it.

" From Yoshiko-san," she said as she handed it to him.

He opened it quickly. Just by looking at the thickness of the roll of paper he knew it was about the incident. He eagerly started to read.

It was in the new colloquial writing style, the penmanship flowing and excellent.

Sensei,

Actually I wanted to talk this over with you, but things happened too quickly so I just acted on my own judgment.

Yesterday, at four o'clock, a telegram came from Tanaka saying he would arrive at Shinbashi Station at six—you can't imagine how surprised I was!

I was really worried because I believed that he wasn't the rash sort of person who'd come about nothing. Sensei, please forgive me—I went to meet him at the said time. When I met him and asked him why he'd come, it turned out that, after reading my letter—in which I explained everything—he'd been really worried that perhaps, because of this incident, I might be taken off back home, and that he'd be to blame. So, he'd abandoned his studies straight away and come up to Tokyo with the intention of explaining everything to you, apologizing, asking for support, and trying to ensure that everything went smoothly. Then when I explained to him about how I'd told you everything, about your kind words, and about how you'd kindly become the witness and protector of our pure and sincere love, he was extremely moved by your kindness and was overcome with tears of gratitude. It seems he was extremely shocked by the over-worried nature of my letter and had come up to Tokyo prepared for the worst. He said he'd come with the intention of, if necessary, getting a friend— who'd gone with us that time to Saga—to act as witness to make it clear that nothing dirty took place between us, and he wanted to explain how we became aware of our love only after we'd parted. He also wanted to ask if you'd be kind enough to tell all this to my parents back home. But seeing how I've just very rashly upset my parents' feelings, how could we do that? We've now come to the conclusion that the best thing to do is wait a while and say nothing, to cherish our hopes and devote ourselves to our studies, and wait for an opportunity to explain things even if it's five or ten years from now. I also told him everything you'd said. And so, things being settled, he should have gone back, but when I saw how thoroughly worn out he looked, I just couldn't tell him to go straight back again. (Please forgive my weakness.) I do try to honor your advice that I shouldn't get involved in practical problems while I'm in the middle of my studies, but, for the time being, I got him settled in a travel lodge, and since he'd taken the trouble to come so far, I ended up saying I'd spend a day sightseeing with him. Please forgive me, Sensei. For all our passionate feelings, we still have common sense, and we won't do anything that might be misunderstood by others, such as at Kyoto when we temporarily forgot ourselves. I swear to you we won't do anything like that.

Best wishes also to your wife,

Yoshiko

As Tokio read this letter various feelings kindled like fire within him. That twenty-one-year old boy Tanaka had actually come to Tokyo. Yoshiko had gone to meet him. Who knows what they did? What she had just told him might be a pack of lies. Perhaps there'd been physical motives ever since Tanaka had first met her at Suma bathing resort during the summer holidays, and so, having sought to gratify his desires in Kyoto, he had now come to Tokyo in pursuit of the woman for whom he could no longer contain his desire. They had no doubt held hands. Their hearts would have pressed against each other. Who knows what they had been doing upstairs in that travel lodge, out of other people's sight? It was only a fleeting moment between purity and impurity. Tokio couldn't bear such thoughts. "This concerns my

52

responsibility as her supervisor!" he cried out angrily within himself. "I can't leave things like this! I can't allow such freedom to a woman of capricious mind. I must exercise supervision, protection. 'We are passionate but sensible'—what's this 'we'? Why did she write 'we' and not 'I'? Why did she use the plural?" Tokio was confused, angry. Tanaka had arrived at six the previous evening. If Tokio went to his sister-in-law's and asked, he could find out what time Yoshiko had returned that night. But what had they done today? What were they doing now?

The dinner, which his wife had so carefully prepared, included fresh sliced raw tuna and chilled bean-curd with *shiso*-plant seasoning, and although he didn't feel much like savoring his meal, he got through one drink of saké after another.

His wife put the youngest child to bed and then came and sat in front of the *hibachi*. Glancing at Yoshiko's letter at her husband's side, she asked:

"What did Yoshiko have to say?"

Without replying, Tokyo tossed the letter to her. As she caught it she gave him a searching look, and knew a storm was brewing.

She read the letter through and then rolled it up.

"He's come, then?"

"Uh."

"Will he stay on in Tokyo, do you think?"

"Isn't it written in the letter! He's going back soon, she says . . ."

"*Will* he go back, though, I wonder?"

"*Who knows?*"

Her husband's tone was harsh, so she kept quiet. Then, after a while:

"Well, it's really too bad. A young girl like her, saying she wants to be a novelist or something—she might well want what she wants, but her parents should act like properly responsible parents too, shouldn't they?"

"But I dare say you were relieved at her affair!" he was about to say, but checked himself. "Well, don't concern yourself about it—people like you just don't understand. . . . Why don't you just pour some saké instead?"

His obedient wife took up the saké-pourer and filled his Kyoto-made porcelain cup to the brim.

Tokio knocked back the saké as though it alone could help

him overcome his depression. At the third bottle his wife grew worried.

"What's the matter with you lately?" she asked.

"Why?"

"Isn't it a fact you do nothing but get drunk?"

"Is there anything the matter, then, if I get drunk?"

"I'd say so, yes. I think there's something on your mind. Shouldn't you stop worrying about Yoshiko-san?"

"Fool!" thundered Tokio.

His wife went on undaunted.

"Well, it's poison if you drink too much, you know, so I should stop while you're still all right. If you lay yourself out again in the toilet, you're too big for me and the maid Otsuru to manage between the two of us!"

"Never you mind—let's just have another bottle!"

And so he drank another half-bottle. He now seemed very drunk. His face had turned a copper color and his eyes were rather fixed. Suddenly he stood up.

"Get my waist-sash out!"

"Where are you going?"

"I'm off to Sanbanchō."

"My sister's?"

"Uh."

"You should forget that idea—you're not in a fit state!"

"What!? I'm all right! You can't be given responsibility for someone's daughter and then neglect to look after her! I can't just look the other way when this fellow comes up to Tokyo and goes strolling about with her! I can't relax while she's over with your sister Takawa, so I'm going to bring her back here today, if there's time. You go and clean upstairs."

"You're going to bring her back to stay here, again . . .?"

"Of course!"

His wife didn't seem keen to get out his waist-sash and outdoor kimono.

"All right, then!—If you won't get my things out, I'll go like this!"

He hurried out, just as he was, without a hat, in his plain white kimono with its dirty muslin under-belt.

"I'm just getting them out! . . . Dear me, what next?" He heard his wife's words behind him.

The summery day was drawing to a close. The birds were chattering noisily in Yarai's Sakai Wood. In the nearby houses the evening meal had been finished, and made-up young women appeared in the doorways as they set out for the evening. Some boys were playing ball. He also encountered several couples strolling to the Kagurazaka—thinly moustached gentlemen, government officials to judge from appearances, escorting their young wives, with their fashionable low-pompadour hairstyles. Tokio was thrown into disorder by his agitated feelings and drunken body, and all his surroundings seemed to belong to a different world. It seemed to him as though the houses on either side were moving, the ground giving way beneath his feet, the sky coming down over his head. Although he had never had a particularly good tolerance for drink he had just drunk heavily and recklessly, and it had gone straight to his head. All at once he recalled how lower-class Russians got drunk and fell flat out asleep on the roadside. He remembered having told a friend that this showed what great people the Russians were—if you're going to let yourself go, then you should let yourself go all the way! "Fool! How could love *possibly* make any discrimination between teacher and pupil?" he yelled at himself.

By the time he had climbed Nakanezaka Hill, gone past the rear gate of the Officers' School, and come to the top of Sanaizaka Hill, the day had drawn completely to a close. Many people in white *yukata* were passing by. The tobacconist's young wife had come out in front of the shop. The hanging curtain in the doorway of the shop selling iced refreshments fluttered in the evening breeze with a suggestion of coolness. Gazing vacantly at this summery night scene Tokio bumped into a telegraph pole and, on the point of collapse, fell to his knees in a shallow ditch. "Drunkard! Stay on your feet!" yelled some workman contemptuously.

Suddenly seeming to come to his senses, Tokio turned to the right from the top of the hill and went into the grounds of the Hachiman Temple. Here there was no one to be seen and all was peaceful. Tall old zelkovas and pines formed a canopy overhead, and in a corner to the left stood a huge, thick coral tree. Here and there the all-night lamps started to come on and cast their light. In terrible distress, Tokio plunged into the shadow of the coral tree and laid himself out on the ground at its base.

His mind was excited, his wild feelings and the pleasure of his sadness mustered all their force, and while on the one hand he was carried away by a burning jealousy, on the other he was coolly and objectively considering his own situation.

Of course his feelings were not the passionate feelings of a first love. Rather than blindly following his fate, he was coolly appraising that fate. Burning feelings and ice-cold objective appraisal fused firmly together like entwined threads, and produced in him an extraordinary state of mind.

He was sad, truly deeply sad. His sadness was not the sadness of florid youth, nor simply the sadness of lovers. It was a more profound and greater sadness, a sadness inherent in the innermost reaches of human life. The flowing of moving waters, the withering of blossoming flowers—when encountering that irresistible force which is deep within nature, there is nothing as wretched nor as transient as man.

Tears flowed down over Tokio's whiskered face.

Then suddenly an idea struck him. He stood up and started walking. It was now full night. The glass lamps erected here and there in the grounds gave off their light, and the three words "all-night lamp" showed clearly on their faces. It upset him to read those three words. Had he not once before looked upon those three words in a state of great distress? When his wife was still unmarried and living just below the high ground where he now stood, he had often climbed to this same spot hoping just to catch the faint sound of her harp. So great had been his passion that if he couldn't win her he had wished only to cast himself away in some colony in the South Seas, and he had often pondered things while gazing at those three words—"all-night lamp"—and at the *haiku* poems on the paper lanterns, at the temple sanctuary, at the long stone steps, at the temple gates. Below, just as in earlier days, stood the same houses and, although the occasional rumbling of a passing train now broke the silence, just as in the old days a light shone bright and clear from the windows of his wife's house. What a fickle heart! Who would have thought that things would change so much after just eight years? Why, with the change of her unmarried *momoware* hairstyle into the rounded chignon *marumage* style of a married woman, had their pleasant life become so bleak? Why had he now come to feel this new love? Tokio could not help feeling an acute awareness of the frightening power of time. However, strange as it was, the facts of the present situation remained completely unchanged.

"Paradox it may be, but there's nothing I can do about it. That paradox, that inconstancy, is a fact, and facts are facts. *Fact!*"

The thought echoed through his mind.

Like a being oppressed by the unendurable forces of nature, Tokio once again laid down his bulky frame, this time on a nearby bench. Chancing to look up, he saw that a large and lusterless copper-colored moon had risen silently over the pines along the moat. The color, the form, the appearance, were thoroughly miserable. Tokio thought how well it matched his own present misery, and once again his heart was filled with unbearable sadness.

By now he had sobered up. The evening dew had started to fall.

He arrived in front of the house in Dote Sanbanchō.

He looked, but could see no light in Yoshiko's room. It appeared that she still hadn't returned. His heart raced feverishly again. Alone with her lover, on a dark night like tonight! Who knew what they might be getting up to? When they acted as stupidly as this, what was to become of their "pure love," their claim to have committed no vulgar act?

Tokio's first thought was to go inside, but then, realizing there was no point in going in before Yoshiko got back, he went straight past. As he walked he looked at the face of each woman he passed, thinking she might be Yoshiko. He loitered—first on the embankment, then in the shadow of the pines, then at the corner of the road—so much that he began to arouse the suspicions of passers-by. It was now nine o'clock, now almost ten. You might well say it was a summer night, but there was no reason for being out quite as late as this. Convinced that Yoshiko must have returned by now, he returned to his sister-in-law's house, but no, she still wasn't back after all.

He went in.

No sooner had he gone through to the small living room at the back than he asked:

"What's happened to Yoshi-san?"

Before answering, in fact before all else, his sister-in-law noticed in surprise the liberal amount of mud on Tokio's clothes.

"Well now, what's happened to you, Tokio-san?"

Under the clear bright light of the lamp he could see, sure enough, on the shoulder, knee, and hip of his plain white casual kimono, not merely a trace but a very large amount of mud.

"What? Oh, I just fell over back there."

"Really? But it's even on your shoulder! You were drunk again, I suppose."

"*What!* . . ."

Tokio tried to turn the comment away with a forced laugh. He continued, not letting up in the least.

"Where's Yoshi-san gone?"

"When she went off this morning she said she was going for a walk with a friend, towards Nakano. She should be back any time now. Anything you wanted with her?"

"Well, yes, a small matter. . . . Was she back late last night?"

"No. She said she was going to Shinbashi to meet a friend, left just after four and came back around eight."

She looked at Tokio's face. "Is anything the matter?"

"Well, really, after all. . . ." Tokio's tone became serious. "I just thought we'd have problems if the same sort of thing that happened in Kyoto were to happen again, and that therefore I ought to have her back at my place and keep a proper eye on her."

"Yes, that would be best. Really, Yoshiko-san has such a strong character, and for uneducated people like me . . ."

"No, that's not the reason. It's just that to allow her too much freedom might turn out to be against her own interests, and so I thought of having her at home and looking after her properly."

"Well, that would be best. Really, even Yoshiko-san. . . . There's nothing really bad about her, and she's bright and intelligent and a rare sort of person, but if she does have a fault then it's this habit of hers of walking nonchalantly around at night with her men friends. I'm often telling her that it's the one thing she should stop, but when I say that she just laughs and calls me old-fashioned. And then I hear how, at the police-box on the corner, they felt it suspicious that she was always hanging around with these men and how a plainclothes detective had been stationed outside the house. Of course those things aren't really going on and so I'm not worried in that sense, but. . . ."

"When was this?"

"The end of last year."

"She's just a bit too sophisticated for comfort." Glancing at his watch, which showed half past ten, he added, "Anyway, I wonder what's happened? Staying out alone as late as this, at her age. . . ."

"She'll be back soon."

"Does this happen often, then?"

"No, it's very unusual. But it's a summer evening, so she'll be out thinking it's still early."

His sister-in-law went on with her needlework as she talked. In front of her stood a cutting-board with broad-based leg-supports, while silk cuttings and threads and scissors lay scattered about in jumbled disarray. The lamplight shone clearly on the beautiful colors of women's clothes. The mid-September night wore on, it grew a little chilly, and a Kōbu Line cargo train passed by along the embankment behind the house, setting up a dreadful shaking.

Every time he heard the sound of *geta* Tokio felt sure it had to be Yoshiko, but eventually, just after eleven had struck, a particular light, mincing sound of a girl's *geta* could be heard resounding through the quiet night.

"This time it *is* Yoshiko-san," said his sister-in-law.

Sure enough, the footsteps stopped at the entrance to the house, and the sliding-door opened with a noisy rattling.

"Yoshiko-san?"

"Yes," replied a charming voice.

A tall, beautiful figure with a fashionable low-pompadour hairstyle came quickly and quietly in from the porch.

"Oh! What a surprise! Sensei!"

Her tone was enough to reveal her surprise and embarrassment.

"Sorry I'm so late," she said as she came to the doorway between the front room and the living room. Then, half-sitting and flashing a searching glance at Tokio, she took out a purple crepe-wrapped package and handed it to his sister-in-law.

"Oh, what's this then? A present? Really, you always go to such trouble over me. . . ."

"Oh no—it's for me too!" replied Yoshiko cheerfully. Although she had looked as if she intended to go into the next room, she was now obliged to sit in a corner of the living room, under the dazzling light of the lamp. Her beautiful figure, her fashionable hairstyle, her colorful flannel kimono tied neatly with an olive-green summer-style waist-sash, her seductive appeal as she casually lay back. . . . Sitting facing this figure, Tokio felt a sort of vague satisfaction, and half forgot his earlier distress and anguish. No matter how powerful your rival in love, if you can just possess the girl you can at least feel some sort of peace of mind.

"I really am late getting back."

She apologized again, quietly, uneasily.

"You went to Nakano then, for a walk?" Tokio asked abruptly.

"Yes . . ." Yoshiko shot another searching glance at him.

His sister-in-law made some tea. On opening the present she found it was her special favorite, cream puffs. "Oh, how delicious!" she exclaimed, and for a moment or two everyone's attention was focused on the cakes.

After a while Yoshiko spoke:

"Sensei, were you waiting for me, then?"

"Yes, that's right—he's been waiting over an hour and a half, you know!" cut in Tokio's sister-in-law.

With this the whole story came out, about how he had come with the intention of taking her back with him, that very night if possible—her luggage could be sent on later. Yoshiko listened with head bowed, nodding assent. Certainly she felt a certain coercion, and yet deep down she had absolute faith in Tokio— and after all, it wasn't so bad to go and live in the home of a teacher who had sympathized so much with her recent love affair. In fact, for some time now she had been unhappy about staying in this old-fashioned house and had wished, if only it were possible, that she could live as she had at the beginning, in Sensei's house; and so, if only it hadn't come about as it had, she would have been only too happy about the plan.

Tokio was anxious to find out about her lover. Where was he now? When was he going back to Kyoto? For Tokio this was a truly important question. But he couldn't reveal everything by asking in front of his sister-in-law, who knew nothing, and so that evening he said not a word about it. The three talked into the night about trivia.

Tokio had mentioned her moving back that very evening, but since it was now midnight his sister-in-law thought it best that Yoshiko go the following day. Tokio considered returning alone to Ushigome, but he felt hopelessly worried and so, on the pretext of it being late, he arranged to stay the night at his sister-in-law's and for himself and Yoshiko to leave early the next morning.

Yoshiko slept in the front room, while Tokio and his sister-in-law slept in the slightly smaller living room. Presently he could hear his sister-in-law's little snores. The clock struck one. Apparently Yoshiko was finding it hard to get to sleep, for from time to time he heard what seemed to be a loud sigh. A Kōbu Line cargo train passed by alone through the still night, setting up a dreadful shaking in the house. For a long while Tokio too was unable to get to sleep.

5

The next morning Tokio escorted Yoshiko to his own house. He had wanted to find out about the previous day's happenings as soon as he was alone with her, but when he saw how she was following dejectedly on behind him with bowed head, he felt rather sorry for her, and walked on in silence, containing his impatience.

When they reached the top of Sanaizaka Hill there were only a few passers-by. Tokio suddenly turned round and asked abruptly:

"Well, what happened?"

"Eh?" Yoshiko frowned as she returned the question.

"I'm talking about yesterday! Is he still here?"

"He's going back on the six o'clock express."

"So, won't you have to see him off, then?"

"No, that's not necessary now."

With this their conversation came to an end, and they walked on in silence.

In Tokio's house in Yaraichō they cleaned the upstairs three-mat and six-mat rooms, which had been used till then as store-rooms, and made them into Yoshiko's living quarters. For ages the storerooms had been left for the children to play in, and were thick with dust, but, after setting to work with a broom and dusters and after repairing the broken, rain-stained sliding paper screens, it became so bright and cheerful one would not have believed it possible. The place was filled with a pleasant greenness by the huge, thickly growing trees of the Sakai Cemetery to the rear of the house, and the view also included the neighbor's grapevine trellis, and the abandoned garden with poppies blooming beautifully amid the weeds. For the alcove Tokio chose a wall-scroll of morning-glory by a certain artist, and placed some late-blooming roses in the hanging vase.

Around noon her luggage arrived—a large Chinese trunk, wicker cases, cloth bags, the bookcase, the desk, her bedding— and it was no small task to carry it all upstairs. Tokio was obliged to take the day off work in order to help.

The desk was placed under the window to the south, the bookcase on its left, and on top were set the mirror, the lipstick-tray, and the bottle. The Chinese trunk and the wicker cases went into one half of the wall-cupboard; then, as he was about to put the set of patterned bedding into the other half, Tokio caught a faint, lingering, feminine smell, and felt rather strange.

By two o'clock the place had achieved a degree of order.

"Well, how about this, then? It shouldn't be too unpleasant living here," said Tokio, laughing and looking very pleased with himself. "The thing to do here is study quietly. Really, there's no sense in getting worried over practical issues."

"Yes . . ." Yoshiko hung her head.

"We can go over things in detail later, but for the moment the two of you just have to settle down to your studies."

"Yes . . ." Yoshiko raised her head. "That's just what we both feel too, Sensei—for both of us to study now, and hold out hope for the future, perhaps even for my parents' consent."

"That's good. At the moment, if you make too much of a fuss, you'll only be misunderstood by everybody, including your parents, and you'll end up unable to make that special dream of yours come true."

"And so, Sensei, I want to devote myself to my studies. That's what Tanaka said, too. He also said that he should definitely meet you and thank you, and he asked me to give you his best regards . . ."

"Really, there's no need . . ."

Tokio was unhappy with Yoshiko's use of the word "we" and
her thinking in the plural, as though they had now openly
pledged their betrothal. He was surprised that a still unmarried
girl of nineteen or twenty and in the budding bloom of woman-
hood could talk like that. He felt, somewhat belatedly, how times
had changed. He was surprised how much the character of
modern girl students differed from that of the unmarried girls of
his own courting days. Of course, from the point of view of
principle and personal taste, he was certainly pleased to see this
character in girl students. Old-fashioned education simply could
not equip a girl to be the wife of a modern, Meiji man. His own
view was that girls too had to stand on their own feet and develop their own willpower. Indeed, he had often preached this
view to Yoshiko. But naturally, when it came to seeing this
new-style sophistication actually put into practice, he couldn't
help showing a certain consternation.

A postcard was forwarded the following day from his sister-
in-law's house in Sanbanchō. It was post-marked Kōzu in Kana-
gawa and was from Tanaka, saying he was on his way home.

Yoshiko, now installed upstairs, would come down as soon as
she was called. The daily meals would all be taken in a happy
family atmosphere. In the evenings, as they gathered round the
bright shining lamp, the conversation would wax lively. Yoshiko
knitted socks for Tokio. She never failed to present a beautiful,
smiling face. Tokio had her completely to himself, and at least
this gave him a certain relief and satisfaction. His wife too,
knowing that Yoshiko now had a lover, completely forgot her
feelings of danger and unease.

It was painful to Yoshiko to be separated from her lover. If
only it had been possible she would have liked him to be there
in Tokyo with her, and just once in a while be able to see him,
speak to him. But she knew this was difficult at the present time.
She realized that, until he graduated from Dōshisha in a few
years' time, they would have to study quietly and wholeheartedly,
only exchanging the occasional letter. And so, in the afternoons,
she went as before to her private English school in Kōjimachi,
while Tokio went to his job in Koishikawa.

From time to time in the evening, Tokio would call Yoshiko

into his study and talk to her about literature, about novels, about love. He would give her advice about her future. His attitude at such times was fair, frank, and full of sympathy, and one would never have thought him the same man who had collapsed blind drunk in the toilet and laid himself flat out on the ground. Even so, it wasn't that Tokio actually planned on adopting such an attitude, but rather that, at moments when he was face to face with his beloved woman, no sacrifice was too great in order to gain her favor.

And so, Yoshiko had faith in her teacher. She even believed that when the time came for speaking to her parents, even if there was going to be a clash between old and new ways of thinking, then it would be enough just to have the support of this benevolent teacher.

September became October. A desolate wind rustled through the wood behind the house, the sky turned a deeper, darker blue, the sunlight came piercingly through the clear air, and the evening shadows gave a new depth to their surroundings. Rain fell all day long on the remaining taro leaves, and mushrooms appeared on display in the greengrocers' shops. The cries of insects in the hedges disappeared with the dew, and the leaves of the paulownia trees in the gardens fell frail to the ground. For one hour each morning, from nine till ten, there was an explanation of Turgenev's novels, and under her teacher's twinkling eyes, Yoshiko would lean across the desk as she listened to the lengthy story of *On the Eve*. How moved she must have been by Elena's passionate feelings and strong, willful character, and by her sad and tragic fate. Yoshiko compared Elena's love story with her own and lost herself in the novel. Her love's fate —the fateful act of placing her future in the hands of someone unexpected, with no chance to love the man she really wanted to—this was just how Yoshiko actually felt at the time. She had never dreamed that the lily-leaf postcard she had chanced to receive at Suma Beach would lead to such a destiny.

As she looked out on the wood, out there in the rain, in the night, in the moonlight, Yoshiko had various thoughts about her affair. The night train to Kyoto, the moon over Saga, the beautiful sunset over Lake Biwa when they had gone to Zeze, the lespedeza blooming in picturesque profusion in the garden of the inn. . . . Those two days of fun seemed now a dream. Her thoughts went further back, to before the time she had fallen in love with him, to swimming at Suma Beach, to the moon over the hills at home, to before the time she had fallen ill—her cheeks flushed instinctively at the particular thought of her distress at that time.

From reverie to reverie . . . The reveries took the form of long letters, bound for Kyoto. And bulky letters would come back from Kyoto, almost every other day. However much they wrote, their feelings were inexhaustible. In fact, their correspondence was so frequent that Tokio waited until Yoshiko was out and then, placating his conscience with the pretext of supervision, went furtively through her writing-case and the drawers of her desk. He read hurriedly through the two or three letters from Tanaka which he found.

They were full of lovers' sweet words. However, Tokio was trying hard to find out something a bit more than that, to discover a certain secret. Was there no evidence anywhere of their lips having met, of sexual desire? Had their relationship not gone beyond the bounds of pure love? But the real state of their love could not be learned even from these letters.

A month went by.

Then one day Tokio took receipt of a postcard addressed to Yoshiko. It was written in English. He read it, nonchalantly. It was from Kyoto, from Tanaka, to the effect that he had saved enough money to support himself for a month and was now wondering if he could find work in Tokyo to keep him going afterwards. Tokio's heart raced. His peace of mind was destroyed at a stroke.

He asked Yoshiko about it after dinner.

She looked upset. "Sensei, I just don't know what to do—Tanaka says he's coming to Tokyo! I've stopped him several times already, but for some reason—he says that after this affair he's sick of pursuing religion and leading a life of hypocrisy, or something like that—anyway, he says he's definitely coming to Tokyo."

"What does he intend to do in Tokyo?"

"He says he'd like to do literature."

" 'Literature'? What's that, then, 'literature'? Writing novels, do you mean?"

"Yes, I suppose so . . ."

"How stupid!" roared Tokio.

"I just don't know what to do."

"Didn't you lead him into this, then?"

"No I didn't!" She shook her head emphatically. "In fact, I told him that for the time being we were in a fix and that he should at least graduate from Dōshisha, and I made him give up this idea of his when he first mentioned it, but now . . . now he's acting completely on his own. And it's too late to do anything about it now, he says."

"Why?"

"Well, you see, in Kobe there's this Christian called Kōzu who's been paying Tanaka's expenses, for the sake of the Kobe Church. Tanaka went and told him that he wasn't cut out for religion and wanted to make his career in literature. And then he asked him to let him go to Tokyo. Kōzu got angry at this and told him that if that was the case then he didn't care any longer and to do what he wanted, and so now he's made all these preparations, and I just don't know what to do."

"How stupid!" Tokio snapped again. "Please get him to stop this time too. This idea he has of making his career writing novels—it's not possible, it's just a daydream, a complete and utter daydream! And besides, if he does come here to Tokyo, I shall be in an extremely difficult position over your supervision. I won't be able to look after you, so please, make sure you get him to stop!"

Yoshiko looked increasingly worried. "I'll try to get him to stop, but my letter may be too late."

"Too late? Is he already on his way, then?" Tokio's eyes opened wide in astonishment.

"He said in the letter I just got that I wasn't to send any further letters because they'd be too late."

"The letter you just got? Did one come *after* that postcard you just got?"

Yoshiko nodded.

"We're in trouble, then. That's why they say young day-dreamers are hopeless."

His peace of mind was destroyed a second time.

6

Two days later a telegram came from Tanaka to say he would be arriving at Shinbashi at six that evening. Telegram in hand, Yoshiko was in complete confusion. She wasn't allowed to go to meet him, however, as it wouldn't have been right to allow a young girl out alone at night.

She met him the next day, saying she would remonstrate strongly with him and somehow or other get him to return to Kyoto. He was staying in a travel lodge called Tsuruya, in front of the station.

When Tokio came home from work, although he had not expected Yoshiko to be back by then, there as usual was her smiling face in the porch. It turned out that Tanaka would definitely not return to Kyoto after having made up his mind to come to Tokyo. Yoshiko had clashed with him almost to the point of arguing, but all to no avail. He had come to Tokyo with his hopes pinned on Sensei, but well, if that was how it was, then that was how it was. He also fully appreciated the inconvenience with regard to supervision. But it was now impossible for him to go back, and so all he could do was try to support himself and try to achieve his objective.

Tokio was disturbed to hear what Tanaka had said. For a time he thought of telling the pair to do as they pleased, and of completely abandoning the matter, but how could he remain totally indifferent, involved as he was?

During the next few days there was no sign that Yoshiko had visited Tanaka again, and she came home punctually from school, but Tokio's heart burned with a jealous suspicion that she might just have said she was going to school while actually going to see her lover. He was greatly upset. His feelings would change from moment to moment. One minute he would decide to become a complete martyr and do everything he could for the pair, while the next he would decide to destroy everything at a single stroke by reporting the whole thing to her parents. But in his present state of mind he was unable to take either course in practice.

His wife suddenly whispered something to him.

"Upstairs—this . . ." She imitated someone sewing clothes. "She's making something for him, you know—a blue and white splash-pattern student's coat! And she's bought lots of white cotton cord as well."

"Really?"

"Yes, really," his wife laughed.

Tokio felt far from laughing.

With blushing face Yoshiko told him that today she would be back a little late.

"You're going there, then?" he asked.

"Oh no! I just have to call in at a friend's for something."

That evening, with a certain desperation, Tokio visited her lover in his lodgings.

"Sensei, really, I don't know what to say . . ." Tanaka made his formal apologies in a drawn-out, flowing tone, as though he were making a public speech. He was of medium height, slightly plumpish, and of pale complexion, and he spoke as if seeking sympathy, with a look in his eyes as if at prayer.

Tokio was heated. "But wouldn't it be best to do that, if you understand? I'm speaking with the future of the pair of you in mind. Yoshiko is my pupil. My responsibilities won't allow me to let her give up her studies. If you insist on staying in Tokyo, then I must either send her back home, or reveal everything to her parents and beg their approval—I must choose one of these two courses of action. I don't imagine you're the sort of egoistic person who would let the girl you love be kept at home back there in the hills just for your own sake. You say that this affair has turned you off religion, but that's just one point of view. If you were just to bear up and return to Kyoto, then everything would go smoothly and there'd be hope for your relationship in the future."

"I fully appreciate what you're saying . . ."

"But you can't do it?"

"Well, I'm sorry, but . . . I've sold my hat and uniform, and even if I wanted to, I couldn't go back now."

"So do I send Yoshiko back home, then?"

Tanaka remained silent.

"Shall I tell her parents, then?"

Tanaka continued to remain silent for a while, but presently spoke.

"My reasons for being in Tokyo have nothing to do with all that. Even now that I'm here it won't particularly affect our relationship . . ."

"That's what you say. But it means I can't supervise her. You can never tell when love will give in to indulgence."

"Well, that's not what I intend."

"Can you swear to it?"

"As long as I can study quietly, there'll be nothing like that."

"In that case it's hopeless!"

They sat facing each other for some considerable time, continuing this roundabout sort of conversation. Tokio proposed Tanaka's returning to Kyoto, on grounds such as hope for the future, the sacrifice of the male, the advancement of the affair, and so on. The Tanaka Hideo that now appeared before his eyes was not good-looking and tough as he had imagined, nor did he look like a genius. When Tokio first met him, there in that cheap travel lodge in Kōjimachi Sanbanchō Road, in that stuffy room hemmed in on three sides by solid walls, the first thing that struck him was the distasteful, unpleasant attitude of one raised in the Christian faith, annoyingly smug and too mature for his years. He spoke in the Kyoto accent, his complexion was fair, and he had a certain gentleness about him, but Tokio could not understand why Yoshiko had chosen someone like him from among numerous young men. What he particularly disliked about him was his formal attitude of trying to justify himself, producing all sorts of reasons for his misdeeds and shortcomings, without the least bit of simple and down-to-earth frankness. But in fact, for all his anger Tokio did feel—not immediately or spontaneously, but on seeing, in a corner of the room, the little traveling-case and the crumpled plain white *yukata*—a certain sympathy for this young man suffering and anguishing for love, and he was reminded of his own past and the dreams of youth.

Facing each other in that stuffy room, not even relaxing enough to sit with crossed legs, the two of them talked for at least an hour. Their talk finally finished without any real conclusion. "Well anyway, try and reconsider things," were the final words with which Tokio took his leave and returned home.

Somehow he felt foolish. He felt as if he'd done something stupid, and derided himself for it. He had spoken words of flattery that he did not mean, and he remembered how, to conceal the secret in his own heart, he had even promised to act as a "kind-hearted guardian" of their love. He also remembered saying he would take the trouble to introduce Tanaka to someone he knew in order to get him some minor translating work. He cursed himself for having no pride and for being too nice a chap.

He thought things over again and again. Perhaps it would be better to tell her parents. But the problem then was what attitude to adopt in doing so. As long as he felt himself to be holding the key to their love, he felt a heavy responsibility. He couldn't bring himself to make a sacrifice of his beloved's passionate love affair for the sake of his own unreasonable jealousy and his own improper feelings of love, and at the same time, as their self-styled "kind-hearted guardian," he couldn't bear to deal with them like some moralist. In yet another respect, he feared Yoshiko's being taken off home by her parents should they learn what was happening.

It was the following evening that Yoshiko came into Tokio's study and, with quiet voice and bowed head, talked about her hopes for the future. However much she reasoned with Tanaka, he would not go back. And yet if her parents were informed, she knew they would not give their consent and might even feel it better to fetch her back at once. Then again, Tanaka had taken such pains to come to Tokyo, and moreover their love wasn't just common and vulgar and she could swear that there would be no impure act or indulgence between them. Literature was a difficult path to follow, and perhaps it was impossible for someone like Tanaka to support a family by writing novels, but anyway, if they were going to share the future together, then they wanted to walk along their chosen path together. She wanted Tokio to leave things as they were for a while, letting them stay in Tokyo.

It was impossible for Tokio simply to refuse coldly this inevitable request. He did have doubts about Yoshiko's chastity during her stay at Saga, but on the other hand he also believed the explanation, and felt it very possible that the young couple's relationship might still be pure. Considered in the light of his own youthful experiences, it was by no means easy for physical love to be realized, even if there was spiritual love. And so, he said it would be all right to leave things as they were for a while, provided they were not given to indulgence, and went on to lecture her with great earnestness and sincerity on spiritual love, physical love, the relationship between love and human life, and on what an educated modern woman should properly preserve. The main points of his lecture were that the fact that people of old paid such heed to a woman's chastity was really, rather than being one of society's moral sanctions, for the benefit of safeguarding that woman's independence; that once a woman gave herself physically to a man her freedom was completely destroyed; that modern Western women well understood such things and so never got into difficulties in their affairs with the other sex, and that modern Japanese women most certainly had to do likewise. He talked with particular earnestness about the new type of woman.

Yoshiko listened with head bowed.

Tokio warmed to the occasion.

"Well, just how does he propose to live?"

"He's come a little prepared, and he'll be all right for a month or so, but . . ."

"It wouldn't be so bad if he had a good job or something . . ."

"Well, actually he was pinning all his hopes on you, Sensei, and came up to Tokyo not knowing anyone, and so he's greatly disheartened . . ."

"Well, he was just too hasty. That's what I thought when I met him the other day. There'll be problems, you know," said Tokio laughingly.

"But please, if there is anything you can do to help him . . . I'm very sorry to have to keep troubling you like this . . ." Yoshiko blushed as she sounded so helpless.

"Don't worry—things will work out somehow."

As soon as Yoshiko had gone Tokio's face adopted a troubled, sullen expression. "Is it possible for me—*me*!—to help out in this love affair?" he asked himself. "Young birds flock only with other young birds—the wings of old birds like me aren't beautiful enough to attract the young ones any more." The thought overwhelmed him, leaving him with an indescribable loneliness. "A wife and children—they call them the happiness of the home, but where's the meaning in that? There's probably some meaning for the wife, who exists for the sake of the children, but what about the husband? He has his wife taken from him by his children and his children taken from him by his wife, so how can he avoid being lonely?" He stared at the lamp.

De Maupassant's "As Strong as Death" lay open on the desk.

Two or three days later, when Tokio came home from work at the usual hour and sat in front of the *hibachi*, his wife said quietly to him:

"He came today, you know."

"Who?"

"You know . . . upstairs—Yoshiko-san's young man," his wife laughed.

"Really?"

"Yes—around one o'clock today, someone came to the porch asking if anyone was at home, and when I went to see who it was, who should it be but a round-faced young student in a splash-pattern coat and white-striped *hakama* trousers. Well, I wondered, is this yet another student with a manuscript or something, when he went and asked if Yokoyama-san lived here. Strange, I thought, and asked him his name, and it was none other than Tanaka. So that's him, is it, I thought. Horrible, isn't he?—She could have had plenty of better students than that for a boyfriend. She's really peculiar, Yoshiko-san. There's no hope for her at all if this is anything to go by."

"So what happened?"

"I suppose Yoshiko-san must have been pleased, but she looked sort of embarrassed. When I took them some tea she was sitting at her desk, and he was there too, facing her, and they suddenly stopped talking and clammed right up. I thought it a bit odd so I came straight down again. . . . But, you know, it really is strange the things young people get up to nowadays. In my day we women used to get really embarrassed if a man just looked at us!"

"Times do change, though."

"Well, however much times change, I got the idea she's just *too* modern. She's no better than some drop-out student. Well, to go by appearances that's how it seems, though I suppose in her heart she's not like that. But anyway, it really is quite extraordinary."

"Never mind all that! What happened next?"

"Yoshiko-san went out and bought some rice cakes and baked sweet potatoes—our maid Otsuru said she'd go for them, but Yoshiko-san said it was all right and went herself—and then they made a right royal feast out of them. . . . Even Otsuru had to laugh, you know. When she went up to offer them some hot water, there were the pair of them, stuffing themselves with these sweet potatoes. . . ."

Even Tokio had to laugh.

His wife continued. "They were talking for quite some time, and very loudly too. It seemed to be some sort of discussion, and Yoshiko-san was really holding her own in it."

"So when did he leave?"

"Just a little while ago."

"And Yoshiko—is she in?"

"No—she said he didn't know the way, so she went out to see him home."

Tokio frowned.

As they were having dinner Yoshiko came in through the back door. She seemed to have been hurrying and was panting for breath.

"How far did you go?" asked Tokio's wife.

"As far as Kagurazaka." With this Yoshiko turned to Tokio, gave him her usual greeting of "Welcome home," and hurried off upstairs. They thought she would come straight back down, but in fact quite a while passed with no sign of her. Tokio's wife called her several times, and she answered with a long, drawn-out "O-kay," but still didn't come down. Otsuru finally went to fetch her and presently she did come down, but she ignored the dinner set out for her and lounged near the wall-support.

"What about your dinner?" asked Tokio's wife.

"I don't feel like anything just now—I'm quite full."

"I suppose that's because you ate too many sweet potatoes!"

"Oh, now really, what a terrible thing to say!" she retorted, looking indignant.

Tokio's wife laughed. "Yoshiko-san really is a strange one."

"Why?" Yoshiko's tone was measured.

"Oh, no particular reason."

"Now really, let's stop this, shall we?" Yoshiko looked indignant again.

Tokio watched this playful bantering in silence. Naturally he was upset. Unhappiness filled his heart. Yoshiko shot a searching glance at him, and immediately realized his unpleasant mood. She promptly changed her attitude.

"Sensei, Tanaka came today."

"So I hear."

"He wanted to meet you to give you his thanks, but said he'd come again. . . . He gave his regards. . . ."

"Oh, really?"

Tokio suddenly stood up and went off into his study.

As long as Yoshiko's lover was in Tokyo, Tokio was unable to relax, despite having her upstairs under his supervision. It was absolutely impossible to prevent the two of them meeting. And naturally neither could he stop them sending letters to each other, nor say anything about Yoshiko blatantly going off with "I'm calling in at Tanaka's today so I'll be an hour or so late." Moreover, he could not now prevent Tanaka from visiting her, however unhappy he might feel about it. Before he knew it, he found that the couple had firmly accepted him as that "kind-hearted guardian" of their love.

He was constantly irritable. He had numerous manuscripts to write. He was pressed by the bookshops. He needed money. Yet he just couldn't get himself into the right settled frame of mind for getting down to writing. When he did force himself to try, he couldn't collect his thoughts. When he tried reading, he lost interest after a few pages. Every time he saw the warmth of their love his heart would burn feverishly, and he would drink, and take his anger out on his innocent wife. He would find fault with the vegetables in the evening meal and kick the table away. Sometimes he would come home past midnight, drunk. Yoshiko was not a little worried about Tokio's violent and extraordinary behavior. "It's my fault because I cause him so much trouble," she would say apologetically to his wife. And so she tried to keep her correspondence as much out of sight as possible; and to make her visits seem less frequent she would, about every third visit, take time off school and go on the sly. Tokio found out about this and became even more unhappy.

In the fields the autumn drew to a close and a cold wintry wind started up. The leaves of the ginkgo trees in the wood behind the house turned yellow and added a beautiful coloration to the evening sky. The fallen leaves, curled and crackly, tumbled along the hedge-lined lanes. The cries of the shrike filled the air. It was about this time that the young couple's love grew just too open for comfort. As supervisor, Tokio could not look upon such a state of affairs, and persuaded Yoshiko to report everything to her parents back home. He himself also sent a long letter to her father about the love affair. Even in this case Tokio tried to win Yoshiko's gratitude. He deceived himself and, telling himself he was a tragic sacrifice, he became that "kind-hearted guardian" of their love.

A number of letters arrived from the hills of Bitchū.

7

January the next year found Tokio on a geography trip to the banks of the Tone River, the boundary between the Kōzuke and Musashi regions. He had been there since the end of the previous year and was therefore anxious about his household affairs, especially Yoshiko. However, he could do nothing to avoid the duties of his work. On the second of January he had briefly returned to Tokyo, to find his second son suffering teething troubles and his wife and Yoshiko busy nursing him. According to his wife, Yoshiko seemed to have become even more indulgent in her affair. Apparently, on New Year's Eve Tanaka had, with no means of support, been unable to return to his lodgings and had spent the night on a train. His wife had also come to a vague exchange of words with Yoshiko over the two of them seeing too much of each other. When he learned of these and various other happenings, Tokio realized what a fine pass things had come to. He stayed one night and then went back to the Tone River.

It was now the night of the fifth. In the wide, open sky the moon was ringed with a halo, and its light sparkled on the center of the river like broken fragments of gold. Tokio opened a letter that lay on his desk, and lost himself in thought over its contents. The inn maid had brought the letter to him a short while before, and the writing was Yoshiko's.

Sensei,

I really must apologize. I shall certainly never forget your kindness and sympathy as long as I live, and even now, when I think of it, tears come to my eyes.

It was typical of my parents to act like that. Despite your writing to them as you did, they're too old-fashioned and stubborn to understand our feelings, and so they wouldn't give their consent no matter how much I begged them. I cried when I read my mother's letter, but I do think it would be nice if they would try to understand my feelings a little, too. I now fully realize how painful love can be. Sensei, I have made up my mind. Just as it says in the Bible that a woman leaves her parents to follow her husband, I think I shall follow Tanaka.

He has still not been able to find means of support, has already used up the money he saved, and saw the year out in the most wretched of circumstances. I can't bear any longer to see him in such a state. Even without support from home, we shall try our best to make a life together.

I'm really sorry for having caused you so much trouble. As supervisor it's understandable that you're worried. But despite your going to the trouble of writing to them to explain things on our behalf my parents just got angry and refused to listen to us, which is most heartless of them, and even if they disown me there's nothing we can do about it. They just go on and on about depravity without actually knowing what's happening, but do they suppose our love is really that insincere? And then they talk of family pedigree, but you will no doubt forgive me, Sensei, for not being the old-fashioned sort of woman who loves in accordance with her parents' convenience.

Sensei, I have made up my mind. Yesterday, there was an advertisement for girl trainees at Ueno Library, and I think I'll try applying. If we both work our hardest, I don't suppose we'll starve. I'm sorry for all the trouble I've caused to both you and your wife, but it's because I'm in your home. Please, Sensei, forgive my decision.

Yoshiko

So the power of love had plunged them into the depths of indulgence after all. Tokio felt he had to do something about it. He considered his attitude as "kind-hearted guardian," a role he had assumed in order to win Yoshiko's favor. He thought about the letter he had sent to her father in Bitchū, in which he had asked for her parents' complete support for the young couple and for consent to their relationship. He knew they would never give that consent. In fact, he had hoped rather that they would completely oppose the relationship. And sure enough, they completely opposed it. Her father had even written back that unless Yoshiko obeyed her parents they would disown her. The two lovers had received due reward for their love. Tokio had argued painstakingly on Yoshiko's behalf, writing how her love had no impure intentions, and he had asked for one of her parents to come without fail to Tokyo to sort the problem out. But they had not come, saying that it was useless to go to Tokyo since Tokio, as her supervisor, felt the way he did, whereas they themselves could definitely not bring themselves to give their approval.

Tokio now considered Yoshiko's letter.

The two lovers' situation now called for immediate action. He took sufficient warning from the bold words with which Yoshiko had expressed her wish to live with Tanaka, away from his supervision. Indeed, perhaps they had already carried the situation a stage further. Yet he was also so annoyed at how they had reduced all his good efforts on their behalf to nothing through this ungrateful and inconsiderate decision that he felt like washing his hands of the whole business.

To calm his agitated mind he went for a walk along the embankment of the river, which was bathed in a misty moonlight. Although it was a winter night, with the moon ringed by a halo, it was quite warm, and a peaceful light shone quietly from the windows of the houses below the embankment. A thick mist hung upstream, broken occasionally by the gentle sound of a passing boat. Downstream someone was calling for passage across the river. The sound of a cart crossing on the ferry filled the air for a while and then all was silent again. Tokio thought over various things as he walked along the embankment. It was the loneliness of his own home that upset him so, rather than Yoshiko's affair. His unhappiness with a life that a man in his mid-thirties should expect rather to enjoy, his unhealthy thoughts about his job, his sexual frustration. . . . He felt terribly depressed by such things. Yoshiko had been the flower and the substance of his banal existence. Her beautiful power had made flowers bloom again in the wilderness of his heart, had made rusty bells peal forth again. Thanks to Yoshiko he had been filled with a new zest for life, been resurrected. And yet now he had to resume that former existence, banal, bleak, and lonely. . . . He felt it was unfair, he felt jealous, and hot, burning tears rolled down his cheeks.

He thought seriously about Yoshiko's love, about her future life. He thought, in the light of his own experience, about the boredom, the tedium, the callousness that would come into the young couple's life after they had lived together for a while. He thought about the pitiable situation of a woman once she had given her body to a man. His heart was now filled with world-weariness, weariness of that dark power lurking in the hidden reaches of nature.

He concluded that a serious step was called for. He felt that up to now his own behavior had been very unnatural and not serious enough. That same evening he wrote with great conviction to Yoshiko's parents back in the hills of Bitchū. He enclosed Yoshiko's letter and gave a detailed account of the young couple's latest situation. Finally he added:

"I believe the time has now come for you, as her father, for me, as her teacher, and for the couple themselves to meet together to discuss this problem properly. You have your point of view as her father, Yoshiko has her freedom as herself, and I too have my opinion as her teacher, and while I appreciate that you are extremely busy, I would be obliged if you would without fail come to Tokyo. I am full of expectation."

Finishing the letter, he put it in an envelope, addressed it "Yokoyama Heizō, Niimimachi, Bitchū," put it to one side, and stared fixedly at it. This letter is the hand of fate, he thought. Making up his mind, he called for the maid and handed it to her.

He imagined the letter being taken to the hills of Bitchū a day or two later. The postman would deliver it to a large white-walled building in the middle of that little hill-encircled country town, and some fellow at the counter would take it through to the rear. The tall, whiskered gentleman would read it. . . . The force of destiny pressed ever closer.

8

Tokio returned to Tokyo on the tenth.

The following day a reply came from Bitchū stating that Yoshiko's father would leave for Tokyo in a few days' time.

It seemed that both Yoshiko and Tanaka were if anything now hoping for this, and they showed no particular sign of surprise when informed.

It was around eleven on the morning of the sixteenth that her father called at Tokio's house in Ushigome, having first found, on arrival, accommodation in Kyōbashi. It was a Sunday and Tokio was at home. Her father wore a frock coat and bowler hat, and seemed worn out after his long journey.

That day Yoshiko had gone to the doctor's. She had caught a cold a few days before, and had a slight fever. She complained of a headache. Presently she came in through the back door, looking unconcerned, and Tokio's wife hurried to speak to her:

"Yoshiko-san, Yoshiko-san! Something terribly important—your father's come!"

"Father?"

Yoshiko was, not unnaturally, a little taken aback.

She went straight upstairs but didn't come down again.

They were asking for Yoshiko in the living room, so Tokio's wife shouted up to her, but got no reply. When she went up to find out what was going on, she found Yoshiko slumped over her desk.

"Yoshiko-san."

There was no reply.

She went over to her side and spoke again. Yoshiko raised her nervous, ill-looking face.

"They're asking for you downstairs, you know."

"But how can I possibly meet Father?"

She was crying.

"Well now, isn't it a long time since you last saw him? Really, you must meet him. There's nothing to worry about—everything'll be all right."

"But . . ."

"Really, it'll be all right, so just face up to him and speak your mind. Don't worry."

Finally Yoshiko confronted her father. When she saw his familiar face, with a hint of gentleness somewhere beneath its heavy whiskers and outward dignity, she could not hold back her tears. He was a stubborn, old-fashioned father, a father who didn't understand the feelings of young people, but nevertheless he was a gentle father. Her mother was attentive in all things and often took a sympathetic interest in her, but somehow Yoshiko still preferred her father. She believed that even he would be moved when she told him of her desperate situation, when she told him in tears how sincere her love was.

"Well, Yoshi, it's been quite a time. . . . How have you been?"

"Father . . ." Yoshiko could say no more.

"Just now, on the way here . . ."—her father was addressing Tokio, who was sitting there beside them—"I think it was between Sano and Gotenba, anyway, the train broke down and we had to wait two hours. The engine exploded."

"Oh?"

"We were going at full speed, when there was this dreadful noise and then the train started going backwards, on an incline. What on earth's going on? I wondered. Well, the engine had exploded, and two firemen were killed outright. . . ."

"It must have been dangerous."

"We had to wait a good two hours for a locomotive to be brought out from Numazu and fixed on, so I had time to think about things. . . . If anything had happened to me on the way up to Tokyo because of this affair, then, Yoshi," (he turned to his daughter) "then you'd have had a hard job justifying yourself to the rest of the family!"

Yoshiko hung her head in silence.

"It was dangerous, that, but it's fortunate that you weren't injured in any way," put in Tokio.

"Well, yes."

Her father and Tokio talked for a while about the engine explosion. Suddenly, Yoshiko spoke:

"Father, is everyone all right back home?"

"Yes, everyone's in good health."

"And Mother . . .?"

"She's fine. I've been busy recently and did ask your mother to come instead, but then I thought it'd be better if I came after all."

"And my brother? How's he?"

"Yes, he's all right, too. Seems to have settled down a bit lately."

As they talked about one thing or another, lunch was served. Yoshiko went back to her room. After lunch, during the tea, Tokio continued with the issue in question:

"So there's no way you'll give your consent, then?"

"Whether I consent or not is not the problem. At the moment, even if I did temporarily agree to the two of them trying to make a go of things together, he's only twenty-two, and a third-year student at Dōshisha . . ."

"That's true, but after you've met him, perhaps then some promise for the future . . ."

"No, I can't make any promises. I haven't met him so of course I don't know for sure, but if he's the sort of man who waylays a girl student on her way back to Tokyo and gets her to dilly-dally with him, and then one morning just ups and abandons his long-standing benefactor from the Kobe Church, then I don't think there's anything to be discussed. In the letter Yoshi just sent to her mother she asked us to appreciate how badly the fellow was suffering, and to provide enough money for him to attend Waseda University, even if it meant reducing her own allowance—I just wonder if Yoshi hasn't been tricked as part of some such scheme?"

"I wouldn't say so, but . . ."

"Well, it's just a bit suspicious. No sooner has he made all these promises to Yoshiko than he suddenly gives up religion and takes a fancy to literature—that's a bit strange. And then he comes following her, and despite your advice stays on here in Tokyo even though he's struggling to find means of support. There's something behind all this, I reckon."

"It could just simply be the infatuation of love, and so it is possible to interpret things in a good sense, too."

"Well anyway, be that as it may, whether I give my consent or not is not the problem. A promise of marriage is no small matter—you have to investigate the person's social standing, consider the balance with your own standing, and you have to investigate his lineage. Then again, the person himself is most important. From what you've seen of him, you say he has ability, but . . ."

"Well no, not exactly that . . ."

"Then, as a person, just what sort of . . .?"

"I understand that your wife knows that better than I do."

"What? She doesn't seem to know him all that well; she only met him once or twice at Suma Sunday School. Anyway, in Kobe they do say that he has a certain amount of ability, and Yoshi has probably known him since her time at the Girls' Academy. They also say that when they get him to preach and to lead prayer he does things even better than adults, but . . ."

Ah, no wonder he talks so formally, as if he were delivering a public address, and uses those horrible upturned eyes—it's the expression he uses at prayer, thought Tokio. He was disturbed to think that this horrible expression could send a young woman into confusion.

"Well anyway, what are we finally going to do? Are you going to take Yoshiko-san back with you?"

"I suppose if that's how it's got to be. . . . If possible I would like to avoid taking her back, but . . . It's not the least bit pleasant when you suddenly bring your daughter back to a country town. My wife and I are involved in various charitable works back home and we hold various honorary positions, and if this sort of affair got out . . . well, we'd be in a lot of bother. So I would like if possible, as you say, to send the boy back to Kyoto, and for my daughter to stay here under your care for a year or two, but . . ."

"That would be best, I agree," said Tokio.

They talked about the couple's relationship. Tokio recounted the circumstances of the Saga incident, and the course of events afterwards, and said that their love was probably a purely spiritual one, with no impure relationship involved. Her father listened, and nodded his head, but added, "Well, surely we must also consider that there is that other type of relationship too?"

Yoshiko's father was now filled with remorse over his daughter. He remembered how they had sent her, out of country folks' vanity, to such a sophisticated school as the Kobe Girls' Academy, how they had obliged her to lead a dormitory life there, how they had let her go to Tokyo, as she had wished, to learn about novels, and how they had, because of her proneness to illness, not been very strict with her and had let her do as she pleased.

An hour later Tanaka entered the room, having been specially sent for. Yoshiko was there too, listening to the conversation with bowed head. From the outset her father didn't take to Tanaka. The figure before his eyes, this student figure with white-striped *hakama* trousers and dark blue, splash-pattern coat, filled him with feelings of contempt and hatred. His feeling of hatred towards this man who had taken away his property was very similar to Tokio's feeling earlier when he had met him in his lodgings.

Tanaka very properly folded the creases of his *hakama* and sat stiffly, staring at the mat a few feet in front of him. He showed, rather than compliance, an attitude of defiance. He seemed somehow just a bit *too* stiff, as though he had a certain right to act freely with Yoshiko.

The conversation was serious and intense. Yoshiko's father didn't go so far as to condemn Tanaka's impudence openly, but would occasionally put a bitter sarcasm into his words. Tokio also spoke at first, but eventually Yoshiko's father and Tanaka took over. Her father was a member of the prefectural council, so his manner of speech was clever and convincing. Even Tanaka, accustomed as he was to public speaking, was occasionally forced into silence. The problem of consent or otherwise was raised, but dismissed as a subject not in need of consideration for the moment, and the immediate question of Tanaka's return to Kyoto was taken up instead.

For the two lovers, and for Tanaka in particular, this separation seemed a bitter matter. He asserted strongly that it was impossible for him to return for several reasons: he was no longer qualified for religion, he had neither house nor home to return to, and now, after enduring abject circumstances for the last few months, he was at last beginning to see some hope for the future here in Tokyo, and couldn't bring himself to give up now.

Yoshiko's father spoke with earnest persuasiveness.

"You say that you can't go back to Kyoto any more, and I'm sure that's true. But things are as they are. If you love a girl, then I don't suppose it's asking too much to sacrifice yourself for her. If you can't go back to Kyoto, then go back to your home in the country. Even if, as you say, you won't be able to accomplish your aims if you go back, I still say that's best. That's to say, even if those aims have to be sacrificed too, then that can't be helped."

Tanaka looked at the floor and said nothing. He didn't seem prepared to agree just like that.

Tokio had been listening quietly, but since Tanaka was being so stubborn he suddenly cut in:

"I've been listening. Don't you understand what Yokoyama-san has been saying? He's not saying anything about your misdeeds, nor about your impudence, neither is he saying that if you're still bound to each other in the future, he will necessarily refuse his consent. You're still young, and Yoshiko-san too is right in the middle of her studies, so the two of you should leave this affair in abeyance for a while and see what the future brings —this is what he's saying. Don't you understand? At the present moment, there's no way the two of you can be left together. One of you will have to leave Tokyo, and since you came here after Yoshiko it's only right that that person be you."

"I quite understand," answered Tanaka. "I'm entirely to blame, so I must be the one to leave. Sensei, you've just said that it doesn't necessarily mean that our love won't be given approval, but I still can't find such satisfaction in what Yokoyama-sama has been saying."

"What do you mean?" asked Tokio.

"I suppose you mean it's unsatisfying not to receive a definite promise," cut in Yoshiko's father, "but I've just explained about that. At the present moment I can neither consent nor refuse. You're still in the middle of your studies and can't be independent, so I just can't have any confidence in what you say about the two of you making your way in the world together. Therefore I think it's best for both of you to study for a few years. If you're serious, then you must understand what I've been saying. I suppose you're also dissatisfied because you think that I'm just fooling you for now and that I intend to marry off Yoshi to someone else. However, I swear before God—and I say it also before Sensei here—that I will not marry off Yoshi for three years. As Jacob believed, sinners can but await that final judgment, and therefore I can't go so far as to promise Yoshi to you—I can't agree at present, because I don't believe that at present this affair accords with the Will of God. We can't tell at the moment whether, in three years from now, it will then accord with his Will or not, but if you're truly sincere and honest in your heart, then I'm sure that it will."

"You see how understanding Yokoyama-san is?" Tokio followed up. "He'll wait three years for your sake. That really is the greatest favor you could wish for, to be told you'll be given three years, enough to prove your dependability. Though no one is under any obligation to discuss anything seriously with someone who's seduced his daughter, and you would've had no cause for complaint in the least if he'd taken Yoshiko straight back home without further ado, Yokoyama-san has said that if you wait three years, until your sincerity becomes clear, then he will not marry Yoshiko to anyone else. Those are really kind words to you, kinder even than if he actually gave his consent. Don't you understand this?"

Tanaka looked down at the floor and, just when everyone expected him to put on a frown, tears started to roll down his cheeks.

The company fell silent, as if cold water had been thrown over them.

Tanaka wiped away his flood of tears with his hand. Tokio thought it the right moment to speak:

"Well, please give your answer."

"I don't care what happens to me! Let me be swallowed up in the countryside, then, I don't care!"

He wiped his tears away again.

"Now that won't do—it's meaningless if you say it so antagonistically. The whole point of this meeting is for everyone to say what they really feel and to bring about a settlement satisfactory to all. If you find it so absolutely unpleasant to go back to the country, then there's nothing else for it but to send Yoshiko back," said Tokio.

"Isn't it possible for the two of us to be together in Tokyo?"

"Impossible! Impossible from the point of view of supervision! Impossible from the point of view of the future of both of you!"

"In that case I don't care if I'm swallowed up in the country."

"No, I'll be the one that goes back!" Yoshiko's voice trembled with tears. "I'm a woman . . . a woman. If you alone make a success of things, then it doesn't matter about me being lost in oblivion in the country—I'll go back."

The company sank into silence again.

Presently Tokio spoke, in a different tone.

"Anyway, just why is it that you can't go back to Kyoto? Wouldn't it be all right if you were just to explain everything to your benefactor in Kobe, apologize for your indiscretion, and then go back to Dōshisha? Just because Yoshiko-san hopes to make a go of literature, it doesn't mean that you have to as well. What about you becoming a religious teacher, a theologian, or a minister?"

"I can no longer enter the service of the church. I'm just not that special sort of person who can preach to people . . . But what's particularly upsetting is that after three months of hardship I've finally managed to open up a path for the future, thanks to the kind help of a friend, so I just couldn't bear to go back to the nothingness of the countryside."

The three talked on again. Finally the conversation came to a vague sort of end. Tanaka left, saying he would talk things over with his friend that evening and come back with a definite answer, either the next day or the day after. It was now four o'clock, the winter's day was drawing to a close, and a patch of light that had, up till then, lit up the corner of the room, now faded quickly away.

Just Tokio and Yoshiko's father were left in the room.

"He's a wishy-washy sort of fellow." Her father made the remark almost casually.

"He's formal, and never gets to the point. It'd be better if he opened up a bit more and spoke frankly . . ."

"Yes, but somehow that sort of thing just doesn't go down with Chūgoku people—they've got very little caliber, and try to worm their way around you. People from this Kantō area and up north in Tōhoku are completely different in this respect. Bad is bad and good is good—they say what's really in their mind, which is how it should be. It just won't do, resorting to petty little tricks like that weeping."

"Yes, he certainly does seem to be a bit like that, doesn't he?"

"You just watch—tomorrow he's bound to find some reason why he can't agree, and why he can't go back to Kyoto."

Suddenly Tokio was seized with suspicion about the couple's relationship, a suspicion aroused by Tanaka's impassioned persistence and by that attitude of his as though he had a right to make Yoshiko his own property.

"So what sort of views do you have about a physical relationship between them?" he asked her father.

"Well, I think we probably have to assume that there *is* a physical relationship."

"At this stage I do think we should make sure about this. Shouldn't we get Yoshiko-san to tell us exactly what happened at Saga? She says they fell in love only *after* Saga, so there should be letters to prove this."

"Well, I don't really think we need go quite that far . . ."

Even though he believed there was a physical relationship, her father seemed to fear this turning out to be a definite fact.

Unfortunately, at that moment Yoshiko came into the room with some tea.

As she was leaving Tokio asked her to show them the old letters she no doubt had from around that time, as these would prove her purity.

Yoshiko suddenly blushed. From her expression and attitude she was clearly greatly embarrassed.

"I've just burned all those old letters," she said quietly.

"Burned them?"

"Yes." She hung her head.

"Burned them? I can't believe that!"

Yoshiko's face grew even redder. Tokio couldn't stop himself from getting furious. The facts struck him with a terrible force.

He stood up and went to the toilet. He was angry and upset, his mind in a daze. He was staggered by the thought that he had been deceived.

When he came out of the toilet he found Yoshiko standing there outside the sliding-door, looking nervous.

"Sensei, really, I've burned them."

"And now tell me a lie, why don't you!" snapped Tokio. Violently slamming shut the sliding-door, he went back into the room.

9

Yoshiko's father went back to his inn after staying for dinner. That night, Tokio's distress was extreme. The thought that he had been deceived made his anger boil. He was furious to think how he had done his serious best to help their love, yet all the while having Yoshiko taken from him body and soul by some student. If things had reached that stage—if she had given up her body to Tanaka—then there was no need for him to respect her chastity as a virgin. It would be in order for him, too, to make a bold move and satisfy his sexual desire. Such thoughts led him to look upon Yoshiko, whom he had formerly worshiped as heavenly, as some sort of prostitute, whose beautiful attitude and expressions, let alone her body, were nothing but contemptible. In such terrible torment, he hardly slept at all that night. All sorts of feelings passed through his heart like dark clouds. Placing his hands on that troubled heart, Tokio thought things over. Perhaps he should . . . Well, for a start it was a fact that she was now soiled, having given her body to a man. Should he simply send Tanaka back to Kyoto, and then exploit her weakness to make her his own? This prompted all sorts of thoughts. What if he were to creep silently upstairs while Yoshiko was asleep there, and then pour out his love for her? Perhaps she would hold herself very prim and proper and lecture him. Perhaps she would call out for help. And yet, perhaps she would understand his pressing passion and sacrifice herself to him. And if she did sacrifice herself to him, what then the following morning? Of course, in the bright light of day they would be unable to face each other. She would stay in bed, ignoring breakfast. He called to mind a short story of de Maupassant's, "The Father." He remembered with particular poignancy the bit about the girl giving her body to the man and then sobbing her heart out afterwards. At such thoughts, however, a force arose within him to oppose this dark imagining, and a sharp conflict followed. Torment followed torment, anguish followed anguish, and he tossed and turned endlessly, hearing the clock strike two, then three.

Undoubtedly Yoshiko was in great distress too. She looked ill when she got up the next morning. She hardly touched her breakfast. She seemed to be trying to avoid meeting Tokio's eyes. Her distress appeared to be not so much that her secret was known as that she realized she had done wrong in trying to hide things. That afternoon she said she'd just like to go out for a while, but Tokio, who had not gone to work, wouldn't allow it. Thus the whole day passed. No answer came from Tanaka.

Yoshiko ate neither lunch nor dinner, saying she didn't feel like eating. A gloomy atmosphere filled the house. Tokio's wife was perplexed at her husband's out-of-sorts mood and Yoshiko's depression. After all, the previous day's talk seemed to have gone so smoothly. . . . She took Yoshiko some food upstairs, thinking she must be terribly hungry as she'd eaten so little. Tokio was spending the miserable twilight hours drinking saké, a sour look on his face. Presently his wife came down. Tokio asked her what Yoshiko had been doing, and it turned out she had been sitting there in the dark at her desk, bent over a letter she had started to write. Letter? A letter to whom? Tokio grew exasperated. He dashed noisily off upstairs, intending to warn her against writing such a letter.

"Sensei, please, for Heaven's sake . . ."

She sounded as if she were praying as she spoke.

She was still bent over her desk.

"Sensei, for Heaven's sake, please, just wait a little longer. I'm writing everything down in this letter for you."

Tokio went back downstairs. Presently, at his wife's directions, the maid went upstairs to light the lamp, and when she came down she was carrying a letter, which she gave to Tokio.

He read it eagerly:

Sensei,

I am a fallen student. I have used your kindness and deceived you. I think my misdeed is so terrible I can never be forgiven however much I apologize. Sensei, please have pity on me as a weak being. I have failed to discharge my duties as a new Meiji-era woman, such as you taught me about. After all, I am an old-fashioned woman without the courage to put the new philosophy into action. I had talked things over with Tanaka and we'd decided that at all costs we would not reveal this one thing. What's done was done, but we pledged to maintain a pure love in the future. But then when I think that all your troubles are due to my shortcomings I just can't rest easy. I've been worried about this all day long. Please, Sensei, have pity on this poor girl. I have no one to turn to but you.

Yoshiko

Tokio felt as if he were about to be swallowed by the earth at his feet. He stood up, letter in hand. His mind was too upset to interpret Yoshiko's reason for daring to make this confession —her attitude of confessing everything and then asking for help. He climbed noisily up the stairs, and sat solemnly beside the desk over which Yoshiko was still bent.

"Well, with things as they are now, I can no longer do anything. I'll give this letter back to you, and I promise I won't say anything about it to anyone. At least, your having trusted me as your teacher is nothing to be ashamed of as a new Meiji woman. But with things as they are now, it's only right for you to go back home. Let's go straight away this evening to your father and tell him everything, so that you can return home as soon as possible—that's best."

And so, after something to eat, they got ready and left the house. Yoshiko was no doubt full of various complaints and grievances, as well as sadness, but she could not disobey Tokio's solemn command. They got on the streetcar at Ichigaya. They sat next to each other, but didn't exchange a single word. Getting off at Yamashitamon, they went to the inn at Kyōbashi, where, fortunately, Yoshiko's father was in his room. They told him everything. He didn't get particularly angry. It seemed that he just wanted, as much as possible, to avoid accompanying Yoshiko back home, but there was nothing else for it. Yoshiko's only emotion appeared to be one merely of being fed up with the irony of fate. Tokio asked if it were not possible for him to continue to look after her, if her parents decided to abandon her, but her father wouldn't allow this as things stood, though he wasn't sure what might happen if Yoshiko herself were to abandon her parents. Yoshiko herself didn't seem resolved to refuse to return home to the point of forsaking her parents, and so Tokio gave her over to her father's care and went back home.

10

The following morning Tanaka called on Tokio. Unaware of what had now been settled, he attempted to explain in detail how his own circumstances were not conducive to his returning home—that is, lovers who had given body and soul to each other could just not bear to be parted, Tokio felt to be his meaning.

A triumphant look spread over Tokio's face.

"Well, the problem has now been solved. Yoshiko told me everything. I know now how the pair of you had been deceiving me. It was some 'pure' love, wasn't it!?"

Tanaka's expression suddenly changed. Shame, exasperation, and a terrible feeling of despair filled his heart. He didn't know what to say.

"There's nothing that can be done about it now," Tokio continued. "I can have nothing more to do with this affair. In fact, I'm now fed up with it. I've given Yoshiko back over to her father's supervision."

Tanaka sat in silence. His ill-looking face could clearly be seen to twitch nervously. Suddenly, he took his leave with a bow, as though he could no longer bear being there in such a situation.

Yoshiko and her father came at about ten that morning. They were going home that same evening on the six o'clock Kobe express and would take only her personal effects, with most of the luggage being sent on afterwards. Yoshiko went up to her room to sort out her luggage.

Tokio was upset, but nevertheless more cheerful than before. He felt indescribably miserable at the thought that he could no longer look upon her beautiful expressions, soon to be separated from him by more than five hundred miles of hills and rivers, but on the other hand it was at least pleasing to have taken her from his rival in love and delivered her to her father. And so it was in quite a cheerful manner that Tokio chatted with her father. The latter was, as is often the case with country gentlemen, very fond of art, particularly of the paintings of Sesshū,

Ōkyo, and Yōsai and the scrolls of San'yō, Chikuden, Kaioku, and Sazan, and he had himself a considerable collection of their masterpieces. The conversation turned naturally in that direction, and for a while the room was filled with banal talk of art.

Tanaka arrived, saying he wanted to speak to Tokio. They met in the eight-mat room, the partition to the six-mat room being closed. Yoshiko's father was in that six-mat room. Yoshiko herself was in her room upstairs.

"Is her father going back home, then?"

"It looks like it, yes."

"With Yoshi-san?"

"Looks that way."

"Could you please possibly tell me what time they'll be leaving?"

"Well, in the present situation, I don't think I can."

"In that case, do you think I could be allowed to see Yoshi-san, just for a moment?"

"No, I really don't think so."

"Well, where is her father staying, then? I'd just like to know that."

"I don't know whether I should really even tell you that."

Tanaka could make no headway. After sitting for a while in silence, he took his leave with a bow.

Presently lunch was brought into the eight-mat room. As this was a farewell, Tokio's wife had carefully prepared something a little special. Tokio was also hoping to have the three of them eat together as a sort of farewell gathering. Yoshiko, however, said she didn't want to eat. Tokio's wife pleaded with her, but she wouldn't come down. Tokio himself went upstairs.

The room was dark, with just one window open to the east. Books and magazines and clothes and waist-sashes and bottles and traveling-cases and trunks were all over the floor, leaving hardly anywhere to walk, and a strong smell of dust struck the nostrils. In the middle of all this Yoshiko was sorting out her luggage, tears in her eyes. What misery and gloom compared with that time three years ago when she had come up to Tokyo with a heart full of youthful hope. It was terribly sad to think that her fate was to return to the country without having produced a single memorable work.

"There's some lunch specially prepared for you, so how about trying to eat? It'll be quite some time before we get the chance to eat together again."

"Sensei—"

Yoshiko burst into tears.

Tokio was moved too. Had he fully discharged his duty as her teacher? He searched his heart scrupulously. He too was miserable enough to want to cry. Here in a dark room among a jumble of baggage and books, his beloved in tears over having to part for home . . . and he had no words of comfort to offer.

At three in the afternoon three carriages arrived. The drivers carried the traveling-cases and the Chinese trunk and the bags from the porch, where they had been placed, and loaded them into the carriages. Yoshiko wore a purple-brown coat, with a white ribbon in her hair, and her eyes were swollen with crying. She took firm hold of the hand of Tokio's wife, who had come out to see them off.

"Well, goodbye then . . . I'll be back again, I'll definitely be back . . . I just have to come back . . ."

"Yes, please, certainly, you must come back, say in a year or so."

Tokio's wife firmly returned the handshake. Tears filled her eyes. With a woman's weakness, her heart was filled with sympathy.

The carriages set off through the residential suburb of Ushigome, somewhat chilly in the winter's day, with Yoshiko's father in the first one, then Yoshiko, then finally Tokio. Tokio's wife and the maid stayed and watched the carriages disappear. The neighbor's wife was behind them watching too, wondering what this sudden departure could be. And behind her, at a corner of the lane, stood a man wearing a brown hat. Yoshiko looked back several times.

As the carriages turned from Kōjimachi Road towards Hibiya, Tokio fell to thinking about present-day girl students. There was Yoshiko in the carriage in front of his, with her high, right-up-with-the-fashion hairstyle, her white ribbon and her rather slouched figure, being taken back home with the baggage by her father, under such circumstances—there were probably lots of other girl students in similar positions. Even the strong-willed Yoshiko, then, had met this fate. There was good reason for the educationalists' constant talk of the female problem. He thought about her father's unhappiness, about Yoshiko's tears, about his own bleak life. There were passers-by who looked meaningfully at this passing spectacle of a flower-like girl student and her pile of baggage, protected by her father and another middle-aged man.

They arrived at the inn in Kyōbashi, gathered the baggage together, and paid the bill. It was in this same inn that Yoshiko and her father had stayed three years before, when they had first come up to Tokyo, and Tokio had visited them there. They were, all three of them, filled with much emotion as they compared that time with the present. Yet they all kept their feelings to themselves.

At five o'clock they went to Shinbashi Station and entered the second-class waiting room.

Confusion upon confusion, crowds upon crowds. The minds of the travelers and those who had come to see them off were filled with restless confusion, and the noise reverberating around the room echoed in their hearts. The station was enveloped in a whirlwind of sadness, of joy, of curiosity. At every moment groups of people would arrive, and in particular there seemed to be a lot of passengers for the six o'clock Kobe express. The second-class waiting room soon became a scene of utter chaos. Tokio bought two packages of sandwiches from the stall upstairs and handed them to Yoshiko. He bought their tickets and a platform ticket for himself. He got a check for their luggage. Now all they had to do was wait.

All three were wondering if Tanaka might not be in the crowd. However, they couldn't see him.

A bell rang. The crowd surged towards the ticket-barrier. Everyone was eager to board at once, everyone impatient, and the confusion was considerable. The three of them just managed to get through and found themselves out on the spacious platform. Yoshiko and her father got into the nearest second-class compartment.

Other passengers flooded in after them. There was a merchant, prepared to sleep through the long trip. An army captain, probably returning to Kure. A group of women, gossiping away in broad Osaka dialect. Yoshiko's father spread a white blanket on the seat, placed his little bag beside it, and sat down with

Yoshiko. The electric light in the carriage made Yoshiko's white face stand out like an engraving. Her father came to the window, repeatedly expressed his thanks to Tokio for all his kindness, and asked him to attend to those things still remaining. Tokio stood there next to the window, in his outfit of brown trilby hat and triple-crested, silk *haori* coat.

The time for the train's departure drew near. Tokio thought about their trip, about Yoshiko's future. If he had not had a wife, of course he would certainly have married Yoshiko himself. And she would probably have been glad to be his wife. She would have comforted his life of ideals, his life of literature, the insufferable torment of his literary creativity. She would probably have been able to save his now bleak heart. He remembered her words to his wife: "Why couldn't I too have been born a little earlier, in your time? It would've been interesting if I had. . . ." Was he then fated never to make Yoshiko his wife? Would there never come a time when he would call her father his father-in-law? Life was long, and fate had strange powers. The fact that she was not a virgin—that she had lost her chastity—might actually be a help towards her becoming his wife, the wife of a man getting on in years and with many children. Fate, life . . . he remembered Turgenev's *Punin and Baburin*, and now realized the significance of the life depicted by that outstanding Russian writer.

Behind Tokio was a crowd of people, come to see passengers off. There at the back, standing next to a pillar, was a man in an old trilby hat, who must have arrived without anyone noticing at the time. Yoshiko now noticed him and her heart raced. Her father was not at all pleased. Tokio, however, standing there lost in his daydreams, had not the faintest suspicion that this man was there behind him.

The guard blew his whistle.

The train started to move.

11

A lonely, bleak existence visited Tokio's home again. It depressed him to hear his wife shouting at the children all the time.

Life fell into the old rut of three years before.

Five days later a letter arrived from Yoshiko. It was not in her usual relaxed, conversational style, but stiff and formal:

I wish to inform you that we arrived safely last night and therefore hope you will no longer be worried. I hope that you will accept my sincerest aplogies for having occasioned you so much trouble when you were so busy. I really cannot apologize enough, and in fact I wanted to thank you and to apologize to you in person, but I hope you will understand how I was too upset to do so even when we finally parted. Each time I go to the glass door here at home I imagine that train window at Shinbashi, and can clearly picture that brown-hatted figure standing on the other side. Snow has fallen in this region from the hills to the north, and along the thirty or more miles of mountain road from Tatai I could think only sad thoughts, being greatly moved as I recalled Issa's* famous haiku, "Is this my old house, buried deep in the snow here, or merely a drift?" Father wished to send a letter of thanks to you, but today is market-day and he is very busy, and he asked to be forgiven for expressing his thanks through me. There is much more I would like to tell you, but I am feeling very upset and so today I shall conclude this letter at this point.

Tokio thought about those thirty miles of mountain road deep in snow, and about that country town there in the hills, also buried in snow. He went upstairs to Yoshiko's room, which was still as she had left it the day of her departure. Overcome with nostalgia and longing, he wanted to recall something of her from those of her things that were left behind. That day the wind from Musashi Plain was blowing fiercely, and the ancient trees behind the house were roaring frighteningly, like ocean breakers. When he opened one of the rain shutters of the window facing east, as on the day of her departure, the light came flooding in. The desk, the bookcase, the bottle, the lipstick-tray, all were there just as before, just as if she had simply gone off to school as usual. He opened a drawer of her desk. An old oil-smeared ribbon had been thrown in there. He picked it up and sniffed it. Presently he stood up and opened the sliding partition. Three large wicker traveling-cases, tied with cord, were waiting to be

* 1763–1827, a renowned master of the seventeen-syllable haiku.

sent off, and beyond them in a pile lay the bedding that Yoshiko normally used—a mattress of light green arabesque design, and a quilt of the same pattern, with thick cotton padding. Tokio drew them out. The familiar smell of a woman's oil and sweat excited him beyond words. The velvet edging of the quilt was noticeably dirty, and Tokio pressed his face to it, immersing himself in that familiar female smell.

All at once he was stricken with desire, with sadness, with despair. He spread out the mattress, lay the quilt out on it, and wept as he buried his face against the cold, stained, velvet edging.

The room was gloomy, and outside the wind was raging.

(September 1907)

The End of Jūemon

1

THERE were some half dozen people in the group and, for some reason or other, the conversation chanced to turn to the works of the Russian novelist I. S. Turgenev. Various interesting opinions emerged about Rudin's fate, Bazarov's character, and so forth, but then one of the men sat excitedly forward in his chair and said, "All this talk about Turgenev has reminded me that I once met a character out in the country who could have come straight from the pages of *A Sportsman's Diary*. It was a really moving experience. He was just like the Russian peasants we find in Turgenev's works, and I can honestly say that in my limited experience I've never had such an obvious revelation of nature's strength and presence. You know, if we look around us, there are quite a few Andrei Kolosovs and Chertopkhanovs here in Japan too." He started to tell his story. . . .

2

Well, I'll begin at the very beginning. It started when I was sixteen and first came up to Tokyo to continue my studies, so it's quite an old story. Anyway, in those days there was a small private school in Kōjimachi, in Nakarokubanchō, called the Sokusei Gakkan—the Intensive Training College. It was a really insignificant school like you often see nowadays in the streets around Hongō and Kanda, a sort of academic general store offering English, German, math, Chinese classics, Japanese—largely the required subjects for candidates taking examinations for the army officers' schools and the military preparatory schools. In fact, only two years after I was there it folded up, and some Supreme Court judge or other renovated the place and made it into a nice house for himself. But the old-fashioned gate's still there, and whenever I think how I used to swagger proudly in through it in my old student-style short *hakama* I get really nostalgic, and all sorts of memories of those days come flooding back. In case you wonder how I came to be going there, well, I wanted to enter the army and my elder brother—who was a terrible moaner—was always after me to stop lazing around and study for a few years at a regular school. Anyone was capable of that, he said, and told me that I wasn't a real man unless I got down to some study right away and got into a military preparatory school within a year or so. So with him on my back like that I deliberately didn't go into the Seijō Gakkō—the Citadel School —in Ichigaya, which in those days was *the* proper place for army candidates, but instead, attracted by the name Sokusei—Intensive Training—I enrolled at that insignificant college. When I think about it now it seems a bit silly, but I was quite impressed by my brother going on about the "Oriental hero," and with this in mind I really got down to work, determined to get into a military preparatory school the following year.

I'll never forget entering the school and starting elementary algebra with a math teacher with a birthmark on his cheek, nor forget two new students who entered a few days later. One of them was a tall, long-haired fellow with a pale complexion and slight pockmarks. He looked sort of rustic, but he had a strange kind of appeal in those gentle eyes of his, and I took to him straightaway. The other fellow was the complete opposite. He was short and thin, with a darkish complexion. His expressions showed only the simplest of thoughts, and his eyes tended to be downcast and didn't give the least suggestion of any imagination. Both these students wore dreadful black woolen scarves with cotton woven in, and old black bowlers that were way behind the times—I see bowlers are still out of fashion with students today, by the way. As well as that they spoke with broad country accents that no one could understand, and the other students all used to collapse in laughter when they heard the pair of them discussing something out loud.

"Itto ezu e dekku," was how they would pronounce "It is a dog" in their *National Readers*, with which they seemed to have all sorts of problems. One day, at the teacher's request, they started to read "The cat ran" . . . "Zū ketto ran."

The whole class burst out laughing.

Their reading of Chinese was also extremely funny. At the time we were reading Han'yu's address to the prime minister in our *Standard Readers*, but they found it impossible to read without adopting this strange sort of incantation, and every time they started the whole class would erupt.

One day, after finishing classes, I was hurrying out through the gate when ahead of me I spotted those two country boys talking very intimately about something and looking for all the world as if they were brothers as they walked along.

I thought about greeting them, but in the end I went on past without saying anything.

The next day too they were walking together, looking very friendly.

Again I didn't say anything to them.

The next day was the same.

Yet again the following day, they were walking ahead talking very intimately about something. I wondered where they were going, and if it wasn't perhaps the same way as I was going myself.

"Where are you off to?" I suddenly asked.

They greeted me politely before replying to my question.

"Us? We're in Yotsuya, in Shiochō," said the taller one rather hesitantly.

"I'm going towards Yotsuya myself!" I said.

At the time I was living in Ushigome, in Tomihisachō, so I had to pass through Shiochō on my way home. In fact, I often used to go out for an evening stroll along the broad streets of Yotsuya, and I was very familiar with the sights of the Shiochō area. There was a toy shop, next door to which was a sugar shop where there was a very nice girl, beyond was a confectioner's called Matsukaze-tei, a blacksmith's, a saké shop, while in front was an impressive new postal telegraph office.

A few yards further on I asked:

"Shiochō, you say? I know it well. Whereabouts exactly in Shiochō?"

"It's . . . well, we board on the second floor of a public bath."

"A bathhouse? That one on the corner with the willows?"

"Yes, that's the one."

"In that case, I've been in there myself. Isn't the lady there on the short side, and always smiling?"

"You really do know the place well!"

They seemed surprised.

"Well, it's the road I always go back along, so how about if we went back together from now on?"

"Fine, if you'd like to . . ." answered the shorter one.

We walked on a few more yards in silence.

"Which part of the country do you two come from, then?"

"Which part do we come from? We come from Shinano."

"Whereabouts in Shinano?"

"From near Nagano."

"When did you come up to Tokyo?"

"We came last December, but being complete strangers from the hill-country we've had a lot of problems."

"Is the bathhouse owner a relative?"

"He's not a relative, but he's from our village, and our parents all gave him a lot of help in the past when he was in financial difficulties back home. He left the village twenty years ago in the middle of the night, but he's made a tidy fortune for himself here, and back home they don't speak too badly of him now— fate's a funny thing."

From this point on I got to know them really well, and as I got to talk to them more I discovered all sorts of really fine characteristics in them. The taller one had talents you wouldn't expect in a country boy, while the shorter one had the same interest as myself in writing Chinese poetry. After walking home with them for a month I felt as though I'd known them for ten years. We talked about our thoughts for the future, about our aims, and we became so friendly that, if by some chance we were unable to walk back together, I would feel terribly lonely. Time and time again, while walking through the dust of the Yotsuya Approach, I would turn to the two of them and encourage their military aspirations, or explain the importance of studying Chinese. I greatly surprised them by reading out some difficult Chinese passages which I was then learning from my brother and by composing some impromptu Chinese verses.

The shorter one in particular, whose name was Yamagata
Kōzaburō, realized that I was quite good at Chinese poetry and
was happy to show me some of his own verses, often giving me
an account of the snow scenes in their village. How my imaginative young mind could picture those snowy village scenes!
This is what they told me . . .

Their village was hidden away in the mountains a dozen or
so miles from Nagano, and the scenery was so beautiful it was
simply beyond the imagination of a city-dweller. In fact, during
classes, Yamagata once opened his old notebook and showed
me a rather amateurish sketch he'd made of the village. He
pointed out his own house, his friend Sugiyama's house, the
village shrine in a thickly wooded spot, and the village temple,
An'yōji, a little to the right in the same wooded spot. He told
me how they'd left the village secretly—their parents hadn't
agreed to it, but they just couldn't hold back the ambitions of
youth—on the night of the thirteenth of December, with the
moon shining crisply and beautifully on the hard frozen surface
of snow that lay some four or five feet deep. What an indescribable scene! He'd made an arrangement with Sugiyama during
the day, and they met up beyond the shrine, then set off together
on foot. So that they couldn't be stopped by anyone following
them they had somehow to get to Nagano during the night and
then get the first train the next morning. And so they pressed on.
But naturally, when they got out of sight of the village they felt
a few misgivings. Their parents would be greatly shocked. Perhaps they hadn't really had to go to such desperate lengths.
Perhaps, if they were to ask with more conviction, their parents
would let them go to Tokyo after all . . .

After hearing this sort of thing my imagination really spread
its wings, my thoughts turned excitedly towards that quiet little
village in the mountains, and I felt I absolutely had to visit it.
When I asked about the place in more detail they told me there
was a crystal-clear mountain river there called the Otani, with
numerous water mills along its banks. In spring there were
azaleas, in summer sunflowers, in autumn pampas grass—it had
more variety than any picture could ever have. And before the
snow, the buckwheat came into full bloom all through the dry
fields on the hillsides, while the autumn wind blew lonely overhead—what marvelous poetry I could make of such scenes, they

told me. What an enchanted place it must be! Mountain upon mountain, crystal-clear waters, a rugged and simple man of the soil heading along the path for home and shouldering his plow-spade, casting shadows in the evening sun . . . When I pictured scenes like this my imagination filled in all the other details, and I could see before me a fairyland from a European story-book.

3

Before long I started visiting their lodgings above the bathhouse in Shiochō. The upstairs consisted of two twelve-mat rooms. In the righthand corner of the room at the top of the stairs was a bright, oblong, zelkova brazier, with two rusting Nanbu kettles on the fire-irons, and behind it a firmly locked paulownia chest-of-drawers stood in obvious ostentation. The general decor of the place was very much in keeping with the tastes of an uncultured merchant, and I would always find, sitting cross-legged in front of the brazier, a fat man of about fifty, with a large head and pockmarked face and wearing a broadly striped dressing-gown, who would invariably greet me politely and jovially. He was the owner, that is to say the former good-for-nothing who had taken off from the village. Twenty years ago he hadn't been able to find a place for himself anywhere in the village but, fate being the unknown thing it is, at twenty-seven he had left secretly during the night for Tokyo, worked pa-tiently as a noodle-dealer's delivery man, a pawnbroker's assist-ant, and a bathhouse attendant, had finally managed to make himself the owner of a bathhouse, put aside a fortune of a few thousand, and was now the sort of man you could probably justly call respectable. He did his best to help fellow villagers, so there were a lot of despairing "expatriates" who came to Tokyo relying on him for support, and not a few who were hoping to work their way up likewise from bathhouse attendant to bath-house owner. Their home region in Shinano bordered on distant Echigo, so it was particularly rich in the spirit of *dekasegi*—leaving your remote country home to find work elsewhere. In-deed, there had been many examples of those who had succeeded in this adventure and returned home with honor, so there had always been others ready and willing to head for the cities, just like their little country streams headed for the ocean; some because they couldn't satisfy their aims in their village, some because they couldn't bear to succumb to poverty, some because they had been reduced to reckless desperation, and others simply because they were filled with the ambitions of youth. What spirit of adventure those country people possessed!

Anyway, I became increasingly friendly with those two country boys and ended up visiting their lodgings almost every day. As spring advanced and the season arrived for enjoying an evening stroll, I would often walk along the broad streets of Yotsuya and would invariably call in on my way back at that bathhouse among the willows. At such times I would hear, floating down from above, the delightful sound of a flute such as you hear at a country procession, the moon would cast its liquid light across the clothes-drying balcony, and there in the bright moonlight would be the sharply silhouetted figure of little Yamagata.

"Hey! Yamagata-kun!" I would call from below.

The flute would abruptly stop.

"Who is it?" he would ask in his country accent.

"It's Tomiyama!"

"Ah, Tomiyama-kun! Come on up!"

That balcony! Up there, bathed in moonlight, how we talked on those beautiful nights! Yamagata would tell me how that same moon would now be shining over Mount Mitsumine near his village and how, down in the village square by the shrine, the young people would be flirting happily in its light. He would describe the darkness of Mount Madarao, the lights spilling faintly from the village houses, and how often he would tell me of his terrible homesickness, how he wanted so much to go back. How I myself could also picture that quiet mountain village!

About six months later the pair of them introduced me to another young man who had also "deserted" the village. He was about twenty-one or two, with a round face and hair sweeping over his forehead, and he was the son of a very wealthy family there. I heard all about his family from Sugiyama, however, and I didn't become as friendly with him as I had with the other two. According to what Sugiyama told me, he was called Nemoto Kōsuke, and his family, despite now priding itself on being the richest in the village, was not well regarded, and in fact until his father's generation had been so poor that people wouldn't readily associate with them. His father, Sannosuke, had blatantly stolen the shrine offertories and was such a rascal that the village elders had considered putting an end to the harm he was always causing the village by wrapping him in rush-matting and throwing him into the Chikuma River. Then he was given a friendly lecture by an old villager called Yamada, himself something of a rags-to-riches success at the time, who had told him that he should act more maturely and that he couldn't go on forever causing problems for the villagers, that he'd certainly have very little hope of making a go of things if he stayed in the village, and that he should think about stirring himself and setting off for Tokyo to show the villagers just what he was capable of. Old Yamada told him how he himself had once been terribly upset at being considered a fool by the villagers, but had eventually managed to make a respectable name for himself, and that now he, Sannosuke, should try to do the same thing. Moved to tears by this lecture, Sannosuke set off for Tokyo, using for his travel expenses the customary parting gift of money. He had his ups and downs in Tokyo, but in the course of twenty years he managed to put together some five thousand, returned to the village, bought land, reared silkworms, and started lending money, and soon doubled his fortune. And so it was that the Nemoto family was not spoken too well of in the village. In fact, in the spot from where the offertory box had been taken, there was still a little inscription reading "Stolen by Nemoto Sannosuke." Sannosuke had offered two hundred yen for the inscription to be removed, but the village elders had steadfastly refused. And now, his eldest son had been fired by youthful ambitions of his own, and had secretly left home. . . . What a fascinating story!

But I only knew these three fellows for a brief two years. Yamagata's family wasn't too well off and he couldn't keep up his tuition fees, so he gave up and went back home. Nemoto got taken back against his wishes by someone sent out from the village. Only Sugiyama kept, like myself, a firm grip on his aims, and the following April we took the examination for military preparatory school. However, I failed the physical, and he failed the academic part, and after that we somehow grew further apart, finally ending up just exchanging letters. It seems that he stayed on in Tokyo for a while, but the news I had of him wasn't at all pleasant—he started going to the Yoshiwara prostitute district, then he got involved with a brush-seller's daughter, then he lost half his money after being swindled by some charlatan at the Employment Office, and ended up in total self-abandonment. I heard that a year or so later, after one failure after another, he drifted back home to the country, but soon got his number called up for conscription and went off to the barracks at Takazaki.

4

Five years went by like a dream.

It was a quiet summer day in that fifth year. I was panting my way along a road threading through the hills. Ahead of me, a hill looking rather like a priest sitting cross-legged rose up into the indigo sky. In the fields won from the hillsides the beautiful white flowers of wheat were just starting to appear. The air was marvelously clear, and from time to time a delightfully cool breeze would come from somewhere in the surrounding hills to refresh my perspiring skin. I drank my fill of this pure mountain air, a true treasure of the mountains. For ten years I had been tainted with the grime of the city and unable to get a single breath of such pure air. When I had got off at Mure, the station beyond Nagano, I had straightaway been captivated by the sight of the clear waters of the Torii River and the encircling blue mountains, and was greatly moved to think that nature could present such a scene. As I crossed bridges over gorges and walked among towering peaks the scenery unfolded before me like a never-ending scroll, the further I went the more exhilarated I became, and I could fully understand why my friends had been so proud.

I crossed a stream running between the hills and climbed up a hill in front of me. As I did so I could see more and more all around. Not only did the mountain road I had just come along now look as clearly defined as on a map, but the scenery ahead of me, which had previously been obscured by the hill I was now climbing, suddenly appeared like a panorama.

The mountain chain fringing the Jōshū region looked just like a screen, neither blue nor purple but a color in between, and it was especially beautiful where soft white fleecy clouds hovered near the peaks. The silver band sparkling in the distance beyond the mountains ahead was no doubt the Chikuma River, while that cluster of dark houses was probably the town of Nakano. I then chanced to look a little to the right, and saw, seemingly near the banks of the Chikuma, a huge, strangely shaped mountain.

For a few moments I gazed entranced at the sight, wondering what the mountain was called.

Just then an old man with a basket on his back happened to come climbing up towards me.

"What mountain would that be?" I asked him, pointing.

"That? Over beyond Mount Iiyama? That's Mount Kōsha!"

So *that* was Mount Kōsha! I had often heard my friends talk about it. The thought of my friends brought memories flooding back, and I felt very nostalgic. I had wondered when I might be able to visit that enchanted land, if indeed ever at all, and now, five years later, there I was. Somehow I felt that fate had brought me there.

"Is it far to Shioyama village?" I asked.

"Shioyama, eh?" He put his basket down on a rock by the roadside and straightened his back. "I'd say Shioyama's still another five miles. You see that group of little hills over there, at the foot of that huge mountain? Well, it's in there in the middle of 'em."

"Is there a family called Nemoto there, in Shioyama?"

"Nemoto! Sure. They're the richest family there!" he answered, then added, "You're a guest of theirs, I suppose."

"Is the son, Kōsuke, still there?"

"He is." He blew the smoke of a cigarette he had just lit out through his rather ungainly turned-up nose. "He's made of sterner stuff than you usually find in rich boys. They say he got through a few hundred when he went to Tokyo, but since then he's got a grip on himself and he's now pretty well thought of in the village."

"And yourself? Are you from Shioyama, then?" I asked him.

"No, not Shioyama, but the next village, Kurasawa."

"I dare say Nemoto's got himself a wife by now?"

"A wife? Well, yes, he did get married. . . . Let me see now. . . . Yes, it must have been about three years ago—a rich girl from Imoko village."

"Any children?"

"Not yet, but the old man reckons it's about time now, and he's getting pretty worried."

"And what about Yamagata? Do you know anyone by that name?"

"Yamagata? That's the schoolteacher. Yes, our kids owe him a lot too—he's a nice, kind man."

"And what about Sugiyama?"

"You really do know the names of the people in Shioyama! You must be the man these youngsters got to know when they were in Tokyo . . ."

He gave me a searching look.

"Young Sugiyama? . . . Well, he got called up and he's now over fighting the Chinese. I can tell you that the village is thoroughly fed up with that swindler. He set up a branch of some shady Tokyo business called Industrial Enterprises over in Nagano, supposedly starting up chemical dyeing, and really swindled villagers who had no idea about such things. Anyway, he made five or six thousand yen, but blew it all on keeping mistresses and having geisha girls in his house and going out on the town every night—made himself into a real wreck after just a couple of months. . . . He's a terrible liar, and nearly swindled me, too!"

"What about his family?"

"His family? Well, they laid out a fair bit on his account, but the old man's still doing all right. He was the richest in the village twenty years back, and he's still keeping his head well up."

Then he suddenly seemed to remember something.

"Shioyama's always produced strange people, you know. It isn't that none of them makes a success in life, but there are a great many who get into difficulties."

"Is there anyone in trouble at the moment?" I asked.

The old man picked up his basket from the rock and set off again, replying as he did so:

"There's a big to-do going on right now!"

With this he hurried off on his way, without explaining what exactly he meant by a "big to-do." I stood there for a while, wondering what sort of a life my friends of some six years ago were now leading, about their wives, their houses, their families. All sorts of thoughts came flooding into my mind, and again I somehow felt a strong bond of fate between myself and this mountain village.

An hour later I was drawing close to that familiar old village. As my friends had so rightly said, it was a case of one mountain after another. There was a stream tirelessly winding its way round the bases of the numerous mountains, and here and there were picturesque wicker-bridges, dark deep pools such as where some strange river-beast might dwell, rushing rapids casting cool pearls of spray through the midsummer air, and roaring waterfalls setting the mountains to tremble and making rainbows of their white hanging veils. Time and time again I was brought to a halt, words of wonder on my lips. With the refreshing sound of running water in my ears I followed the winding river for about half an hour, when suddenly and unexpectedly the countryside opened out in front of me to reveal, amidst gentle undulations, paddy fields of yellowing rice, dry fields of white flowering wheat, a densely grown grove around a shrine, and miscanthus-thatch cottages scattered like counters on a *go* board.

I remembered that sketch I had seen in Yamagata's notebook.

What a peaceful village!

How my feelings, prone as they were to romantic inclinations, were stirred by the sight! After half a dozen years of imagining, now it was actually before my very eyes!

Above all, being stained by the dirt of worldly things I had long since yearned for the beauty of nature, and now, at last, I could have my fill of it. And there in that peaceful village could I not also find two friends to comfort me in my world-weariness?

I looked around and saw that the evening sun was already low in the sky, with the shadows of the mountains behind me reaching away to the grove around the shrine. The sky was turning a deeper but still clear blue, and the huge cryptomerias in the fields towered up in sharp outline against it. I understood that Yamagata's house was in the shadow of those cryptomerias, and strained my eyes in that direction.

What a peaceful village!

5

Just at that moment, I caught sight of something. In the shadow of the cryptomerias was a dark cluster of some ten houses, and beyond, on a slightly raised section, was a large building that looked like the primary school. And there, in what appeared to be its playground, two white jets of water were gushing out through the deep blue sky, just like a huge fountain.

They sparkled beautifully as they moved through the evening sunlight.

"What's that, then?" I asked curiously of a disheveled child of about ten who had chanced to draw near, carrying an infant and with a runny nose.

"That's the pump!" came the reply as the child ran off, frightened at my being a stranger.

Indeed, it was clearly a pump. But a pump like that, in a peaceful village like this?! Fire-drill, in a country spot like this where they probably hadn't had a fire in ten years? I couldn't help but be perplexed. Anyway, assuming it was indeed nothing more than a rather pointless fire-drill, I went on into the village. I came first to a picturesque little bridge, with a constantly turning waterwheel next to it, then a cheap sweets-shop where an old lady worked at her spinning wheel when she wasn't actually selling, a wide-fronted house with a pile of silkworm trays, and next a little cottage where a young girl was singing as she busily worked her loom. As I walked past these various sights I noticed that the dips in the cobbly street were full of water, as if a flood had just receded, and that the roofs of the houses were glistening as though it had been raining.

That wasn't all. Some twenty yards away I saw a large new

red pump, with a fabric hose leading down to the Otani River and two nozzles, of five-inch diameter, sending jets of water into the air with a tremendous noise.

There were about thirty young men of the village gathered around the pump practicing enthusiastically, their cheeks wrapped and their trousers rolled up. Some were attending to the water in the pump, some were handling the feeder-hose, some were manning the nozzles trying to gauge the distance, then someone would yell for more effort, or to go over a bit to the side, or yell that it was leaking, or that it was cold—there was an almighty commotion going on. A man of about fifty, dressed in a workman's coat, seemed to be in charge and was busily giving instructions, but nevertheless it looked as though they were all still inexperienced with the pump and they were clearly having great difficulty in training the jets onto the spot they were aiming at. They were trying to hit the school roof, and had the two nozzles turned in that direction, but first they greatly overshot, then next they hit the thatch roof of a cottage in the foreground, before, at the third attempt, they got the water to smack against the school's rain-shutters.

"Hurray!" went up a shout of applause behind me.

I saw with some surprise that what must have been almost the entire population of the village, young and old, men and women alike, were gathered to watch this rare spectacle of fire-drill, lining the roads, watching from windows, roofs, and treetops. They roared when things went right, they roared when things went wrong, and they gave enthusiastic opinions about the operation or someone happening to get drenched.

I stood there watching, fascinated. I did wonder whether my friends were among the group of young men, but I was so absorbed in what was going on that I didn't give them all that much thought. The hose leading to the river was coiled in front of me like a wriggling snake, and the water must have been passing through it with tremendous force for an extra little jet was spurting with a great hissing sound out of a little hole. The group finally got their cold torrent onto the target of the school roof and suddenly, one of the group—wearing an old towel round his head and a striped *yukata* with the tail hitched well up—came hurrying in my direction, as though he'd got something to attend to. . . . We looked at one another. . . .

"Well, look who it isn't!" I said.

"Why . . . Tomiyama-san!" Nemoto Kōsuke called out in surprise.

It was a good six years since we had met, but his looks and his manner were just as they had been in the past, and on seeing this I felt right away the tranquility of the countryside.

His placid features full of joy, he looked deeply into my face. Then, suddenly, he turned to a boy of about fourteen or fifteen who was standing nearby—apparently his houseboy—and asked him to show me politely to the house. He then turned to me:

"I'm sorry, but the young men in the village have got all this to attend to. . . . Would you mind going back ahead of me? I'll be through in a short while, and then I'll come straight over."

The boy then led me to Nemoto's house. We scrambled up a narrow path between on the one side paddy fields of what looked like a bumper crop of rice, and on the other dry fields of deliciously ripening muskmelons. On a sort of shelf where one hill rose up from another I could see a detached, miscanthus-thatched house with a small whitewashed storehouse. Behind it stood a still rather sparse wood of zelkovas, probably planted some ten years ago, while around lay fields of wheat, cucumber, pumpkin, and corn. As we drew closer I saw a rather unpleasant vat of manure, just like anywhere else in the countryside, a little shed stacked with firewood, an old well with weeds growing all around the rim, and a well-bucket hanging high in the evening shadows. In front of the well a pond about six feet square had been dug, for washing hoes and plowspades. This sort of pond was a feature of the region, where it was known as a *taneke*, and it was about shoulder deep. Apparently they kept carp and roach in such ponds, occasionally even rearing the fish to several feet in length. Weeds such as miscanthus and pampas grass grew profusely round about, while at the water's edge candocks and wild pinks cast their beautiful reflections on the unfortunately rather muddy water. Yamagata had once told me that when he was fifteen or sixteen and full of mischief, he and Sugiyama would often come here to take carp, and that one night they'd stolen several dozen, almost more than they knew what to do with. I'd never have dreamed that the pond he was talking about was this muddy little thing. Nor, indeed, that his friend's house—the richest in the village—was so small and humble.

Suddenly I saw, at the side of the pond, a woman wearing a white towel round her head, busy sharpening a scythe.

"Ma'am, the master just told me to bring along this visitor from Tokyo," the boy suddenly yelled.

The woman looked up in surprise. I have no grounds for criticism, but her face was dark-complexioned, insensitive looking, with blackened teeth, and was quite aged. I realized at once that this was my friend's wife and I couldn't help thinking how tall and sturdy she was compared with her small and youthful husband. Or perhaps it was just that in Tokyo I had grown too used to seeing older men with young wives.

She straightaway led me to be introduced to my friend's father. At the time he happened to be sitting with his back to us on the verandah, sorting some vegetable seeds and surrounded by a confusion of saws and sickles and pumpkins and threads, but when he saw me and realized I was the man his son had talked about, he greeted me with great friendliness:

"Well now! The young man from Tokyo! And here in the middle of nowhere!"

He had of course gone through hardship in Tokyo when he was younger, and I knew straightaway from his affable way of talking and his beaming smile that he was no ordinary character. He had rounded features and twinkling eyes but a rather pointed nose, and was so heavily built—at least a hundred and seventy-five pounds—that you might have taken him for a sumō wrestler. When I realized that this was that rogue of old, that dreamer, that adventurer, that man whom the villagers had found too much to handle and had considered throwing bound into the Chikuma River, then I couldn't help feeling how strange was the infinite depth of human life.

Just then a dirty looking fellow of about thirty, and apparently a servant in the house, came running up:

"Sir, it's so hot the horse has got tired out and lain down, and now he just won't get up! What shall I do?"

"Lain down again?! That's no good! It's because you work him too hard."

"I don't know about working him too hard—the last time he lay down I lightened his load from four bags to three!"

"Where's he lying down?"

"On the slope by Magoemon's fence. He just won't get up.

I tried going to Magoemon's place for help, but there were only some little girls there, so I couldn't get anything done."

"You're all useless!" the old man yelled at him, then spoke to his daughter-in-law standing nearby.

'Well, it's extremely rude to our guest, but I've got to go and move the horse, so just take him through into the house and look after him till Kōsuke gets back."

He then spoke to me:

"I'm sorry, young sir, but please excuse me."

He didn't wait for my reply.

"Oy, Saku! Let's go! What are you waiting for?!"

He set off at a run.

I was led through into the house, to the guestroom. As I expected, this room was quite presentable. In the alcove hung a landscape by Bunchō that was obviously a reproduction, even to an amateur, while up on the crossbeam were fastened two lances that had no doubt been bought from some broken-up aristocratic family in Iiyama. The lances were blackened and austere, just as if they were the symbols of lamented fortune. Unlike city houses, however, the place was structurally very solid, and the ceiling was high so the circulation of air was naturally good. If it hadn't been for the flies that came in from the stable, it would have been a very pleasant and restful room.

Nemoto's wife brought in some tea things. She sat nervously in front of me and then drew some cheap tea from a Kutani-ware teapot.

"It's so nice and quiet here in the country," I said nonchalantly.

"Oh, no, far from being quiet, we've had a real to-do of late . . ."

"Oh?" I asked curiously.

"Yes, we've had a lot of fires recently, and we can't even sleep at night."

"What's the cause, then?"

"Well, there isn't really a proper explanation . . ."

She hesitated.

"Is it arson?" I asked.

"Yes."

"You have a troublemaker around, then?"

"Yes, there's a troublemaker all right, and it's a real problem."

114

There was silence for a while.

I sipped a cup of the lukewarm tea.

"So that's why they were practicing with the pump just now?"

"You saw it then? Yes, we've been having fires almost every night, a real uproar, and there was nothing else for it but for the whole village to get together to buy a pump. It arrived yesterday, from Tokyo."

"A pump from Tokyo?"

"Yes, just arrived yesterday. There hadn't been a fire in the village for years and years, so there wasn't a pump. But, well, there was nothing else for it this time. There's nothing to say we won't have a fire tonight, either, so the young men have been practicing fire-drill at the school all afternoon." She paused. "But anyway, they seem to have spread a fair bit of water around, and they should be finishing soon."

She changed the subject.

"Well, you must be worn out, so please feel free to lie down. It's a good seven or eight miles from Mure, after all."

She gave me an old black-lacquered pillow and then politely retired to the adjoining room.

The view from the room was very good. The house was on high ground, so the whole village looked almost as if you could pick it up in your hands. There was the sparkle of the fast-flowing Otani River in the evening sun, the blue of Mount Mitsumine, shaped long and low like a cow at rest, the deep purple of the distant range of mountains on the Jōshū border, and I was particularly moved by the ever-changing, cloud-enshrouded beauty of the wonderfully shaped Mount Kōsha, which presented an even more impressive aspect when seen from here. What a peaceful village! What beautiful nature! However, at these thoughts I suddenly called to mind what Nemoto's wife had just told me. A pump, here in this peaceful village! Arson, in this beautiful village! A village, moreover, where previously they hadn't had a fire for years! Something unnatural was going on. There had to be some explanation. My imaginative feelings were struck all the more by the thought of the intensity of the ceaseless maelstrom of human life that reached even here into the mountains.

6

"What's all this I hear about arson?" I asked my friend Ne-moto.

He had got back from his fire-drill about an hour before, and we'd talked about the past, about the last six years, he'd told me how glad but how surprised he was to see me, and so on and so on. We'd already finished off several bottles of local saké, not that it was particularly good, and my bowl was piled high with noodles of the famous local wheat. In country-feast style, his wife was hovering around with her Nikkō-lacquered tray, waiting to cut in with more should an opportunity present itself. Having already been forced into submission by her several times, this was something I greatly feared. My friend seemed to be getting rather drunk and had been staring at the gathering darkness outside, but at my sudden question he seemed to return to his senses.

"Yes, it's a real problem. We can hardly sleep at night."

"Don't you know who's doing it?"

"Yes, well, we do know who it is all right, but . . ."

"Then why don't you get him arrested?"

"Well, this is the country, you see . . ." he said slowly, as if by way of explanation. "There's a policeman at the local station, sure enough, but these country police are pretty easy-going, and they won't make any arrests on suspicion alone. . . . The offender has to be caught in the act—or, at least, that's what he says. He's pretty timid, you know, and that delinquent's having a fine time as a result. He's already burned down fifteen or sixteen houses."

"Fifteen or sixteen!"

"There are only about a hundred houses in this entire little village, so with fifteen or so houses affected it's the biggest trouble the village has ever had."

"I dare say it must be."

There was silence for a while.

"Well, just who is the troublemaker?" I asked. "Is he one of the villagers?"

"Yes, he's a villager."

"Then if he's a villager, there must be a reason why he's doing such a terrible thing."

"Well, it's all pretty stupid, really. . . . He's a real rake, he's got a bad character, and the villagers have had nothing to do with him for the last five or six years."

"Is he still a youngster?"

"Oh, no, he's in his early forties now."

"In that case he should certainly know what he's doing . . ." I was deep in thought as I spoke.

"Perhaps the noodles aren't to your liking, but we have nothing else so please do try and have some more," said my friend's wife, offering me another dishful.

I replied that I had now had my fill, and put the dish to one side "for later." She then took up the saké decanter, and I declined this too, only to end up draining my cup for a refill.

"Even so," I said, continuing the conversation, "if he's lit so many fires, there must surely be someone who's caught him at it at least once."

"Yes, of course that would be the case if he did it himself, but he gets this little hussy to do it for him, and she's so damn quick—just like lightning—that the villagers simply can't catch her."

"His daughter, is she?"

"No, she's been his mistress since spring this year. From the Imosawa area, so I believe. She's a bit of a handful, I can tell you—no family since she was a little child, and raised in the wild just like some animal, so they say. Apparently Jūemon— that's the rogue's name—taught her the facts of life for the first time in Iitsunahara, and she came back with him to the village afterwards to replace his wife. She's a real handful, all right! Jūemon doesn't start any fires himself but gets this animal of a girl to do it for him, so even though we know he's responsible we can't get him arrested. And as for the girl, well, she's just too quick for us, so we're in a real mess."

"About how old would she be?"

"Only around seventeen, I'd say."

"And you can't catch her? Just *one* little girl?"

"It's only natural you think like that, but you don't know her! It sounds ridiculous, I know, to say you can't catch one

little girl, but if you only knew her, you'd be in for a real surprise. One minute you think she's here, but then the next she's
miles away somewhere else! The lads often encounter her in the
middle of the village and throw stones at her, but you can't do
anything if there's only one or two of you—quite often people
have got hurt when she's thrown stones back at their heads.
And then when you get a larger group, of half a dozen or a
dozen, she just disappears on the spot—she climbs roofs and
trees like a cat, and you can't tell whether she's in the woods or
the fields or down by the river or what. She's just amazing!"

"Hi there!"

Just at that moment we heard a shout, and someone came in
from the garden. It was my old friend Yamagata Kōzaburō.
He'd just heard about my arriving and had dropped everything
to rush up and see me. The summer sun had now set, and the
sky stretched clear and dark like a sea. Stars were twinkling,
almost seeming to fall, and the two-week-old moon rather slowly
started spreading its light from behind the blackened form of
Mount Kōsha, sending an advance band of light across the now
misty fields. All around it was quiet and soft. Occasionally a
wonderfully cool and pleasant breeze gently swayed the large
leaves of the corn plants out front, while even the cries of the
insects that one usually heard fell silent. However, if I listened
carefully, I could just hear the Otani River babbling in the
distance, sounding like delicate music from another world.

By the time lights could be seen twinkling here and there
across the little wood around the shrine, a beautiful moon had
appeared above the black and impressive figure of Mount Kōsha,
and its cool flowing light skimmed first over a copse on top of
Mount Mitsumine, then went straight on to illuminate the village at the foot of the hill, missing out the waters of the Otani
that hugged the shadow of the mountain. From there the light
played on the edge of the wood by the shrine, then finally spread
to the wheat fields in front of us. If it hadn't been for the lamps,
no doubt our little gathering too would have found itself bathed
in that moonlight.

Now that Yamagata had come the conversation livened up,
and we talked with renewed enthusiasm about Tokyo, about the
school, about English, and poetry, and literature, and so on and

so on. I got rather carried away by it all, and recited, in a very low voice, my favorite Chinese poem—the one about Emperor Hsüan Tsung's boundless grief."

"What about this wonderful evening, then, eh?" said Yamagata with great feeling.

Just then, from the darkly wooded shrine, the click-clacking sound of wooden clappers guarding against the night could be heard spreading gradually afar.

"Who's attending to the clappers tonight? Isn't it meant to be you?" Nemoto asked Yamagata.

"It was supposed to be me, yes, but when I heard that Tomiyama-kun had come I asked Matsumoto-kun to take my place. In return I've got to go on patrol for two hours from ten o'clock tonight."

"And I'm going to be woken up at two myself," said Nemoto, then quickly added, "I've heard that that little hussy was watching the fire-drill today. Is it true?"

"It's true all right! She was watching from the corner of Sōzaemon's house, with a broad grin all over her face. The cheek of the girl! I hear she was grabbed by half a dozen lads and they were just going to give her a good thrashing when she slipped away from them nice as you like and skipped off like some fox. And then, would you believe, Jūemon himself came along to watch!"

"Jūemon too?"

"That wretch! . . . How impudent can he get?! While he was watching it seems he got into some sort of argument with Constable Yamada. He actually had the cheek to mouth off about how he wasn't afraid of the police and how it would be more useful for the villagers to present him with saké than mess around with pumps. He seemed pretty drunk."

"I wonder who let him get at the drink, then?"

"Who? The wretch threatened Hyōei the saké-dealer again into giving him a couple of pints."

"What a hopeless case!" muttered Nemoto with considerable emotion.

"Oh, I forgot to mention it earlier, but when I was on my way here I heard a rustling as I was going past the wood, and it turned out to be that hussy, looking for something. She's up to no good, I thought, so I yelled to her—'Hey! What are you doing?' She glared at me with eyes like a cat, then disappeared into the wood. She's just like an animal! I then went to the meeting-hall and told them what had happened and to be on the look-out for trouble."

While I was listening to their conversation my thoughts were rambling on about the tranquility of the countryside and the maelstrom of human life. The moon had gradually risen up on high, and its liquid light filled the sky and set the evening dew sparkling beautifully on the ground. The village seemed particularly lonely, being, apart from the crying of the insects, the whispering of the wind, and the murmuring of the river, deep in silence.

An hour or so went past.

Suddenly, unexpectedly, the silence was broken by a singularly unpleasant noise, like that of a gong being struck. It was the panicked ringing of a bell!

My two friends gave a start.

"He's done it again!" yelled Nemoto's father as he went racing past, cursing.

"It's Kume-san's place! Kume-san's place!" yelled someone else, racing along the ridge between the paddy fields.

Yamagata gave a quick glance then shouted, "What? It looks more like my place!" He dashed off in a panic, in his bare feet.

Nemoto dashed off after him.

Down in the dark shadow of the wood round the shrine I could see a white column of smoke rising up like a mirage, sending out red tongues of flame, and I could hear the terrible crackle of a house on fire. The temple at the foot of the hill also started furiously ringing its bell.

I set off too, as fast as I could.

7

Across the ridge between the paddy fields, over the hill, over the river, from front and rear, from left and right, a vast sea of people flocked towards the path through the wood near the shrine, and the little hill behind it, which people normally rarely visited, was completely overrun. I too was one of those running, but, being a stranger and not wishing to cause any problems through my lack of familiarity with the place, I was unfortunately unable to do anything but stand on a patch of raised ground a little way away and look helplessly on my friend's burning house.

And what a scene lay before my eyes! The burning house was a large one, facing the eastern edge of the wood. The flames were already reaching up to the roof, but the whole house wasn't yet on fire. Terrible black smoke billowed out from the half-burned windows. If the whole house were to catch fire, then the storehouse out front and several houses below would also be in danger. However, the fire-team was still nowhere to be seen, and the new pump with which they had been practicing during the day still hadn't been brought to the spot. A few moments later the smoking flames set the roof ablaze with a sudden and terrible force, lighting the area up like the middle of the day. I could clearly see figures standing there, a few items of furniture that had barely been saved, and similar tragic sights. But, fortunately, though the whole house was now ablaze there wasn't the terrible problem of sparks flying high into the air, for there was no real wind and the fire wasn't spreading as fiercely as it might otherwise have done. Even so, the houses down below still looked anything but safe.

"The pump!" people were yelling.

"Hey! What's happened to the pump?!" called others, more deliberately.

However, for some reason or other, there was still no sign of the pump coming. Every time a part of the roof collapsed it sent up a shower of sparks as if in a firework display, and eventually the fire did catch a little breeze and now turned towards the storehouse. It looked as if some half dozen people got up onto the storehouse to try to keep the flames at bay, but every one of them had to give up and come on down again.

"It's just too hot to bear!"

"It's burning right down while they're messing around!"

"What's happened? Where on earth's that pump?! Useless so-and-so's, that team!"

Just down below me I could hear the remarks of the people coming down from the storehouse.

Just at that moment a group of some fifteen or sixteen people appeared in a slight dip in the ground, struggling to bring along the new pump I had seen during the day.

Presently I could see a powerful stream of water being directed towards the fire.

"Use the pump right!"

"Get it right!"

"The pump!"

Voices were raised all round.

The water went right and left and mostly missed the mark, but nevertheless a considerable volume did go in the right direction, and, with there being no real wind, the fire was brought under control before it spread to the storehouse out front or the houses below.

It was exactly twenty past ten.

I was tired and thought about going back and sleeping, but the sky was very clear after the fire, and the beauty of the moon over the mountains was out of this world, so I decided to go for a little stroll along the river bank. I set quietly off towards the village, going around the aftermath of the fire and following a narrow path next to a brushwood fence.

Down in the village there wasn't a single house that wasn't up and about. Despite the relief that the fire had been put out, an atmosphere of anxiety filled the whole village, disturbed as it was almost every night by fires. Groups had gathered at corners —women and old folk—and they were talking noisily.

"Really, we can't get any peace to sleep, with these fires almost every night. We've got to get something done quickly."

"I wonder what on earth he was playing at over at the police station?! It's no good at all!"

The first voice, an elderly one, replied:

"He can't handle it at the station here—it'd be better if we went off to Nagano to get something done. And if they can't do anything for us at Nagano either, then there's nothing for it but to get the village council together and throw the trouble-maker in the Chikuma River or something!"

"It really does look as if we'll have to do something like that . . ."

I went on a bit further.

"If we don't get something done, it may be my turn next to have my house burned down. What on earth can we do?"

"Yes, it's a real problem."

They sounded terribly worried.

I continued walking.

"I never dreamed Jūemon could act like this. I'm sure you remember how he wasn't such a bad lad at all when he was young . . ."

The speaker was a wrinkled old woman in her mid-sixties. Standing facing her was another old woman of about the same age. The moonlight revealed the distressed look on her face as she answered, "That's true. Jūemon's a distant relative of mine, and I don't say it for that reason, but, well, if he'd been brought up properly, he wouldn't have turned into a scoundrel like this. His grandfather's to blame—he spoiled him too much!"

"That's why it's not easy bringing up children," replied the first old woman.

I went on past.

Then, on the corner, I saw what seemed to be a saké bar. It was brightly lit inside and there were seven or eight young men there, drinking and talking loudly.

I stopped and listened.

"Where did you say Jūemon was during the fire?"

"That wretch! He went straight down to the houses below Yamagata-san's, said he'd come to offer his sympathy over their predicament, and then enjoyed himself drinking saké, the impudent swine!"

"He should be allowed to drink to his heart's content—then we could finish him off!"

"I've always said that's the quickest way, but it looks like no one's prepared to do it."

"Damn the wretch!" someone in the group said.

I walked on again. The road now turned down to the river, so I followed it round to the left. About half a block further on I came to a cliff forming the bank of the Otani, and the sound of the water dashing against the rock was almost like heavenly music to my ears after hearing all that unpleasant talk. The moon was now on high, and half of the river was sparkling in its light while the other half remained in darkness. I rested against the cliff, thinking about what had happened that night. Putting together what my friends had said and what I'd heard in the village, there was no doubt that this Jūemon, who was at the center of the trouble, had really fallen into a state of self-abandonment. But just why had he sunk to such a dismal state? According to what

the old woman had said just a short while ago, it was because
his grandfather had been to blame by spoiling him, but could
a simple excess of affection result in a man going to such terrible
and desperate lengths as to burn down the houses in his own
village? Moreover, this village was filled with a particularly
strong spirit of adventure, and if it was simply a question of not
being able to fit in here, then, like Nemoto's father or the bathhouse owner in Shiochō, he could simply have given vent to his
anger by leaving the place—there were after all many examples
of people doing this and redeeming themselves. There had to be
some reason why he hadn't chosen to do this, but was fighting
instead against the villagers. Was it the character he'd inherited,
or perhaps something to do with the environment?

I let my thoughts wander freely, but since I hadn't yet even
seen the man in question it was impossible for me to come to
any conclusion. Eventually I gave the matter up and set off on
the road back. I had been led along the way by the boy during
the day, so I wasn't in any particular danger of getting lost, and
soon I reached that path up the slope, which was rather dark
as the moonlight found it hard to penetrate the thickly growing
foliage. It seemed that there was still quite a fuss going on down
in the village, and from time to time I could hear voices, but
here all was quiet, with not even a rustle from the leaves. I
walked through the crisscrossing shadows cast by the moonlit
trees and drew near to a farm-house that happened to stand
halfway up the slope along my path.

As I did so I saw, in front of the fence around the house a
small figure bending down busily attending to something. Of
course the figure was in the shadow of the house so I couldn't
be absolutely sure, but, judging from what I could make out, it
definitely didn't look like an adult. I stopped. Hiding in the
shadow of a tree, I watched for a few moments to see what was
going on.

Suddenly I heard a match being struck!

"Who's there?" I yelled at once, and ran towards the figure.

But it ducked and ran past me as quick as lightning, with
superhuman agility, and was lost in the wood. The match fell
onto something that had been soaked in oil, which burst into
flame.

"Fire! Fire!" I yelled for all I was worth.

124

8

I was told that Fujita Jūemon's family was, up until his grand-father's time, a family of considerable substance, owning some twenty-five acres and with some seven or eight tenant farmers. The family house was on a stretch of flat land running alongside the Otani. It was particularly finely built, and, along with the storehouse and shed, was ringed by oaks. Whenever anything arose in the village, Jūemon's grandfather would invariably be chosen as the village representative or delegate, such was the family's repute. In fact, the grandfather was also said to have been one of the councillors those years back who had decided to throw the troublesome Nemoto Sannosuke into the Chikuma River. He was an easy-going, kind-hearted man of few words, a man whose formal penmanship, if not exactly erudite, was the best in the village, so much so that it was invariably he who was asked to handle dealings with the other villages, correspon-dence with the samurai of Iiyama Fief, and such like. He married a woman from a place called Ōmata, on the far side of the Chikuma, and she too was much liked, giving food and money to the poor and in her later years spending all her time seeking salvation at the temple. Nevertheless, somehow, in the short space of two generations, such calamity as this had befallen the Fujita family. How on earth could this have happened? How could such people have had such a wild and ruthless grandson as Jūemon?

The more concerned villagers were always saying that if this gentle, upright couple had had a child to inherit their blood, even a girl, then this trouble would never have happened, but unfortunately they had no such child and were obliged to adopt a son in order to maintain the family lineage. Jūemon's father was the second son of some rich playboy over in Imosawa, while his mother was the third daughter of a villager called Sugizaka Shōgorō. Neither of them was what you could call a bad person, and in fact, upset over their son's behavior and too ashamed to face the villagers, they had hidden themselves away in the moun-tains, so they were if anything rather upright people. Even so, they fell far short of the adoptive grandparents in terms of character, and on Jūemon's mother's side there was even the black mark of an uncle who had been beheaded for murder. This was the couple, then, who gave birth to Jūemon. The old couple, having no children of their own, showed the child the most extraordinary degree of affection, never letting him from their thoughts. But, there was one unfortunate thing about this beloved grandson—he was born with part of his intestines pushed down into his testicles. The grandparents had gone as far as Nagano to get the boy's oversized scrotum seen to by various doctors, but in those days medicine wasn't very advanced, and even if the doctors got the boy's intestines back temporarily into the abdomen they fell again at the next movement. Sad as it was, there was nothing that could be done.

The problem became increasingly inconvenient, while his grandparents continued to spoil him, and before they knew it their beloved little grandson had grown out of infancy and reached five, then six, and his character had started to emerge. When he was young, however, he was merely very strong-willed but otherwise seemed not particularly different from any other youngster, though some old folk in the village still said they had noticed something odd about Jūemon even from his childhood, in that he had a definite air of distraction about him that seemed out of place in a child. In any event, it was usually felt that he wasn't in general greatly different from other children. Yamagata's eldest brother used to be one of his playmates, and apparently they'd often go off together to catch dragonflies, or gather plants, or pick wild grapes. His brother could especially remember how they would play tag in the grounds of the shrine, and how, because his oversized scrotum would prevent him from running properly, Jūemon would always end up being caught; how Jūemon had once got stung on his scrotum by a bee when they'd gone to Mount Mitsumine to pick berries, and how he'd cried all the way back home; and how they'd make up all sorts of nicknames and say all sorts of nasty things about his big scrotum and how he'd always pull a face and run off home whenever they started saying such things, even if it was right in the middle of a game. But it was a fact that this congenital deformity was a great tragedy in his life. There could be few born to such misfortune. And it was certain that the excessive affection he received had also helped bring about his unhappiness, for until he grew up his kindly old grandfather spoiled him, referring to him so often as his "dear little grandson" that at one stage even his playmates used to call him this and no one would use his proper name. There were those who certainly felt that this was an important factor in his fate.

The years rolled by, and soon he was seventeen. In the spring of that year his grandmother died of old age, and it turned out to be a most unlucky year for the Fujita family. In the early summer his father greatly expanded his silkworm business in an attempt to reverse a string of losses he had suffered over previous years, but the whole thing failed through the weather, and he was forced to sell off half the land. To add to it all his mother was laid up with a recurrence of a chronic womb complaint, and to drown his sorrows his father went off to the red-light district of Nagano, incurring debts he could ill afford. The old grandfather, now approaching seventy, was left alone with his worries and pinned his hopes on his "dear little grandson," imploring him all the time not to end up in the same hopeless state as his father but to restore his grandfather's land to what it used to be.

Nemoto Kōsuke, who was telling me all this, went on to tell me that there was a young people's meeting-place in the village, where everyone used to get together after the day's work and the evening meal to gossip idly about things like girls and quarrels and gambling, as well as to eat and drink. Nemoto was saying how nowadays, what with the school being built, everyone was aware of the importance of education, so such a trivial form of amusement had lost popularity, but how in his younger days it was very popular indeed. They'd talk about how pretty Heiemon's second daughter was, how Sōsuke's youngest girl had just reached the age of interest in boys, and so on and so on, and if things had stopped there then it wouldn't have been too bad. However, rivalries over girls would emerge between the young men, then quarrels and disputes would start, and fights would often break out with people getting hurt and things getting smashed, and a lot of bad things would happen. What was particularly bad about the meeting-place was that leaders would naturally emerge within the group, who would lead the less assertive teenagers into trouble. Nemoto remembered similar experiences of his own, how they'd get really worked up in the meeting-place and then pool all their money to go off to the red-light district at Yudanaka, although it was seven or eight miles away and the middle of the night. There would always be some lad in the group for whom it was the first time, and they'd really enjoy making fun of him as they walked along. Their parents had given silent approval to this sort of business, realizing they couldn't really stop it, and some of them had even said to the group, "My youngster's just come of age, so I dare say he'll be off to Yudanaka before too long. Just keep an eye on him, will you, and see that he has a good time without getting into trouble." Such parents would treat the elder boys as though they were their own lads' elder brothers. All the young men in the village, without exception, went off to Yudanaka, and the following morning the first-timers would always be made to tell the group about their experiences, much to their embarrassment.

Apparently it was a lad called Katsugorō—quite a name at the time, but now a failure who'd disappeared somewhere or other—who had led Jūemon off to his first night, and he had loved to talk about Jūemon's experiences. . . . "Well, Jūe has this deformity, so the girls there wouldn't have anything to do with him. We went four or five nights in a row and tried him with different girls, but they all got upset and wouldn't consent. And the morning after, as I walked back between the paddy fields, Jūe would always be there waiting, looking so depressed. 'How was last night?' I'd ask. 'Hopeless!' he'd reply, shaking his head. Anyway, this went on for so long that I started to feel sorry for him. After all, he's a human being. Just because he was born deformed, it didn't mean there was anything wrong with him as a person. But, because of his deformity, he couldn't have fun with the girls, and that made me feel sorry for him. I decided to help him as best I could, and I went and explained everything to the madam of a house I knew. Naturally, having a head for business, she readily agreed, and so Jūe was able to spend the night there. And his face the next morning?! Full of smiles! I slapped him on the back and he started chuckling away like nothing on earth—I just can't describe how pleased he looked! But really, I tell you, I've taken a lot of lads off to Yudanaka, but I've never had anyone as difficult as Jūemon!" Katsugorō used to burst out laughing at this point in his story, and would add: "But it's just so funny to think about! With that huge bag of his, struggling to have it off with some girl! . . ."

It seems that after that Jūemon frequently went off to Yudanaka, but one thing he wasn't spoiled in was money, so he never quite got to enjoy himself as much as he would have liked to.

Meanwhile the Fujita household went from bad to worse. The old grandfather was the only one really concerned, but he couldn't do much about things. More and more of the land got sold off, and by the time of the old man's death, when Jūemon was twenty-two, barely a couple of acres remained. In fact, there was a particularly sad story about the old man's death. At the time Jūemon was greatly infatuated with some woman over at Yudanaka, and paying not the least heed to the decline of the family, he'd take whatever money he could lay his hands on, five or ten yen from the sale of rice or silkworms or whatever, and race off to Yudanaka to stay as long as his money lasted, sometimes for days on end. Jūemon and his parents had never got on well together, and at the time the parents were off in Nagano, on some sort of business or so they said. The old grandfather was left alone in the house, dying. Although he had loved his grandson dearly in the past, here he was left alone to die, not a single person to attend him!

He had been ill for two days and unable to get his twisted old body out of the house, and on the third night a neighbor had gone in, worried at how quiet the house was, and found him slumped in a curled-up position against the foot-warmer.

"Old man Fujita! What's wrong?!"

There was no answer.

"Fujita-san!"

Again there was no answer.

The neighbor rushed to his side in concern, but the old man was already dead, tears in his eyes.

Alarmed, the neighbor reported it to a village official, and a messenger was sent off to Jūemon in Yudanaka. He found Jūemon upstairs in the brothel at the height of his pleasures, huge scrotum in hand. On hearing what should have been the saddening news of his grandfather's death he showed not a sign of a tear, and replied, "We can't do anything for the dead, so I'll go back tomorrow, when I'm ready, and see to the funeral arrangements. And now you can go!" The messenger was disgusted.

Anyway, from here on Jūemon's standing got steadily worse, and those who knew of his grandfather's affection, even those in other villages, said to themselves that he was bound to be in for a nasty end.

With the old man's death, Jūemon's parents returned to the village and lived in the house for a while. But, perhaps because of the grandfather's excessive affection, the relationship between Jūemon and his parents was extraordinarily cold. They argued over the least thing and started coming to blows. Even people who tried to intervene got hit and injured, so eventually no one had anything to do with them. There was quite a feud, then, between father and son, but Jūemon was a big man with tremendous strength, and extremely strong-willed in the bargain, and when he had drink inside him you could hardly tell father from son, so, not unexpectedly, his parents finally got sick of living with a son like that and only a year later went off back to Nagano.

From this point on Jūemon's story was far from pleasant. With his grandfather dead and his parents chased off, there was now no one to curb his selfish ways, and he began by mortgaging family property to raise money for his continuing debauchery. However, it seems that he hadn't lost all his powers of reason nor failed to show any thought about his situation, for from time to time he seemed to worry about the future and think about how he might restore the declining family fortunes. As evidence of this, about a year later he completely gave up his whoring and, just like a new man, started tilling his neglected fields, led horses, and helped with silkworms to earn money, and worked so hard that for a time he caused the villagers to take notice.

Around this time, then, Jūemon had redeemed himself a little. There were people in the village prepared to help him, and he seemed to have turned over a new leaf and, indeed, to see him working so hard, there seemed hope for the future. There were those who thought that finding him a suitable wife might help him further in his self-reform, and not a few people agreed with this idea, so it was decided that a suitable wife should indeed be found.

Who was this woman to be?

At that time there was a woman who eked out a living with her old mother in a cheap sweets-shop on the edge of the village, selling "tortoise crackers" and such like to the children. She'd been born over in Echigo, so it was said, and had come to the village about seven or eight years before. At first she'd lived with her father too—a stooping old man with a dirty, dark complexion —but he'd soon died and she was now left with just her old mother. The young men had paid her an occasional visit, but she was plain and rather unobliging, with a bit of a stutter in the bargain, so no one was interested in courting her, and till her present age of twenty-five she'd never got to embrace any male other than a tomcat. But she was said to be not a bad girl as far as personality went and seemed very kind towards children, so Jūemon was reminded of the saying that looks weren't everything and was urged to consider taking her as his wife.

Jūemon was naturally taken a bit aback, but, recognizing that he should act for the best in view of his deformity, he agreed, and before a month was out a woman's laughter could occasionally be heard coming from his lonely house.

The villagers were happy to think that this meant that Jūemon had settled down. But that was a rather shallow and mistaken opinion of Jūemon's kind of character and congenital defect. He was a selfish, brazen man who badly wanted his own way, a man moreover of intense passion. If this passion had been directed to good ends he could have been capable of tremendous undertakings and astonishing achievements, but, unfortunately, he lacked the inner resources to direct his passion in such fashion. It was a faculty he lacked from birth. "I'm deformed, a freak who just can't be like other people"—the thought had been in his mind since childhood, and would, sadly, immediately take over whenever he thought about doing something really worthwhile. This awareness of being deformed would come on, like ice, bringing unspeakable misery into the very midst of his passion. There was nothing so trying for him as the onset of this unhappiness, nothing so cursed. Why was I born deformed like this?! Why wasn't I born normal like other people?!

He hated his parents, those parents who had given him his birth to deformity. At such times a terrible rage would consume his whole being, feelings of hatred and resentment and jealousy

would prevent him being calm even for a second; he would feel
vexed and bitter, and basely wish to destroy the world, to plunge
it into darkness before tumbling headlong himself into the black
depths of the pit and thereby gain at least some measure of
satisfaction.

At these times he just had to drink, even if he hadn't any
money at all. He would rush off in desperation to the saké bar,
and drink one glass, two glasses . . . four pints, eight pints . . .

A wife was not necessarily a good thing for Jūemon, but perhaps, if there had been a child born to them early on, he might
have solved his problems. Unfortunately, however, a year went by
without a child, and gradually the relationship between Jūemon
and his wife became unruly, violent, inconsiderate, with crying
and shouting and scuffling. These scenes became as commonplace
as dogfights, and things reached a wretched state, with his wife's
face hardly ever free from bruises.

As a perhaps inevitable result, Jūemon once again started
visiting the brothels he had recently gone to such lengths to
avoid and completely gave up the recovery of his neglected
land, which he had just set about.

If his wife had had any wits about her it wouldn't have been
too difficult for her to stop the recurrence of this trouble before
it got under way. Fate, however, denied even this small blessing
to poor Jūemon, and his extraordinarily stupid wife met the
crisis by, of all things, spitefully taking advantage of her husband's absence to start up an affair with some wild-living hunter
from the hills.

When Jūemon found out about this she merely babbled to
him:

"Well, it's only natural. You go off doing whatever you like,
so there's no need to blame me for it!"

"You slut!" yelled Jūemon, in a terrible rage.

He suddenly grabbed her by the hair and dragged her to the
floor, pummeling her till his fists hurt. Then, with a contemp-
tuous glare at the half-murdered woman, he went hurrying off
to Yudanaka. And it was back to his old drinking . . .

From then on Jūemon let himself completely slip. Not only
did he visit the brothels, he also fell in with the hunter, and
went gambling, getting into brawls, whoring even with tea-house
waitresses, and in next to no time had sold off all his farmland.

To raise money for his debauchery he even tried to mortgage his house and the land it stood on as well, but everyone was afraid to lend such a scoundrel any money for fear of trouble when it came to trying to claim the mortgaged house, so no one dealt with him and for a time at least he was left with the house as his sole possession.

An interesting story is told of those days.

Jūemon had been in Yudanaka for three days, indulging in his favorite pleasure. However, when he came to leave, he found that he couldn't pay the account. Amid much complaining and bitterness, he was obliged to take the brothel's debt-collector the seven or eight miles back to his house, only for the collector to get angry when he found that most of the furniture had been sold off and that not a single thing of any value was left. Just as Jūemon was in a fix, wondering what on earth he could do, he heard the whinnying of his three-year-old chestnut horse, which had been left in the stable in the rear during its master's absence with nothing to eat for those three days. It had whinnied at the sound of voices.

"Ah! There's still the horse!" said Jūemon.

Nonchalantly he led it out and handed it over to the debt-collector, not bothering to give it anything to eat. Then, with the surplus money he received from its sale, he went straight off again to Yudanaka.

Somehow the villagers got to hear of this episode, and the story went round about how "little grandson" had come back leading one "nag"—the nickname for a brothel debt-collector—and had had another nag led away.

Three years then passed, till Jūemon eventually did manage to mortgage his home. He was dispossessed of it; then in a fit of pique set fire to it, only to be caught and put in prison in Nagano. His behavior during those three years before his imprisonment was largely a history of darkness and iniquity, with no sign of improvement. However, on one occasion, the following incident took place. . . .

Apparently, it was after Jūemon had mortgaged his house. One day, thinking to borrow some money, he visited the home of a man called Ageo Teishichi in Kamishioyama. Ageo Teishichi was, rather like Nemoto Sannosuke and others, a man who at one time had fallen into great adversity and, unable to get on in his village, had gone off indignantly to Tokyo. There he had somehow weathered twenty years of life's vicissitudes and had returned to Kamishioyama with a fortune of some ten thousand yen, and was now the richest man there. When Jūemon came calling he greeted him cordially, listened to his request, and duly gave him fifteen yen. Then, in a serious tone, he said:

"To tell you the truth I've already heard about you. But, you know, the village where you were born is only a small place, and you just can't do what you like there. I know from my own experiences, once you've lost the respect of the people in your village you simply can't get on there, however much fuss you make. You're spoken of very badly in your village, so how about trying to make a real go of things somewhere else?"

Jūemon was silent.

"You know," continued Teishichi, "I had a really bad time of things, too. I was abandoned by my parents and spat on by my brothers, and no one in the village would have anything to do with me. And so one night I set off away from the place. I'll never forget how sad I was. You know that spring just outside Kurasawa? Well, I sat down on a rock there, and when I realized that I might never return to the village I got really miserable and started crying. I might just as well die where I am, I thought. And yet, I started to change my mind. . . . If I was going to die, then I might actually just as well die in Tokyo. And I might just as well try working first, seeing as I had nothing to lose if I was going to die. With these thoughts in mind I slowly set off on my way. It was the start of my change of fortune, and, well, I got to be where I am today. . . ."

"In my case it's hopeless . . ." replied Jūemon.

His head was downcast, and tears fell onto his lap.

"There's no such thing as 'hopeless'! When I was in your position I also thought it was hopeless, but that 'hopelessness' turned into my present-day fortune. You've got to have spirit, that's the thing!"

There was no reply from Jūemon, so he continued:

"Let those villagers say whatever they like. The world's a big place, and there's no reason why you have to stay in the village. You're born a man, so go off to Tokyo or somewhere and take life by the horns . . ."

Jūemon was almost overcome with emotion and was biting

his lower lip in a desperate attempt to keep back the flow of tears.

"It's true!" Teishichi went on. "I'm not talking about something I don't know about. Really, you just try giving it a go, and I'm sure things'll work out for you."

"In my case it's hopeless . . ." Jūemon was still fighting back the tears. "I just can't do what you did, not with a body like mine . . ."

"Nonsense!" Teishichi was about to say, but then he realized that perhaps, after all, Jūemon wasn't able to give things a proper go, and he felt really sorry for him.

"I don't really think that's true. There are many people around who've got far greater physical handicaps than you yet have made a real success in life. What about the blind scholar Hanawa Kengyō, and the crippled millionaire Sōshichi from Ōmata? With a body like yours there's no reason to say such wishy-washy things. Really, why don't you try giving it a go? I know quite a lot of people in Tokyo, and they'd help you if you wanted to go . . ."

"I'm very grateful. You're the only person to talk to me like that. I certainly . . ." Jūemon's voice was choked with tears. " . . . I certainly won't ever forget how kind you've been. But it really is hopeless in my case. If only my body hadn't been like this, I wouldn't be messing around in the village like this . . . it's hopeless!"

Tears fell once more.

Teishichi had spoken about this later and said how he felt very sorry for Jūemon and wondered why the villagers treated the poor man so callously. After all, it was just that he was highly spirited, and acted so wildly because his body was handicapped. . . . Teishichi really felt the deepest sympathy for Jūemon.

In fact, as I listened to my friend's story, I couldn't help feeling myself that Jūemon was a human being after all, and that even though he was now acting so badly it might still be that deep down he had at least some measure of tenderness. I was sure that his congenital deformity was partly the cause of the trouble, and that his disposition had also greatly influenced his misdeeds.

Jūemon's subsequent story was indeed one of simply astonishing troubles. Having his mortgaged house taken from him and in vexation setting fire to it, he was imprisoned in Nagano and came out after six years; but, although the villagers were now hoping for some improvement in him, he continued to be roguish and profligate and in fact, far from any repentance, he grew even bolder in his wrongdoings, almost to the point of sheer defiance. The following year he was caught red-handed gambling and sent back to prison in Nagano for another year. When he came out for a second time he returned to create more trouble in the village and, having no home to go to, built himself a beggar's sort of shack down by the embankment. A gang of similar villains would gather there around him, and when he needed rice he'd brazenly go off to get some from some nearby house. If people showed any unwillingness he'd start making threats about fire and, fearing arson, they'd be obliged to give him what he wanted, and he'd go happily off with his huge cloth-bundle full of rice. He was almost too much for the village to cope with, but even so, if things had stayed like that it still wouldn't have been too bad. However, he had suddenly started going on about his feelings being hurt, and got terribly angry, walking around like a drunkard yelling "If this lousy village isn't prepared to look after this Jūemon, then I'll burn the whole damn place down!"

Hence the present fire-setting.

9

The day after Yamagata's house got burned down, precautions were greatly increased. Not only were Jūemon's actions watched but also those of the girl, even down to her minute-by-minute whereabouts—not the least detail was overlooked. Also, the fire-team was increased in number, as, too, the young men on night-watch, and those on patrol duty and clappers' duty were now to be changed every fifteen minutes. Such extraordinary caution was exercised that even a supernatural demon would probably have found it hard to get up to anything. Nevertheless, this resolute line of defense was somehow cleverly penetrated, for shortly after ten that night there was a strange smell and then a strange crackling sound. I drew back the sliding-door to the outside, having just settled down to sleep, and saw showering sparks filling the air—a not perhaps unexpected scene of late. From the windows of a house just down below, darkish yellow smoke and long red tongues of flame . . .

"Fire! Fire!" came loud and utterly despairing cries.

In some confusion I ran out into the garden in my bare feet. The house below was no more than twenty yards away, so there was already great alarm in the main section of Nemoto's house, and I could clearly hear the old man yelling instructions at the top of his voice to bring water and buckets and so on. I too thought to help in the emergency and went towards the main section, but then I realized that, not knowing the place, I could do little, and it would be better to keep out of people's way, so I went and stood in a piece of open ground in front of the store-house, merely watching what was happening.

Just like the previous night, the moon was as if floating in a liquid sky, the mountains were stark and black, and I could still hear insects singing in a clump of grass a few yards in front of me. Black and yellow smoke billowed up over that sleepy village, mingled with the crackle of burning timber. Then I could hear the temple bell, the frenzied ringing of the fire-bell, people shouting, people running! . . .

Soon the village was in seething turmoil.

10

In the large main room of the main section of Nemoto's house I heard someone shout, in a terribly sharp voice:

"What?! What did you say you were going to do to me, to Jūemon?!"

My friend came up to me.

"Jūemon's here! He sets fire to the place, and then comes playing the innocent to drink with the helpers! Isn't that just the height of impudence?!"

The fire had, fortunately, been contained to the one little house down below and had not spread to the main section of Nemoto's house, and now the villagers who had come to help, the young men drenched by the pump, and worried relatives who had come to do what they could, were all gathered in that large, fifteen-mat room having the customary "helper's drink." Disheveled and in no real order, people were drinking from beakers or teacups or whatever they could find, others were busy chomping hungrily away at rice, while still others were sitting cross-legged, smoking cigarettes. I had peeped in at the scene a little while before, but it had seemed to me somehow indescribably brutish, like a gathering of demons. Everyone was pleased that the fire hadn't spread to the main section of Nemoto's place, but what with the disturbances continuing every night, the exhaustion from lack of sleep, and a sort of wild excitement, every face seemed to show, without exception, signs of a terribly stressed agitation.

An hour had passed since then, and it seemed that the saké had had its effect on the gathering. I could hear a dreadful racket going on in that next room.

"He's come, then, has he?" I quickly replied to my friend's comment.

"He's here all right. The swine enjoys it, drinking this helper's saké—that's half the reason he sets fire to places!"

A few moments passed, then:

"What?! What did you say I did?! What did you say Jūemon did?! . . ."

A raised and very angry voice could be heard in the next room.

"The fool's drunk again," said my friend.

Now we could hear them arguing.

"I didn't say you set fire to places—whether you do or not is decided by the law, and you've already been in its care on that account!" said a thick, hoarse voice.

"What? It's none of your business whether I have anything to do with the law or not! . . . You lousy lot!" There was a short pause before he went on, "I bet there's no one prepared to take me on—not me, Jūemon!"

He seemed to have rolled up his sleeves.

"We're not saying you're no good, we're just saying you're too much for us and that we're having a rough time because of your being in the village."

"Rough time? . . . Of course you're having a rough time—I, Jūemon, am deliberately making things rough for you!"

He seemed hopelessly drunk.

"Give it up—it's no use trying to talk to a drunkard!" said a restraining voice.

There was silence for a few moments.

"But Jūemon, isn't it a fact you were born a villager, too? Do you think it's a good thing to get hated by everyone like this, getting up to nothing but trouble—don't you feel bad about it?"

The voice was a different, rather more elderly one.

"What do I, Jūemon, care if you lousy lot have nothing to do with me?! Damn it all, look at people like Nemoto Sannosuke— a real somebody now, but he's had his hands in the offertory box in the past!"

"Thump him!" yelled a hot-blooded young man, unable to control his anger.

"Hit him! Hit him!"

"Get him!"

Voices were raised all round.

"Hit me, eh?! That's a laugh! Let's see, then, who's going to try and hit me—me, Jūemon!"

It then sounded as though a whole crowd of people had gathered round him and were about to start hitting him. My friend tried to hold me back but I dashed over to the door leading to that next room, which was slightly ajar, and peeped out. Everyone there was too busy to notice me. Through the smoky, horribly stuffy atmosphere I could see, beneath the dim light of an old-fashioned mercury-lamp, a terrible, nightmarish spectacle. A middle-aged man was sitting up against the pillar in the center of the room, and three young men, with eyes blazing and fists clenched, were just on the very point of laying into him for all they were worth, while an old man was trying his best to stop them. The middle-aged man was wearing a tattered white *yukata*, his hair was disheveled, his hairy legs indifferently exposed. It was my first sight of Fujita Jūemon, and in his red face, with its blazing eyes, I could indeed see signs of terrible iniquity and depravity, with the wretched history of his half-lifetime etched in those furtive wrinkles. I have always believed that a man's life is visible in his face, and nothing moves me as much as the sight of a face etched with misery, but my immediate thought was that I had never seen a face as full of wretchedness as was Jūemon's. His rather aged facial skin was quite flabby, and his piercing eyes, while harboring infinite sadness, glared fixedly at the young men who had now come to attack him—he looked for all the world like a starving wild beast about to hurl itself on someone.

"It's no good taking on a drunkard—forget it!" said the old man, trying to hold back the youths.

"It's a real laugh! These striplings, saying they're going to hit me, Jūemon! Let 'em try!"

Jūemon had his sleeves rolled up and held himself ready for action.

"We can't let him get away with this to gloat. This swine's thrown the village into turmoil and stopped us getting our sleep at night, and there's no reason at all for us to give him drink and let him talk like he is! If they're too spineless at the police station, then we'll just have to settle things ourselves! It's you elders who should leave things alone!" So saying, a plumpish, excited young man in his early twenties shook his sleeve free and immediately started hitting Jūemon on the side of the face.

"Why, you wretch!" yelled Jūemon, standing up and adopting a fighting pose. The youth displayed enormous strength, and not surprisingly Jūemon was immediately pinned to the ground by such youthful vigor, while a hail of clenched fists rained down on his face and head.

Five or six elders, unable to bear to watch any longer, rushed up and eventually broke up the scrimmage, but Jūemon, dazed from the punches, would have nothing to do with this peace-making and, staggering about, now came back at his adversary, who was temporarily forced to retreat into an adjoining room.

"Hey! What's all this business of getting someone to hit me and then disappear! Are you going to get someone to take me on, or not?" yelled Jūemon fiercely.

They placated him with the promise that someone would see to that later, and got him to sit down again, only for him to gulp down his saké and yell again:

"Well, isn't anyone going to take me on, then?"

There was no adversary, so for a while he sat in silence, his head slumped. Then, as if he'd suddenly remembered:

"No one? What about Nemoto Sannosuke? Is Sannosuke here?"

Then, again in a loud, angry voice:

"Saké! Saké! Bring me saké!"

Saké was duly brought forth, and Jūemon proceeded to knock it back by the cupful, as if he had completely forgotten his anger at having been hit. But everyone knew that things couldn't be left as they were, and one of the village delegates stood up and went over to him:

"Jūemon! You've had enough now, so why don't you think about going home? Too much drink isn't good for the body . . ."

"No good for the body?" His head was slumped. "What do I care if it's no good for the body? And if anyone should go home, then you lot go! Leave me here with Nemoto Sannosuke!" His words were slurred.

"Well, talk is talk, and we can see to all that later. But you've got a bit of a nerve, haven't you, getting hopelessly drunk like this and then saying you're not going back home?"

With these words the delegate grabbed the drunken Jūemon by the arms and tried to get him to stand. Jūemon, however, was set in his place like a rock, showing no signs of moving, and eventually two or three others had to be enlisted to drag him from where he was sitting.

"What are you doing?!" Jūemon yelled, and tried to kick out as he was being dragged. But he was terribly drunk and lacked control over his feet, crashing against the table before slumping to the ground.

"Control yourself!" yelled the delegate. Some five of them then just managed to raise Jūemon, who made not the least effort to get up, and, carrying him by his outstretched limbs and ignoring his protests, they tottered across the room and finally out of the door.

The room was plunged into sudden silence. No one said anything, but at that moment they all had the same thought— that if it were not for that wild Jūemon, the village would be forever peaceful, and houses and property would be safe, but as it was, with him there, the village was being caused more trouble than it had ever known before.

It would be better to . . .

Everyone seemed to have his thoughts in tune, and they all looked meaningfully at each other.

What a moment!

I felt a kind of wave of darkness—a frightening, saddening,

disgusting wave—pass with tremendous rapidity through the silent gathering.

Again everyone exchanged looks.

"Right!"

One of the delegates, sitting against the great black pillar, seemed to give sudden directions with a jerk of his chin, and four or five young men sitting near the main door dashed straight outside, as if some emergency had cropped up.

It was twenty minutes later.

I could scarcely believe it. You probably all remember that field-pond I saw when I first came to Nemoto's house—that little pond no more than a few feet square and surrounded by those beautiful candocks and wild pinks, and where his wife was washing the hoe and the plowspade and so on? Well, now I heard that a group had gathered there by the pond, carrying dimly shining lanterns from the Nemoto house despite the bright moonlight, and I dashed there to find a truly sad and moving sight. For floating there face down, and almost filling that tiny ditch-like pond, was the man who had just been carried out drunk, Fujita Jūemon, drowned like some dog.

"What happened?" I asked excitedly.

"Well now, sir, he was very drunk, you know, and ended up falling in here!" answered someone in the group.

"Why didn't you get him out?!" I then asked.

No one answered my question.

But I realized at once that I didn't really have to ask, and I looked in silence at the pathetic corpse. The moon shone bright and clear on the pond, and the little ripples around the drowned man's floating hair sparkled beautifully in its light. In a clump of grass a few feet away bell-ring insects and crickets sang a joyful tune to the beautiful night. And over there were the dark forms of the mountains, seemingly ignorant of such tragedy in the human world.

"Is this, then, the end of Jūemon?"

For some reason the thought brought stinging tears of indescribable sadness and sympathy welling to my eyes.

For some time I stood there beside the pond.

11

"If man is completely natural, then it's bound to end in tragedy. For then nature necessarily comes into conflict with the conventions of the present day. In which case, does not nature itself end up, in this world, as unnatural?"

I was thinking to myself.

"Six thousand years of history and customs—that goes a very long way towards making a second nature. As a result of this history, society sometimes dominates nature, or embellishes it. But can nature remain always subjugated by six thousand years of history?

"Perhaps it could be argued that this isn't a subjugation of nature, but an improvement of it? But then, to just what extent could man, with his superficial knowledge and petty mind, possibly be able to improve nature?

"There are gods, and there are ideals, but they are all less than nature. There are principles, and there are imaginative visions, but none is greater than nature. And to those who would ask me on what grounds I say this, I believe I would answer the analysis of the innate individual."

I pondered the matter further.

"After all, isn't that what Jūemon's fate amounts to? He lived his life as he thought and wished, that is, in accordance with the dictates of his faculties. Perhaps if he had been born without that self-centeredness or that physical deformity, he would have been perfectly able to preserve those long-standing human traditions and customs, without ever displaying the unbridled workings of nature. But, sad as it was, he was born into this world with a body and character incapable of harmonizing with this world's customs and traditions.

"In particular, he was fated to be unable to get away from the place where he was born—a mountain village that, although thought of as particularly natural, in fact greatly respects customs and traditions."

At this thought I fully realized how silly I had been to yearn for the peace and nature of the country while I was in Tokyo. The mountains were as primeval as ever, the waters were as pure as ever, but in contrast, I could not help feeling sad to think how much man had lost of nature in a mere six thousand years.

"And yet . . ."

I thought further for a while.

"And yet, why do I feel that the villagers' final act towards Jūemon should not be counted among those things we ought to consider as illegal, as immoral, as crimes? Is it not perhaps because of nature, because it was the workings of nature that so clearly appeared from deep within the feelings of the villagers?"

Suddenly there flashed before my eyes the scene of that purposeful, silent gathering. Then I pictured that night, the following morning, and in particular the shock of Jūemon's girl, who had rushed to the spot when she heard what had happened.

"What a terrible thing for you, old man! But I'll get whoever did it!" she had said in a strange tone of voice as she clung tearfully to the corpse. A truly sad sight!

I can still hear the sharpness of her voice.

Eventually, in the afternoon, a magistrate and attorney had come from Nagano with the policeman, and conducted an investigation. Things seemed to be getting difficult, since they felt that, however much Jūemon was drunk, the pond was simply too small for him to have fallen in and drowned by himself, and that there was something more to it. It even looked as if several of those who had been present might have to go off to Nagano. However, the body bore no suspicious marks and was handed over just as it was to the girl, who had come forward as the recipient.

The sight of the body had made me instinctively cover my eyes with my hands. It had been left in the water for half a day, and the face was horribly swollen, the eyes were fixed in a terrible stare, mucus ran down from the nose to the half-open mouth, and that huge scrotum dangled down.

"But what did she do with the body?" I wondered as I looked outside. "They were saying in the village that it certainly wasn't going to be buried in the temple while it was in her possession."

The weather was very different from the clarity of the previous night, and it had been cloudy and threatening rain since morning. Sure enough, I now saw that it had already started to rain, and the greenery was glistening moistly all around, while ashen clouds hung halfway down the mountains. It was not like normal summer rain, but was an utterly miserable drizzle.

Suddenly Nemoto came in.

He had been kept busy by the investigation, having to rush off all over the place, but he told me that things now seemed to be settled after a fashion, and he'd come back for a bit of a rest.

"How are things, then?" I asked him.

"Oh, nothing to worry about. The policeman knows that Jūemon was up to no good and in his own mind he also knows that he was bound to end up like he did, but I guess he has his job to do and couldn't let things pass just like that—that's why he was making such a fuss."

"What happened to the corpse?"

"Jūemon's corpse? That hussy of his took receipt of it, but she didn't find things easy—no one in the village gives a damn, and his relatives all keep clear of the place, so there was no one to help her. Anyway, from what I just heard on my way back, she took the corpse away on her back and carried it up the hill behind their shack, and she's now cremating it using floorboards and door-panels and so on that she's broken from that shack of theirs. We might be able to see the smoke from here."

He looked out.

I looked out again too, and sure enough, atop a little green hill beneath Mount Mitsumine, I could see a thin column of smoke rising faintly up amid the misty drizzle and being blown westward by the easterly wind till it suddenly mingled with the cloud.

"There—that's it!" my friend informed me nonchalantly.

When I realized that this was the smoke from the burning of the corpse of Jūemon, the man who had been too much for the village to handle, I was overcome with infinite sadness and almost moved to tears in my sympathy. "They say that death reconciles all enemies," I said to myself, "and yet these villagers are refusing even to bury his corpse—how heartless of them! How sad and wretched that that poor girl, that child of nature, should be forced to rip up the doors and floorboards of their shack to use as his funeral pyre!"

I could clearly see before me that animal-like girl, that child of nature, burning the corpse with tears in her eyes. Below lay the village which these two had opposed, and I wondered what her feelings were as she now gazed down upon it.

"And yet," I thought to myself, "for Jūemon this might be the most appropriate thing, being cremated by the familiar hands of this child of nature, the one person in the wide world to have shown him any sympathy. Indeed, it may have been impossible to find a more suitable 'priest' to see him off from this world.

"What cold hearts those cruel villagers must have, not making peace even with the dead! How could Jūemon's spirit possibly be reconciled with such cold hearts? And with that being the case, how much better for him to be in the tender care of that natural-living girl than sleeping his eternal sleep in the temple of cold-hearted villagers with whom he would never know peace . . ."

I was moved to silent tears.

"The child of nature simply cannot exist in this impure world. Woe to those who are born full of nature into the world, for are they not children of nature born into the world of man, to die in oblivious defeat? . . .

"No, no, no . . .

"To die in defeat! Such might be the sad fate of the child of nature. And yet, like the death of the warrior on the battle-field, does not this defeat possess infinite life? Does it not show infinite tragedy? Does it not call for infinite reflection upon man's life?"

I thought the matter over deeply for a while.

"Considered from a broader point of view the whole life of this poor child of nature is a question of living in accordance with how he is born and what he has to do, and just because Jūemon died like an animal, with no one to bury him, it doesn't mean his life was in vain!"

I was unaware how much time had passed, but my friend was no longer there with me.

The rain outside was increasingly miserable, and the mist was all around and as depressing as grief itself. The pathetic smoke from the hilltop fluttered so faintly I almost thought the fire had gone out, and tears again welled up within me at the realization that down in the village there was not a single sympathizer.

Ah, that smoke in the rain! How can I ever forget such a scene!

12

No, indeed . . .

Well, everyone, that night I was again witness to a startling and unforgettable incident. I had never dreamed of such a tremendously terrifying manifestation of nature's power and will. That evening I had gone to bed early and, what with the thought that the troublemaker was now dead and with the fatigue of successive nights without sleep, it took little to lead me into the land of slumber, and I was very soundly asleep. Sleep . . . sleep . . . but if I had remained asleep just a little longer, I would probably have ended up burned to a crisp! When I opened my eyes the room was full of flames, and black smoke that almost entirely obscured vision. In surprise and alarm, and still in my nightclothes, I kicked at the sliding-door to the outside, which fortunately, being a country house, was not set in a very deep groove and came out immediately, and I dashed outside together with clouds of black smoke.

Outside, I was again in for a surprise.

I wondered if it wasn't a dream.

I tell you, everyone, the whole village was in flames!! There was a fire in the wood by the shrine. A fire in a corner of the lower ground just below. Another behind. One over to the right. There were terrible tongues of flame leaping up in some half dozen spots, reflecting on the grey rain-clouds and seeming to my eyes as if heaven and earth alike were on fire. The rain had stopped and a slight wind had sprung up in its place, and the black-smoking fire was gradually spreading with a terrible ferocity. There was the temple bell, the fire bell, there were shouts, yells! . . .

I climbed up the little hill behind me and gazed alone upon the sad sight, full of all sorts of thoughts.

Actually, I had had a certain range of experiences but had never been moved by such a sad and impressive spectacle as the scene that night. There was the fury of the fire as the wind spread it from house to house, there were the occasional cries of despair from those battling it in vain—I felt that at that moment I had truly encountered the presence of nature.

Well, everyone, that brings me to the end of my story. But, there's still one more thing I must tell you. The next day, amid the smoking ruins of the village—which had been almost entirely burned down—they found the half-burned corpse of the young girl, just as she had fallen, with her head in her hands. Had she been caught by the villagers and thrown into the flames in a fit of hatred, or had she cast herself laughing into those flames? Probably no one will ever know.

I left that hellish arena the next day, full of a myriad thoughts.

Since then seven years have passed.

I'm still in contact with the villagers, and in fact only recently one adventurer left there and visited my house. I asked him if things were quieter in the village nowadays, and he told me, "Oh, there's nothing like that going on now! The village just couldn't get along when all that was going on. Fortunately, since then we've had nothing but bumper years, and the village is now a lot richer." He also told me that graves had been made in the temple for Jūemon and the girl, and that the villagers occasionally made offerings of flowers and incense.

Well, everyone, nature finally went back to nature!

(May 1902)

One Soldier

HE started walking.

His rifle was heavy, his pack was heavy, his legs were heavy, and his aluminum mess-tin rattled as it knocked against the bayonet at his hip. The noise really got on his already strained nerves, and he tried time and time again to stop it, but the rattling just went on and on. Finally he gave up in disgust.

His sickness hadn't really cleared up, and he found it very difficult to get his breath. Hot and cold flushes passed constantly through his whole body. His head burned like fire, and his temples throbbed violently. Why had he left the hospital? Why, when the army doctor had told him how serious the consequences would be and had tried so hard to get him to stay, had he left the hospital? Yet in spite of such thoughts he didn't really regret leaving. There had been fifteen of them, sick and wounded soldiers, there in that small, bare-boarded room in a dirty, Western-style building abandoned by the retreating enemy, and for twenty days he had managed to put up with the decay and the filth and the groaning and the oppressive air, and the horrid swarms of flies as well. Their food had been barley-rice gruel with just a pinch of salt, and he had often had to put up with hunger. He shuddered as he remembered the latrine behind the hospital. The hastily dug pits were shallow, and their stench struck powerfully at the nose and eyes. Flies buzzed around you. The filthy, grey-stained lime was nauseating.

It was far better being here on this broad open plain than in there, unimaginably better. The Manchurian plains were bleak and deserted, with nothing in the fields but the rows of ripening sorghum. However, there was fresh air, there was sunshine, there were clouds, there were mountains—suddenly he could hear a dreadful din, and he stopped and turned to look. That train was still there, in the same place. Long, boiler-less, and funnel-less, it was surrounded by hundreds of Chinese coolies, all pushing it furiously, just like ants moving some enormous prey.

The evening sun slanted across the scene like a picture.

That N.C.O. was still on board. That was the bastard up there, standing on that big pile of rice-bales. "I'm in agony and I just can't walk at all—could you give me a lift as far as An-shan?" he had asked. "This train's not for soldiers! Is there any regulation then that says infantrymen should ride on trains?!" the so-and-so had yelled back. "You can see that I'm sick. I've got beriberi. If I can get to Anshan my unit will be there, I'm sure of it. Fighting men should look after one another, you know, so please, give me a lift!" He had begged, but to no avail. He felt as though he'd been mocked, just because he was only a private and didn't have many stripes. It was thanks to com-mon soldiers that the battles at Chin-chou and Te-li-shih had been won! Fool! Swine!

Ants, ants, really just ants. They were still there. When it gets to that state even a train's had it! At this thought another train, the one in which he had set out for the war from Toyohashi, passed before his mind's eye. The station was buried beneath a mass of flags. There were resounding cheers of *"Banzai!"* Sud-denly he pictured the face of his beloved wife. It was not the tearful face he had seen as he left his gate, but a beautiful, smiling face from a moment—he forgot the exact circumstances—in which he had felt it truly dear to him. And now his mother was shaking him, telling him to get up or he'd be late for school. His mind had somehow flown back to his childhood. The boatman in the inlet behind the house was yelling at a group of children, his bald head glinting in the evening sun. He himself was one of that group of children.

While he could still clearly distinguish such images of the past from the painful anxieties of the present, the two were very close to each other. His rifle was heavy, his pack was heavy, his legs were heavy. From the waist down he was just like some other person, and he didn't even know for certain whether it was he himself who was doing the walking.

The brown road, its mud now dried hard as stone and deeply set with the ruts and marks of gun-carriage wheels and boots and straw sandals, stretched away before him. He had little love left for Manchurian roads like this. How far must he go before this one came to an end? How far before he could stop walking? He longed for the pebbly roads of home, the sandy roads along the coast, wet after the rain, all smooth and pleasant. This road was big and broad, but there was not a single smooth level spot. After a day's rain it would get as soft as wall-plaster, and you'd sink in halfway up to your knees, let alone just your boots. The evening before the battle at T'ai-shih-ch'iao he had come through some eight miles of this mud in the darkness. He had been spattered from his back to the hair on his head. That was when they had been assigned to convoy the gun-carriages. These would bog down in the mud, and they had had to keep pushing and shoving them along. If the Third Regiment's guns hadn't advanced to occupy their positions, then there could have been no battle the following day. And so they worked all that night, and fought on the morrow. The enemy's shells and their own shells alike passed steadily overhead with their nasty sound. And from almost directly overhead the hot midday sun blazed scorchingly down. After four o'clock the two sides' infantry came to close quarters. Rifle fire sounded, like beans being fried. Occasionally a shot whizzed close past his ear. Someone in the line gasped. Looking round in surprise, he saw a soldier suddenly fall forward, oozing blood vividly colored by the strong evening sun. He had a bullet in his chest. That soldier was a good man. He was cheerful, unconstrained, outward-going. He was from the town of Shinshiro and must have had a young wife. After landing they had often gone out together on requisition duties. They had rounded up pigs together. But that man was no longer in this world. It was somehow impossible to believe. But whether he believed it or not, it was a fact.

A column of carts, laden with provisions, came along the brown road. There were mule-carts and donkey-carts, and the old Chinese drivers could be heard yelling "C'mon! Giddup!" Their long whips flashed in the evening sun, filling the air with their distinctive sound. The road was badly pitted, and the carts looked as if they were crashing through waves as they lurched and rattled forward. It was painful, his breathing was painful. He couldn't go on in such pain. He started to run after the carts, to ask for a ride.

His canteen rattled. It rattled something terrible. The odds

152

and ends in his pack and the bullets in his ammunition pouch bounced noisily about. Occasionally the butt of his rifle struck his shin, and he almost leapt with the pain.

"Hey! Hey!"

He hardly had any voice.

"Hey! Hey!"

He put all his strength into his shouts. They heard, without doubt, but didn't turn to look. They probably realized there was nothing in it for them. He momentarily gave up, but then started running again. This time he eventually managed to catch up with the last cart.

The bales of rice were piled up like a mountain. The old Chinese driver looked back, his face round and unpleasant. But he leapt up on the cart before the man could say anything, and laid himself out among the bales. The Chinaman urged on his mules, as if resigned to what had happened. The cart rattled joltingly on.

His head reeled, and heaven and earth seemed to spin around him. His chest hurt. His head hurt. His calves felt as if they were being squeezed, and it was horrible, really horrible. He felt he was going to be sick at any moment. Feelings of anxiety invaded his whole body with a terrible force. At the same time, the dreadful lurching started again, and all kinds of voices came whispering into his ears, into his head. He had experienced this sort of anxiety before, but nothing as bad as this. He felt as if there was no refuge for him anywhere.

They seemed to have left the open plain and entered a village. The green of thick willows swayed above him. The rays of the evening sun slanted through the willows and picked out clearly each tiny leaf. Low, unsightly roofs passed before his eyes, swaying as if in an earthquake. Suddenly he realized that the cart had stopped. He raised his head to look.

They were in a spot shaded by willows. He saw five carts, drawn up one behind the other.

Suddenly someone grasped him by the shoulder.

It was a Japanese, a fellow countryman, an N.C.O.

"You there--what's going on?"

He raised his pain-racked body.

"Why are you riding on this cart?"

It was too much effort to explain why. He found it too hard even to speak.

"You can't ride on this cart. Even if it was permitted, the load's already too heavy. You're from the Eighteenth Regiment, aren't you? From Toyohashi—yes?"

He nodded.

"What's the matter?"

"I was sick in hospital at T'ai-shih-ch'iao until yesterday."

"Are you better now?"

He nodded again, meaninglessly.

"I know it's rough when you're sick, but please get down. We've got to get a move on. The fighting's started at Liaoyang."

"Liaoyang!" This single word was enough to set his nerves off.

"Has it started already?"

"Can't you hear those guns?"

From some time before he had imagined that a sort of rumbling had started towards the horizon, but he hadn't thought that it was Liaoyang yet.

"Has Anshan fallen?"

"It fell to us the day before yesterday. It now looks as if the enemy will put up some resistance this side of Liaoyang. It started today, at six, so they say."

There was a distant, faint rumbling, and sure enough, if you listened carefully, it was indeed the sound of gunfire. Unpleasantly familiar sounds were flying overhead. The infantry was advancing, weaving its way through. Blood was flowing. These thoughts made him feel a sort of fear, yet at the same time a sort of attraction. His comrades were fighting. They were spilling their blood for the Japanese Empire.

He could imagine the scenes of carnage. He could picture too the scenes of heroism amid the exploding shells. But here on this lonely Manchurian plain, some twenty miles away, there was nothing but the lonely autumn breeze as it fanned the evening sun, while the village, having suffered the tide-like passage of the great armies, was its usual peaceful self.

"It'll be a big battle, I suppose?"

"It sure will!"

"Not over in a day, I guess?"

"Course not!"

The N.C.O. was now talking away with his colleague, the sound of gun-fire in their ears. The old Chinese coolies had drawn up their five provision-carts and were chattering away over something or other, forming a vague circle. The sun shone slanting onto the long ears of the donkeys, and every now and then piercing brays would fill the air. Over beyond the willows was a row of half a dozen or so white-walled Chinese houses, and he could see tall pagoda-trees in the gardens. There were wells. There were sheds. An old woman with tiny feet hobbled unsteadily by. Looking through the willows he could see, beyond, the vast, bleak plain. The N.C.O. pointed out to him a line of brown hills. Beyond that was a meandering range of tall, purplish mountains. It was from there that the gun-fire sounded.

The five carts moved off.

He was left behind, alone again. He had been told that the next supply depot, after Hai-ch'eng, Tung-yuan-t'ai, and Kan-hsien-po, was located at Hsin-t'ai-tzu, still another three miles on. There was, however, nowhere for him to shelter for the night unless he went on to there.

He made up his mind to go on, and started walking.

He was thoroughly worn out so it was hard going, but on the other hand it was better than the cart. His chest was as painful as ever, but there was nothing else for it.

Again the same brown road, the same fields of sorghum, the same evening sunshine, and even that same train passing by again over on the track. This time it was on a down-grade, and moving at quite a speed. It raced giddily across the dip, quicker even than a train with a boiler could have done. A Japanese flag fluttered on the last wagon, flashing in and out of sight in the spaces between the sorghum fields. Even when this finally disappeared, the rumbling of the train could still be heard. Mingled with that rumbling was the incessant rumbling of the gun-fire.

On the road there had been no village for some time now, but over to the west were numerous gloomy, thick clusters of willows, among which he could make out the odd white and brown houses. There was no sign anywhere of people, but thin blue threads of kitchen smoke rose up cheerlessly from the houses.

The evening sun made long shadows of everything. The tall shadows of the sorghum fell right across the road—some four yards wide—and then onto the sorghum on the far side. Even the shadows of the small clumps of grass by the roadside were enormously long, while over in the east the hills appeared in sharp relief. The lonely, sad evening came on with a sort of indescribable, shadowy force.

He came to a break in the sorghum. Suddenly, there before him, he saw his own astonishingly long shadow. The shadow of the rifle on his shoulder was away out over the grass on the plain. He was stricken with a sudden profound melancholy.

Insects were singing in the clumps of grass. Their cries were not at all like the cries of the insects he used to hear in the fields back home. This dissimilarity, and the vast plain, somehow distressed him. The reminiscences that had briefly stopped came flooding back.

His mother's face, his young wife's face, his younger brother's face, various women's faces, all spun round him as in a kaleidoscope. The old house in the village, surrounded by zelkova trees, the peaceful, happy home, then his youthful departure to study in Tokyo . . . he remembered it all. He pictured the busy night-life of Kagurazaka. Beautiful flowers, magazine shops, new books, and, around the corner, the lively variety halls, assignation houses, the sound of the *shamisen,* coquettish female voices . . . those were the days! The girl he loved was in Nakachō, and he often went to see her. She was a sweet, round-faced girl, and he was still fond of her even now. He was the young sir of a wealthy country family, with no worries about money, so he had done many very enjoyable things. His friends from those days were now all gone out into the world. Only recently, at Kaip'ing, he had bumped into one of them, now a swollen-headed captain in the Sixth Division.

The thought suddenly struck him that there was nothing crueler than the restrictiveness of army life. But today, strangely, instead of his usual thoughts of rebellion, martyrdom, or the like, he was filled with fear. When he had set off for the war, he had pledged without regret to offer himself for his emperor and country. He had made a heroic speech at his village school about how he had no wish to return. At that time he was in the prime of health and vitality. Of course, despite his words, he had had no wish to die. In his heart he had dreamt of a glorious, triumphal return. And yet his present feelings were anxious ones, about death, about the disturbingly very real possibility that he might not return home alive. Even if this sickness, this beriberi, cleared up, the war itself was still one great prison. Struggle, yearn for freedom as he might, there could be no escape from this prison. He remembered the words spoken to him by a fellow soldier, who died in action at Te-li-shih: "There's no way out of this hole. You've just got to resign yourself to it and die a good death."

Overcome as he was with exhaustion, sickness, and fear, how could he hope to escape from this dreadful calamity? Desertion? Fine, but if he were captured he would die anyway the following dawn, and into the bargain his name would receive the ultimate disgrace. And yet, if he pressed on, it was certain that he would have to take his place in the arena of battle. And once he entered that arena, he would have to come to terms with death. For the first time he fully realized his stupidity in leaving the hospital. It would have been better if he'd tried to get himself invalided home from there.

It was now hopeless, all was in vain, there was no way of escape. A nihilistic pessimism overwhelmed him with frightening force. He lost even the will to walk. He couldn't stop the tears flowing. If there is a God in this life, then please let Him help me! Please let Him show me the way out! I'll suffer any hardship afterwards! I'll do all sorts of good deeds! I won't turn my back on anything!

He broke into a loud and bitter sob.

His chest kept heaving. Tears flowed down his cheeks as if he were a little child. The thought of dying was painfully sad to him. Up till now he had been, on numerous occasions, fired by patriotic thoughts. On board ship, when they had sung their songs of war, he had been filled with thoughts of heroic sacrifice. Even if an enemy warship suddenly appeared and sent them down with a single shell, leaving him a corpse tangled in the weeds on the bottom, he would have no regrets, so he had thought. At the battle of Chin-chou he had advanced bravely, flat out on the ground, through the very middle of the screaming death of the machine-gun fire. It wasn't that he hadn't been affected by the blood-spattered figures of his comrades, but he had felt it was for the sake of his country, that it was an honor.

But the blood that had flowed had not been his own. Face to face with his own death, even the bravest man trembles.

His legs were heavy, he was worn out, and he felt sick. The twenty-five miles from T'ai-shih-ch'iao, with the two days on the road, the evening dew, and the bitter cold, had certainly aggravated his chronic beriberi. The dysentery had gone, but the beriberi had become acute. He shuddered, realizing the terrible danger of heart failure. Was it really impossible to escape? He couldn't relax, his body was numb, his legs seized with cramp. . . . He wept aloud as he walked.

The plain was peaceful. The huge red sun dipped to the horizon, and the sky was half golden, half deep blue. A section of cloud moved through the sky like the wings of some golden bird. The sorghum cast shadows over shadows, and an autumn wind sprang up over the bleak plain. The gun-fire from Liaoyang, which he had heard clearly till then, now died completely away.

Two upper-privates overtook him, brushing past. A dozen or so yards on, one of them turned and came back.

"Hey, what's up with you?"

He came back to his senses. He was ashamed to have been weeping out loud.

"Hey there!"

The soldier spoke to him a second time.

"I've got beriberi."

"Beriberi?"

"Uh."

"That must be rough. Is it very bad?"

"It hurts."

"That really is rough. If beriberi gets to your heart it's a very serious matter. How far are you going?"

"I think my unit's beyond Anshan."

"Well, you won't get there today."

"I guess not."

"Look, come with us to Hsin-t'ai-tzu. There's a depot there, so you can get seen to by a doctor."

"Is it far?"

"Just over there. You see that hill there? On this side there's the railroad. There where the flag's flying, that's the Hsin-t'ai-tzu depot."

"Is there a doctor there?"

"There's one army doctor."

His spirits revived.

He walked along behind the pair. They were both feeling sorry for him and carried his rifle and pack.

As they walked along in front they talked about the day's fighting at Liaoyang.

"I wonder how things are?"

"They're probably still at it. I heard at Yuan-t'ai that the enemy is putting up a stand a few miles this side of Liaoyang. I heard the name Shou-shan-po or something."

"There're a lot of reserves moving up."

"We've not got enough troops. I'm told the enemy defenses are really good."

"It looks like it'll be quite a battle."

"Well, the guns were going all day, that's for sure."

"Do you think we can win?"

"It'll be hard on us if we lose."

"The First Army's set out too, I suppose."

"Naturally."

"It'd be good if we could just get a chance to cut neatly in behind them."

"It'll go all right this time, you just watch."

They listened. The gun-fire started right up again.

The supply depot at Hsin-t'ai-tzu was now in a state of tremendous bustling confusion. A regiment of the Reserve Brigade had arrived, and everywhere—on the rails, in the shadow of the buildings, beside the piles of provisions—it was a mass of soldiers' hats and bayonets. Some five barracks, which the enemy's rail-support troops had used, stood flanking the rails. Now a Japanese flag fluttered above the depot headquarters, where the confusion was particularly great—a swarm of soldiers had gathered there, and countless officers, with long dangling swords, were going in and out. Fires were blazing under the depot's three huge cauldrons, and thick clouds of smoke curled into the dusky evening sky. The rice in one cauldron had already cooked, and the mess-sergeant was yelling vociferous orders to his subordinates and busily distributing the rice to the soldiers around him. However, it was utterly impossible to cater for all those many soldiers' evening meals with just these three cauldrons,

so the majority simply took the polished rice in their mess-tins and
scattered on the plain to cook it themselves. Soon the surrounding
plain was dotted with innumerable sorghum-fires.

Over by the buildings they were working through the night
loading boxes of ammunition for the front onto the freight
wagons. In the feeble evening light you could just make out
groups of infantrymen and transport troops moving about,
working frantically. A single N.C.O. stood high on top of one of
the loaded wagons, busily directing operations.

The day had ended, but not the war. Saddle-shaped Mount
Anshan grew dark, while the firing could be heard intermittently
from beyond.

Having arrived, he tried to find the doctor. The doctor, however, seemed to be the last person he could expect to find there.
It wasn't the time or place for worrying about whether one
soldier lived or died. It was all his two helpers could do to get
him a mere mess-tin of boiled rice. "Look, we can't do anything
at the moment. Just hang on a bit. As soon as this regiment's
moved off we'll find the doctor and bring him along. For the
time being, just take it easy. If you go straight on from here a
few hundred yards or so, you'll find a Western-style building—
there's a canteen in the entrance, just been opened this morning,
so you'll soon recognize it. Go into the back there and get some
sleep."

He no longer had the will to walk. He took back his rifle and
pack, but looked in danger of collapsing when he put them on
his back. He felt dizzy. He felt sick. His legs were weary. His
head was spinning violently.

But it wouldn't do to collapse there. He had to find somewhere
quiet and private in which to die. Yes, somewhere quiet and
private. . . . Any such sort of place would do. He just wanted to
sleep somewhere quiet, just take a rest.

The road stretched on and on through the darkness. Here and
there he came across groups of soldiers. Suddenly he remembered
the barracks at Toyohashi. He had often hidden himself away
in the canteen there, drinking saké. Once he had got drunk and
had struck a sergeant, and had been given a long spell in the
cooler. The road just went on and on. However far he went he
couldn't see anything like a Western-style building. A few
hundred yards, they'd said. Let alone a few hundred, he'd now

come at least a thousand! He turned round, wondering if he hadn't made a mistake. The night air behind him was broken by the shouts of the men carrying the ammunition boxes, and he could see the black shapes of groups of soldiers passing by in the gloom, the lights from the campfires, the lamplight from the depot.

It was so quiet there around him. Not a person nearby. Suddenly his chest seized painfully. If there was no refuge to die in, then he would die there where he was. He collapsed. But strangely, his earlier sadness had gone, so too his memories. He noticed the stars twinkling in the sky. He vaguely raised his head and looked around.

He was surprised to see the elusive Western building right there in front of him. He could see the lamplight inside. He could see a round red lantern. He heard voices.

He just managed to get to his feet by leaning on his rifle.

Sure enough, it looked like there was a canteen in the entrance. It was dark, so he couldn't be certain, but it looked as though there was a cauldron in a corner outside—he could see the glowing red embers. A thin wisp of smoke curled lightly up around the lantern. For all his terrible pain, he could clearly make out the writing on the lantern—"Bean soup, 5 sen a bowl."

"Soup's finished, is it?" asked a soldier standing there out front.

"Finished, I'm afraid," came a voice from inside.

Peeping inside, he saw bright light, two candles, cans and various odds and ends piled in a heap, and among them, sitting on a raised spot, a plump, grinning, thickly moustached man of about thirty. In the shop a soldier was examining a towel.

Looking to the side, through the darkness he could make out some low stone steps. This is the place, he thought. As he realized that now he could at least rest, his first feeling was one of indescribable satisfaction. Quietly and stealthily he climbed the steps. It was dark inside. He wasn't sure, but it seemed to be a corridor. He tried pushing what he thought to be the first door, but it wouldn't open. A few paces further on he tried the next door, which wouldn't open either. He pushed a door on the left, but also to no avail.

He went further inside.

The corridor came to an end. There was no turning either

side. In despair he pushed against the wall on his right, and suddenly the darkness was broken as a door opened. He couldn't make out the inside of the room, but somewhere there was starlight, and he knew there must be a window in front.

He set down his rifle, lowered his pack, and fell straight down, flat out. He drew a deep, painful breath. Well, he'd found his resting place, he thought.

Along with his contentment, a new anxiety welled up within him. Weariness, fatigue, and a feeling akin to despair weighed painfully down like lead on his whole being. Recollections came to him all in fragments, sometimes with lightning speed, sometimes with ponderous slowness. He was in a state of constant restlessness.

He was well aware that a sort of painful pressure had come over his heavy, weary legs. He had a throbbing pain in his calves. It wasn't a normal sort of pain—it was exactly as if they'd been turned inside out.

He writhed about almost automatically. His utterly exhausted body couldn't bear up to this pressure.

He tossed and turned instinctively.

It wasn't that he didn't think about home, or feel upset about his wife and mother. It wasn't that he didn't regret having to die like this. However, such grieving, such memories, such dreams, such things mattered little now. What he had to do was fight against the pain, that pain, that immense force.

It came over him like a tide. It raged like a tempest. He lifted his legs and brought them down again on the hard wooden boards; he tossed his body from side to side.

"The pain! . . ." he cried out, unthinkingly.

Yet in fact he didn't feel the pain to be as bad as all that. It was bad enough, that was for sure, but it was lessened somewhat by his strenuous mental efforts to prepare himself for a still greater pain that was yet to come. A strength of sorts flowed through his entire body.

Rather than feeling sad about dying, his strongest thought was to overcome the pain. While he was on the one hand filled with a negative, tearful, prideless sort of despair, he was at the same time firmly possessed of a strength, a positive strength, the right of a human being to survive.

Like a tide the pain came and went, fell away and advanced

again. As it came on he would bite his lip, grit his teeth, clutch his legs with both hands.

He wondered whether he hadn't now developed some sort of sixth sense. He could clearly see the room, despite the darkness. There was a tall table up against the dark wall. The white on top was sure to be paper. The window was half-broken, and he could make out the twinkling stars that lit up the sky. In a corner to the right something or other had been set down in a jumble.

He was no longer aware of the passage of time. He wished the doctor would come, but he didn't have time to pursue this thought. A new pain had come on.

A cricket was chirping somewhere near where he was lying. "Ah, a cricket . . ." he thought, amid his agony. Its melancholy notes seemed to him somehow to pierce his whole being.

The pain returned, and he started rolling about again.

"The pain! The pain! The pain!"

He was screaming.

"The pain! . . . Is there . . . is there no one here?!"

That fervent power of survival was now considerably weakened. His cries for help were now more subconscious than conscious, the cries of distress of a man overcome by the forces of nature, like the leaves that rustle on the trees and the waves that roar.

"The pain! The pain!"

His voice echoed frighteningly around the empty room. Up until a month ago that room had been occupied by officers of the Russian rail-support detachment. When Japanese troops had first entered they had found a figure of Christ, stained black with soot, fixed on the wall. During the previous winter those officers had drunk vodka, looking out through that window at the wind-driven snow falling steadily on the Manchurian plains. Soldiers had stood outside in their furry winter uniforms. They had talked big, bragged about how the Japanese troops were too pathetic to do anything. And now that room echoed with the groans of a dying soldier.

"The pain! The pain! The pain!"

Things were quiet for a moment. The cricket was chirping the same sad, soft song. A late moon had risen over the vast Manchurian plain. It was brighter, and the area outside the window was bathed in moonlight.

He squirmed there in the room, groaning, moaning, despairing. The buttons had come off his uniform, his chest and neck were scratched, his cap was crushed, still fastened about his chin, and stale vomit streaked his face.

Suddenly he was aware of a bright beam of light penetrating the room, and standing there at the door, like some embossed carving, was the figure of a man holding a candle. It was that same face, the plump moustached face from the canteen. However, the face was no longer smiling amiably as before, but was serious and concerned. The man came silently into the room and looked at the moaning, writhing, sick soldier by the light of the candle. The sick man's face was terribly pale, like that of a corpse. Vomit was smeared all around.

"What's the matter? Are you ill?"

"Aah, the pain! The pain!"

He screamed, writhing.

The man from the canteen stood there a while looking at him, reluctant to touch, and then, fixing the candle on the table with its own wax, he hurried out of the room. With the light of the candle the room grew bright as day. He noticed it was his own pack and rifle there in that corner.

The candle flame flickered. The wax ran down in drops, like tears.

After a while the man came back with a soldier. He had woken him from his sleep in a building across the way, one of those troops soon due to continue on the march again. The soldier looked at the sick man's face and around the room, and then inspected his shoulder insignia.

The sick man could hear their conversation clearly.

"He's from the Eighteenth Regiment."

"Oh?"

"How long's he been here?"

"I haven't the faintest idea—no idea at all when he arrived. I was fast asleep around ten, and then I suddenly woke up hearing groans. 'The pain! The pain!' someone was yelling. Strange, I thought, there shouldn't be anyone in the back, and

so I listened carefully for a while, and sure enough, the cries
gradually got louder—'Won't somebody come?!' I could hear,
and so I came. It's beriberi. It's got to his heart."

"To his heart?"

"There's nothing we can do."

"That's a real pity. I suppose there's an army doctor here in
the depot?"

"There is, but . . . he won't come out at this hour!"

"What time is it?" Taking his watch out, the soldier looked
for himself. He put it back in his pocket, a knowing look on his
face.

"Well, what is the time, then?"

"Two-fifteen."

The two stood in silence.

The pain came on again. The groans and cries grew into an
unbearable screaming.

"It's a pity, isn't it?" said the soldier again.

"It really is a shame," agreed the other man. "Where do you
suppose he's from?"

He felt the soldier searching his pockets, and drawing out his
regimental tally-book. He could see the soldier's dark, strong
face, see him move over to the candle on the table in order to
read the book. "Katō Heisaku, from Fukue Village, Atsumi
District, Mikawa Province"—he could hear the soldier reading
the words out loud. Once again he could picture the scenes of
home. His mother's face, his wife's face, the big house surrounded
by zelkovas, the smooth shore out back, the blue-green sea, the
familiar fishermen's faces . . .

The two stood in silence. Their faces were somber. Occasionally
they exchanged words of sympathy over the sick man. He had
already fully realized he was going to die. But he didn't feel
particularly sad or distressed about it. It was some other, in-
animate thing, not himself, that the two were discussing. He
just wanted to escape from this pain, this unbearable pain, that
was all.

The candle flickered. The cricket chirped the same sad song.

The depot doctor came at daybreak. But the sick soldier had
already died, an hour earlier. As the first train set off for Anshan

amid rousing cheers, up in the sky the lingering morning moon hung wan and pale and lonely.

Soon the sound of steady firing could be heard. It was the first of September, and the attack on Liaoyang had begun.

(January 1908)

The Girl Watcher

1

A S the 7: 20 A.M. Yamanote Line train passes through Yoyogi
Station on its way to the city, shaking the embankment,
a man walks on his way between the paddies in nearby Sendagaya. He goes the same way every morning, whatever the
weather. Rainy days find him plowing his way through the
mud in his old waterproof boots, while on windy days he has
his hat clamped on the back of his head, warding off the dust.
The people living along the way spot him coming, and one
woman even wakes up her husband, a military official prone to
sleep late on drowsy spring mornings, by telling him he'll be late
for the office as "that man" has just gone past.

He had first appeared on the scene some two months earlier.
It was a time of suburban development, and new properties
would appear on the top of a hill or at the edge of a wood, with
the huge mansions of major-generals and company directors
scattered picturesquely among the great rows of charcoal oaks
that were spared from the development of the area. Rumor had
it that beyond these oaks half a dozen or so houses had been
built to let, and that the man had probably moved into one of
these.

Somebody passing by is not usually anything to start talking
about, but in the lonely countryside people are something of
a rarity, and this particular man's figure was, moreover, de-
cidedly peculiar: he walked in a strange duck-like fashion, and
there was just something odd about him which caught the attention of the people of leisure living along the way.

He was about thirty-seven, with rounded shoulders, a pug

nose, protruding teeth, a swarthy complexion, and tangled side-burns that covered half his face. He was quite fearsome to look at, enough to upset young ladies even in broad daylight. But, in contrast, he had something kind and gentle about his eyes, which always seemed as if entranced by something. His legs set determinedly wide apart, he would scurry along at an amazing pace, even putting to shame a certain soldier who went out training every morning.

He mostly wore Western-style clothes—an old brown suit of thread-bare Scotch wool, and an Inverness cape faded to a dull purplish yellow. In his right hand he carried a walking-stick with an easy-grip dog's-head handle, while he kept his left hand in his pocket, with an ill-becoming maroon cloth bundle clasped under his arm.

"He's off now, then, I see," mumbled the gardener's wife to herself as he passed by their trellis fence on the corner. The gardener's place was also a newly built detached, with the spindly pines, oaks, boxtrees, eight-finger trees, and so on that were for sale planted untidily around outside. Beyond it, along the high-way, lay the broken skyline of Sendagaya's new residential area, with the rays of the morning sun glittering on the upstairs' windows. To the left lay the numerous factories of Tsunohazu, with the smoke of the morning's work, already under way, coiling low and thick from the narrow flues. In the otherwise clear sky he could make out the tops of telegraph poles above the woods.

He walked on his way.

Crossing the paddies he entered a narrow pebbly lane with neat rows of brushwood fences, oak hedges, and hawthorn hedges, punctuated by glass doors, crossbarred gates, and gas lamps. Some gardens still had ropes fastened to the trees to prevent frost damage. A few blocks further on he came to Sendagaya Road, where he invariably encountered the soldier racing along on his exercises. He continued past a foreigner's large Western-style house, the huge gate of a doctor's new house, and an old thatched cottage that sold cheap confectionery. Now he could see the raised track of Yoyogi Station, and from here he could usually hear the train whistle from Shinjuku, the next station, which would prompt him to forget any semblance of dignity and race ahead at full tilt, bulky as he was.

Today as usual he arrived at the spot and listened, but could not hear the train coming and so continued at his same brisk pace. However, turning the corner at the T-junction with the track, he caught sight ahead of him of an attractive woman with a fashionable hairstyle and a smart purple coat. A green ribbon, satin sandal-straps, crisp white socks. The sight made his heart race. He couldn't put it into words, but just seemed to feel, in a happy, flustered sort of way, that it would be a pity to overtake her. He already knew the woman by sight, and they had traveled in the same train carriage at least five or six times. In fact, one wintry evening he had deliberately made a detour to see where she lived—a large house to the west of the Sendagaya paddies, surrounded by oaks. He knew she was the eldest daughter of the family. She had beautiful eyebrows, a pale complexion, and plump cheeks, and when she laughed her eyes were expressive beyond words.

He enjoyed thinking about her. "She's in her early twenties, so she can't be going to school—I know that anyway since I don't see her every day. But I wonder where she does go, then?" He was terribly excited by the beautiful figure ahead of him. "I wonder if she's engaged yet?" This thought, however, caused him a twinge of sadness. "If only I were a bit younger . . ." But then his thoughts changed again. "How absurd! I'm not only too old, I have a wife and children as well!" He was left feeling somehow sad, somehow happy.

As it happened, he did overtake her, at the steps up to Yoyogi Station. The rustling of her clothes and the fragrance of her perfume made his heart miss a beat, but he refrained from turning round and raced up the steps with giant strides, almost at a gallop. The station-master clipped his red return-ticket and gave it back to him. Like all the station officials, he was now quite accustomed to the man's bustling, fast-talking manner.

As he was about to enter the wooden waiting room, the man's sharp eyes caught sight of the familiar figure of a girl student standing there. She was a sweet-looking girl, with plumpish features and rosy cheeks. She wore a bright, striped top and a maroon *hakama*. She carried a slender parasol in her right hand and a bundle wrapped in purple cloth in her left. He noticed straight away that her ribbon today was white, different from her usual one.

"Surely she can't have forgotten me, not *this* girl?" He looked towards her, but she was facing away, with a blank expression. "She's probably just shy," he thought, and this somehow seemed to endear her to him. He pretended not to look, but in fact did so frequently and intently. And then, looking away, his gaze now fixed on the woman he had just overtaken on the steps.

He hardly seemed aware of the train's arrival.

2

There was a reason for his thinking that the girl might not have forgotten him, for a rather interesting incident had taken place. She had always got on the train at Yoyogi at the same time as he did, to go as far as Ushigome, so he had known her by sight for some time. But even so, he'd never gone so far as to speak to her. He would just sit opposite her, thinking about what a plump girl she was, how fleshy her cheeks were, how big her breasts were, and what a wonderful girl she was. As the days passed, he'd come to notice all sorts of things about her, such as how beautiful her smile was, how she had a little mole just below her ear, how white her slender arms were as she clung to the straps in the crowded carriage, how she talked saucy girl-talk with some schoolfriends who joined her at Shinanomachi. It got to the point where he wanted to find out about her home and family.

But for all that, he didn't seem prepared to go quite as far as to follow her to find these things out. Then, one day, as he was coming out onto the paddies of Sendagaya in his same old way along his same old route, with his same old hat and his same old Inverness cape and his same old suit and his same old shoes, he suddenly saw, walking towards him, that very same plumpish girl. She was wearing a white top fastened loosely over her jacket, was smoothing her hair with her hand, and was chatting about something with a girl friend. Whenever we meet a familiar face in an unfamiliar setting we always seem to feel a sort of friendship, and this is what he too seemed to feel. He suddenly slowed, as if intending to say hello. The girl also glanced towards him, as if she were thinking, "Ah, it's that man from the train." However, she passed by without a word. He spoke out instinctively, but to himself: "No school today, then? Exam-leave perhaps, or spring holidays?" He hurried on a dozen or so yards without thinking, then suddenly spotted—quietly fallen there on the black, soft, beautiful spring soil, and looking just like a silver pine needle on a gilded screen—an aluminum hair-pin.

It was hers!

He turned round quickly and called out to her.

"I say! Hey! I say!"

She'd only gone a few dozen paces, so she undoubtedly heard him. But, not thinking that it was she herself that he was calling, she carried on walking and chatting with her friend, not even looking round. The morning sun shone beautifully on the blade of a farmworker's plowspade out in the fields.

"I say! Hey! I say!"

He called out again, as if reciting a verse.

This time the girl did turn round. She saw him looking towards her, in a strange pose with his hands up in the air. With a sudden realization she clasped her hand to her hair—the pin was gone. "What? Heavens! I've dropped my hairpin!" she exclaimed, and dashed off towards him. He waited, holding the pin, hands still held high. She panted as she ran.

"Thank you very much . . ."

She thanked him, blushing with embarrassment. A grin spread over his big, square-cut face, revealing his obvious delight as he returned the pin to her beautiful white hand.

"Thank you very much indeed."

She thanked him again politely, then turned on her heels. He was deliriously happy. It was simply marvelous. "From now on she'll remember me! From now on, when we meet in the train, she'll think of me as the man who picked up her pin for her!" His thoughts rambled. "If I were a little younger, and if she were just a little prettier, then there'd have been an inter-esting tale to tell about this episode . . ." One thought gave rise to another. He had idly wasted away his youth. His wife, whom he'd once loved, had passed her prime. He had children. His life was bleak. He was behind the times, with no hope for the future. Such thoughts were tangled and twisted, almost with-out end. Then suddenly, into the midst of this reverie floated the sullen face of the editor-in-chief of the magazine house where he worked. At which, hastily abandoning his daydreams, he hurried on along the lane.

3

We might well wonder where this man comes from. Across the paddies of Sendagaya, beyond the rows of charcoal oaks, through the area lined with the gates of the splendid new mansions, past a meadow with lowing cows, along a little path by the rows of great oaks, and beyond that, down in the shadow of a gently sloping hill, you find a small detached house, and it is from here that he emerges every morning. Its appearance—low roof, three rooms, surrounded by a low hawthorn hedge—tells you that it is a crudely built rented house. The garden and parlor can be fully seen from the road, without having to go in through the little gate. And in the garden, down at the foot of five or six dwarf-bamboos, several small daphnes are in bloom, with half a dozen or so potted plants laid out untidily nearby. A woman in her mid-twenties, clearly his wife, is busily at work, with her sleeves tied up out of the way. A boy of about four and a girl of about six have come out onto the sunny verandah of the room next to the parlor, and are happily playing and chattering away.

On the south side of the house is a well with an upturned bucket, and, around ten o'clock and weather permitting, his wife takes the tub out there and busily sets about the washing. You can hear the peaceful, splashing, watery sound of clothes being washed, while a nearby white lotus, sparkling beautifully in the spring sunlight, spreads an aura of indescribable serenity. Naturally his wife is now somewhat faded, but even so she gives the impression that in her day she was better looking than average. She has her hair done up in a rather old-fashioned pile, with her puffy front locks taken up; she wears a striped cotton kimono, the ends of her maroon waist-sash hang to the ground, and, as she busies her hands with the washing, her sash-bustle moves delicately. Presently her young boy comes up to her, calling "Mama! Mama!" and no sooner does he reach her than he gropes for her breast. "Now just wait!" she says, but the child pays not the least attention and so, hastily drying her wet hands on her apron, she sits down on the front verandah, and takes the child in her arms. The girl also comes along and stands there.

The study, which doubles as the guestroom, is a six-mat room, with a small, glass-fitted Western-style bookcase set up against the west wall, and a chestnut desk against the opposite wall. A bowl of spring orchids stands in the alcove, and the scroll there is a reproduction of a landscape by Bunchō. The spring sunlight comes into the room, and it all seems very warm and pleasant. There are two or three magazines on the desk, the yellow wood-graining of a Noshiro-lacquered inkstone case stands out quite noticeably, and some paper—probably copy-paper from his company—flutters in the spring breeze.

The hero of the piece is named Sugita Kojō, and it goes without saying that he is a literary man. When he was younger his name had achieved a befitting degree of prominence, and two or three of his works had even been quite well received. Indeed, neither he himself nor anyone else had thought that at his present age of thirty-seven he would have come to be employed in an insignificant magazine house, commuting day after day and even doing trivial tasks such as proofreading magazines, nor that he would have sunk banally below the horizon of the literary world. But there was a reason for this course of events. He had been the same for years, actually, but he had this bad habit of getting obsessed with young women. Every time he saw a beautiful young woman, his otherwise quite sharp powers of observation lost all discrimination. When he was younger, he wrote a great number of so-called girl novels, and for a time quite captivated the youth of the day; but for how long could such novels, devoid of proper observation and ideology, be expected to hold people's interest? Finally he and his thing about girls became the laughingstock of the literary world, and his novels and other writings were all laughed down. To add to it, as has already been remarked, his features were unsurpassably uncouth, and this made things worse by the contrast which they created: with a face like that, how could he have turned out as he had? When in fact, judging from appearances, he had the looks and build of someone about to do battle with the beasts? Rumor had it that it was all doubtless a freak of nature.

His friends were once discussing his case.

174

"I don't know—I just can't make it out. Perhaps it's some sort of illness. The thing is, he does nothing but *think* about girls —just thinks about how good-looking they are, and nothing more. Now if it was us, well, we wouldn't be satisfied with just *thinking* about them—the force of instinct would soon raise its head, wouldn't you say?"

"You know, perhaps he's got something physically missing somewhere."

"It could be a character defect rather than a physical one."

"No, I don't think so. I just wonder if he wasn't too self-indulgent when he was younger."

"Self-indulgent?"

"Oh, you know what I mean! He abused himself too much. They say that if you go on with that habit for too long then you get certain physical deficiencies, and that the physical body and inner being don't harmonize properly."

"How absurd!" someone laughed.

"But he's got children, hasn't he?" remarked somebody else.

"Yes, he has got children," the first speaker conceded. "But I did ask a doctor about this, and he told me that the consequences could take a number of forms. In extreme cases there's a loss of reproductive ability, but apparently there're also lots of people who end up just like Sensei. That doctor told me all sorts of things, you know, and I really think my diagnosis is correct."

"Well, I still think it's his character."

"No, look, he's ill I tell you! He should do something to get rid of his desires, like going off to the coast or somewhere and getting some good air or something."

"But it's just too much to believe. If he were eighteen or nineteen, or even in his early twenties, then what you say might well be true. But he has a wife and children, and he's almost thirty-eight, isn't he? You're just giving some sort of physiological 'catch-all'—it's just too conclusive to be true!"

"No, listen, it can be explained! You're saying this sort of thing can't happen once you're out of your teens. But the point is that there're any number of cases. I'm sure that Sensei's still going on with the habit even now. You see, when he was younger he was silly enough to pretend to believe that love was pure and sacred. But, whatever he might say, he couldn't fool his instincts, so finally he had to resort to self-abuse for his pleasures. Then when this got to be a habit he became ill, unable to satisfy those instincts. I'm sure that's the way it is! In other words, like I said before, his body and his inner being don't harmonize properly. But it really is interesting, isn't it? He'd pretend to be so clean-living, and even convince other people, but now he's ended up degraded, an example of decadence, just because he wouldn't respect his instincts. You lot are always criticizing me for believing in the force of instinct, but really, instincts are terribly important in people. You can't live unless you follow your instincts!" he argued, waxing lyrical.

4

The train left Yoyogi.

It was a pleasant spring morning. The sun shone gently overhead, and the air was exceptionally clear. Untidy rows of new houses in the low land of Sendagaya and the dark rows of charcoal oaks, topped by the beautiful form of Mount Fuji away in the distance, passed quickly by like a kaleidoscope. But our man, preferring the figure of a beautiful girl to the beauty of mute nature, was almost completely entranced with the faces and figures of two girls opposite him. Gazing upon living beings, however, is more troublesome than gazing upon mute nature, and so, sensing he might be discovered if he stared too openly, he was pretending to look to the side, while flashing furtive sidelong glances at the girls. As someone once said, when it comes to girl watching on trains, it's too direct to watch them face-on, whereas from a distance it's too conspicuous and likely to arouse people's suspicions; therefore, the most convenient seat to occupy is one diagonally opposite, at rather an oblique angle. Being an obsessive girl watcher, Sugita had not, of course, had to be taught this secret and had naturally discovered the technique for himself, never wasting any suitable opportunity.

The expression in the elder girl's eyes was infinitely beautiful. Even the stars in the sky, he felt, lost their sparkle in comparison. Slender legs under that crepe kimono, a brilliant mauve hem, white-stockinged feet in fashionable high sandals, a beautifully white neck, beautiful breasts at the swelling of her chest—it was too much for him to bear. The other, plumper girl, on the other hand, took a notebook from her pocket and began to read it with great interest.

Soon they arrived at Sendagaya Station.

He knew from experience that he could expect at least three girls to get on here. But today, for some reason—perhaps it was a little too early, or a little too late—not one of those familiar three appeared. Instead, a plain young woman got on, the sort you normally wouldn't look twice at. So long as it was a young woman, even a rather ugly one, he would usually find some attractive feature on which to fix his gaze, such as nice eyes, a nice nose, a white complexion, a pretty neck, shapely legs, or something of the sort. However, with this woman he could not, search as he might, find a single attractive point. This ghastly creature—with its protruding teeth and frizzly hair and dark complexion—promptly came and took the seat next to him.

The next station, Shinanomachi, was a place where relatively few girls got on. He could remember that on one occasion an absolutely beautiful girl, who had all the air of being the demoiselle of a noble family, had traveled next to him as far as Ushigome, but since then he had not seen her again, to his great disappointment. He was disappointed again today. The train took on a whole crowd of gentlemen and military men and merchants and students and the like, and then sped off like some flying serpent.

Coming out through the tunnel, the train started to slacken speed, and from this point he strained to get a good look at the next waiting room. Suddenly his face lit up and his heart raced. He'd spotted a ribbon he recognized. There was a girl of about eighteen who got on here at Yotsuya and went to the Ochanomizu Girls' School. She was a very attractively dressed girl with particularly charming features and so beautiful he felt there could be few to equal her even in Tokyo. She was slimly built, not at all fat but neither too skinny, her eyes sparkling clear, her mouth firm, and her cheerful face invariably flushed with a healthy crimson. Unfortunately, that day there were a lot of passengers so she just stood there by the door, but at the conductor's request to move down inside to ease the congestion she soon came and stood right in front of him, reaching up for the strap with her white arm. It wasn't that he didn't think about standing up to give her his seat, it was just that, if he did, then he would not only be unable to look at her white arm, it would also be very inconvenient to have to look down on her from above, and so he didn't get up.

Beautiful girls in crowded trains—there was nothing he enjoyed quite so much, and he had already experienced this pleasure countless times. The feel of soft clothing, the elusive perfumes, the touch of warm flesh—he was stirred to indescribable thoughts. In particular, the smell of female hair aroused a sort of violent desire in him, giving him inexpressible pleasure.

Ichigaya, Ushigome, and Iidamachi passed quickly by.

The two girls from Yoyogi had both got off at Ushigome. The train took on a new look as it got more and more crowded. In spite of all this, he just gazed, like a man with a lost soul, in rapt admiration at the beautiful face in front of him.

Presently they arrived at Ochanomizu.

5

The magazine house where he worked, Seinensha, was in Nishiki-chō in Kanda, in the very next street to the School of Proper English. In front of the glass door facing the road stood a row of some half dozen signboards advertising the latest publications, and, on going in through that door, there was the grave face of the owner of the company, waiting at the desk of a room cluttered with magazines. The editing room was upstairs at the back, a single, ten-mat room with the west and south blocked off and therefore very gloomy. There were five desks lined up there for the editors, and his desk was in the dark spot nearest the wall, so dark, in fact, that on rainy days he could have done with a lamp. To make things worse the telephone was right at his side, and its incessant ringing tormented his nerves.

Our hero felt thoroughly depressed as he changed onto the Sotobori Line at Ochanomizu and got off at the corner of Nishikichō Sanchōme. It was as though his pleasant daydreams had been shattered, and he immediately pictured the chief editor and his own gloomy desk. Another day's agony! He went straight on to thoughts about how trying life was. He came to the gloomy conclusion, as the yellow dust of the road danced before his eyes, that the world was worth nothing. He could clearly see how mean a chore it was to proofread, and how petty it was to edit magazines. It was almost endless. If it had been that alone, however, it wouldn't have been too bad, but those beautiful visions from the train, which still lingered on in vanishing, appeared vaguely in that wretched yellow dust, making him feel that his one real pleasure in life was thus somehow being destroyed by it all, and that was even more depressing.

Into the bargain, the chief editor was a sarcastic man who thought nothing of making fun of people. Even when he, Sugita, really tried and wrote something elegant, the chief would dig in with, "Ah, Sugita-kun, you've produced another love affair, I see!" At the least opportunity Sugita was mocked because of girls. Occasionally he would get angry and snap back that he wasn't a child, that he was thirty-seven, and that there was a limit even to making a fool of somebody. But his anger soon died down, and he never learned, and went on writing spicy poems and composing new-style poetry.

In fact, apart from gazing at the beautiful figures in the train, he liked nothing better than composing flowery, new-style poetry, and while he was at the office, whenever he had no work to attend to, he would take out some paper and write beautiful things as if his life depended on it. It goes without saying that many of his thoughts involved girls.

That day there was a lot of proofreading to be done, and our hero worked busily on it all by himself. Around two in the afternoon he managed to get some of it out of the way, and let out a sigh.

At this point the chief editor called over to him:

"Sugita-kun."

"Yes?" he replied, looking over to the chief.

"I've read your latest work, you know," said the chief, laughing.

"Oh, really?"

"As usual, it's beautiful. Just how do you manage to write so prettily? You know, I don't think it would be an exaggeration to say you were a lady-killer! There was even one reporter I remember who said how surprised he was when he actually saw how well-built you are—quite beyond what he expected, he said."

"Really, is that so?" Sugita could do nothing except laugh.

"Three cheers for girls, eh!?" chimed in one of the other editors, mockingly.

Sugita got angry but, considering it beneath his dignity to take up the challenge, he finally looked away. "It's all so annoying—how can you understand the mentality of people who want to make fun of me, a man of thirty-seven?" he thought to himself.

He smoked a cigarette, unable to stand the misery of the gloomy, dismal room no matter how he tried looking at it, and the purplish-blue smoke trailed upwards in a wispy, soothing way. As he stared at it, the girl from Yoyogi, and then the girl student, the beautiful figure from Yotsuya, and all the others appeared in mixed-up fragments, and seemed to blend into one person. He realized this was a bit silly, but he didn't seem to find it unpleasant either.

When it turned three o'clock and got closer to the time when he could leave, his thoughts turned to home. He thought about his wife. It was so useless, getting old like this. He was full of regret. To have spent his youth worthlessly and now to regret it—what use was that? It was absolutely pointless, he thought to himself again. Why hadn't he made passionate love while he was young? Why hadn't he tasted his fill of the delights of the flesh? What good was it to think of this now? He was now thirty-seven. It irritated him to think like this, and made him feel like tearing his hair.

He went out through the glass door. His mind was completely worn out with his day's labors, and he had a bad headache. The yellow dust being blown about by the westerly wind was miserable, so miserable. For some reason or other, today was a particularly miserable and trying day. However much he was attracted to the fragrant scent of beautiful girls' hair, his days for loving were past. And anyway, even if he tried, he no longer had the wings to lure any beautiful bird. As he moved his bulky frame along, such thoughts made him feel life was no longer worth living, that he would be better off dead . . . better off dead . . . better off dead. . . .

He looked ill. His clouded eyes were a sign of his gloomy heart. It wasn't that he didn't think about his wife and children and peaceful home, it was just that such things now seemed far removed. Better off dead? If he were dead, what would his wife and children do? Even this thought now dwindled away, his spirit having sunk so low it failed to respond. Loneliness . . . loneliness . . . loneliness—was there no one who would save him from this loneliness? Any one of those beautiful figures from the train would do—was there no one who would embrace him in her white arms? If only someone would, then he was sure he would be resurrected. He was sure that then he would discover life in hope, in challenge, in hard work. Fresh blood would flow through his veins. . . . At least, that was what he believed, but in reality it was doubtful if his spirits could be revived in this way.

The Sotobori train came and he got on. Straightaway his sharp eyes sought for the colors of beautiful clothes, but unfortunately there was nothing on board to give him satisfaction. However, he felt more relaxed just being on the train, and from now until he got home he would be at his ease, as if in his own little paradise. The various shops and signboards along the way passed before his eyes like a kaleidoscope, and this prompted various beautiful, pleasant memories.

When he came to change onto the Kōbu Line at Ochanomizu he found the train almost full, due to an exhibition being held at the time. He managed to wedge himself in at the guard's section; or, at least, he managed to position himself on the outside of the right-hand door, where he took a firm hold of the brass pole. Glancing inside the carriage, he gave a surprised start. For there, just beyond the glass window, almost overwhelmed by felt hats and college hats and Inverness capes—in fact looking just like a dove surrounded by a flock of crows—was the beautiful demoiselle from Shinanomachi, the one he had wished so much to see again. Such beautiful eyes, beautiful hands, beautiful hair . . . How could such a pretty girl exist in this vulgar world? Whose wife would she become? Whose arms would hold her? He was overcome with sadness and misery. It will be a fateful day all right when she gets married, he thought. Taking advantage of the crowd of passengers and the glass between he poured his heart, his very soul into her beautiful figure, with her white neck, her black hair, her olive ribbon, her dainty white fingers, her gold, jeweled ring.

Suidōbashi, Iidamachi—more and more passengers got on. When they got to Ushigome he was on the verge of getting pushed out of the carriage. He clung to the brass pole, never taking his eyes off the girl's figure, lost to all else. At Ichigaya another half-dozen or so passengers got on, and he pushed and shoved back in his turn, but still appeared to be right on the point of getting pushed from the carriage. The electric wires could be heard humming in the distance, and somehow everything seemed to get noisy. The whistle blew, the carriage moved forward a few yards, and then, as it suddenly gathered speed, a few nearby passengers somehow lost their balance and started to fall. The hand of the man ogling the beautiful girl came away from the brass pole, and his large frame described a perfect somersault as it tumbled rolling onto the track, just like some large ball. "Watch out!" yelled the conductor, but at that moment a city-bound train came along, shaking the ground, and in a mere instant the big black mass was dragged slitheringly for some ten yards or more, and a crimson trail of blood stained one of the rails.

The emergency whistle rent the air with a piercing blast.

(May 1907)

The Railway Track

1

THE train had hardly gone any distance from the station when, with a light jolt, it came to a sudden but gentle stop. The emergency whistle blew.

"What the—?"

"What's happened?"

The passengers looked at one another. Some stuck their heads out of the windows. "Has someone been run over or something?" asked others, as they, too, went to the windows. It was a typical edge-of-town area, with a line of low, dirty houses stretching away on either side. Faded napkins and other bits of washing were hung out to dry. Huge advertisements decorated long corrugated-iron hoardings. At the intersection of track and road a low hedge of *karatachi* orange was vigorously putting out new buds. On the far side an open stretch of grass lay like a green carpet.

2

"A child's been run over!"

The word spread from carriage to carriage.

In no time at all groups had started to form. Some passengers even got down from the carriages and ran off to look. From beyond the far side of the stretch of grass a saké-roundsman— to judge from appearances—came hurrying to where several children were standing. He appeared to ask them something very anxiously and then came up to the train.

Others followed in quick succession.

A flustered policeman came running up, sword in hand, and plunged into the crowd as if to tell someone off.

The atmosphere inside the train developed into one of general commotion. The passengers were all looking worried. They seemed particularly upset that it was a child who had been run over.

"How on earth could a child come to be playing in such a spot?" asked one middle-aged woman in a coat, with a sweet little girl of about seven at her side.

"The parents couldn't have been paying proper attention," said someone else.

"How old? Five? Five, they say? Well, they don't know any better at that tender age, do they? Must have come with someone else, wouldn't you say?"

"Those are the playmates over there, so I heard," said a man over to the right.

The women looked over towards three children in the middle of the group on the far side of the grass. They seemed between about seven and ten years old. The eldest had her hair done up in the "brazier" style and was wearing a red muslin apron.

At first she appeared to say something or other and was pointing as if to explain, but then her young mind suddenly seemed to realize exactly what had happened and she burst into tears, hiding her face with her sleeve.

3

The train gently started to move.

The passengers' faces could be seen pressed against the windows on the left.

Slowly, gently, the carriages moved forward.

The first thing to appear was the dirty greyish water of a canal. A boat full of mud was moored there. You could just hear the sound of the train starting to cross the bridge over the canal. Presently a small grassy slope between track and canal came into view. Green grass . . . a scattered bunch of flowers . . . crimson blood . . . a small crimson lump with dismembered hands and feet . . . the policeman's sword . . . the group . . .

4

"Oh, how terrible!" said one of the women, covering her face with her hands and sitting rigid.

"Just what sort of a train is this that we've got on?"

"And the parents—what about them?"

Such comments could be heard mingled with the rumbling of the train.

"Oh, why did I have to see it? I do wish I hadn't. How horrible!" said one distressed young woman.

There were women in the train who were sighing, as if relieved to have so narrowly escaped persecution by some terrible fate. Without exception all those who were mothers were thinking of their own young children left at home. Those who had their children with them drew them closely to their sides.

"You really can't afford to relax, can you?"

"No, it's a lesson to us all."

The comments went endlessly on.

"So the child got out onto the track? Fancy coming to play in such a spot! Came to pick flowers, they say. . . . But then, at that age you don't realize it's dangerous, do you?"

Even several stations later the conversation was going strong. Long afterwards, people could still clearly picture that little crimson lump.

5

The view on both sides of the train showed run-down country towns, cottages with iris blooming in the thatch, and splendid new villas up on the higher ground.

Some of the people in the train took hold of the new passengers to tell them expectantly, "Do you know, this train's just run over a five-year-old child?" The new passengers would listen with curiosity, with expressions such as to say, "What a terrible train I've just got on!" Some of the new women passengers would sympathize with comments like "Oh, what a shame!" The scene they had left behind would be created anew.

However, as the train entered a pine thicket near the coast, one of the mothers, who up till then had been keeping her own five-year-old girl clasped tightly on her lap, sat the child down near the window and, taking an orange from her bundle, proceeded to peel it carefully and pop segments into the child's mouth. A girl of eleven or twelve with pigtails went over to the window and gazed out at the shimmering sea.

"Well, thank heavens I can get off soon. You can't imagine how worried I've been, hoping that nothing else happens. Where there's one thing there's always another! What a horrible, horrible train!" With these words the middle-aged woman who had covered her face at the sight of the corpse took down a cloth bag from the rack overhead, and got off presently at the station among the pines. The China pinks were in splendid crimson bloom in the station's little flower bed.

The number of new passengers gradually increased, and one man who had been repeating the story of the incident with particular enthusiasm also got off somewhere. Presently the new passengers started gossiping and laughing about some new topic.

(June 1912)

The Photograph

THE soldiers on the mountain would get bored and would often go down to the Gyōkeikan for something to do. The guestrooms there stretched out in a row facing the sea, and from each of them the view was the same: the towering Inubo lighthouse, the angry breakers on the rocks, and casually dressed holiday-makers strolling about. It was late spring and there weren't actually very many holiday-makers, but nevertheless most of the rooms fronting on the sea were occupied and the young maids were always busy, hurrying along the connecting balcony in their red sleeve-bands and muslin waist-sashes.

The soldiers would invariably spend their spare time visiting the rooms and chatting with the guests—a dignified, white-haired old chap who had come with his grandchild, an almost transparently pale young woman with consumption, a well-to-do young man from a merchant family, who also looked rather ill, an old lady from the Yōkaichiba area, taking advantage of the relative quiet of the resort to visit for her health, and a robust, attractive young woman in her late twenties, who spent her days traveling around the resorts in carefree style while her husband, a naval commander, was away at war. There was a harmonica and hand organ in her room, and almost every day a small, fat, and rather simple private would come and play them.

It was just before the Battle of the Japan Sea, and the rumor was everywhere that the Russian Baltic Fleet had left Kamuran Bay and was headed north. The newspapers carried all sorts of reports in large print, and the cry of "Extra! Extra!" was heard even in this remote fishing village. Everyone was wondering whether the fleet would go via Tsushima or the Tsugaru Strait, or whether it might perhaps go round the Sōya Strait.

But the fat private just said, as if there were nothing to worry about:

"What can the Russkies possibly do? For all their trouble, they'll just end up blowing bubbles as they sink to the bottom!"

"It's not very nice for you fellows, though, having to keep watch every day, and even having to report any unfamiliar boats in the area," a guest would remark.

"Well, at least something unfamiliar would be something interesting. At the moment there's nothing but the sea to look at, day in and day out."

With this he would nonchalantly carry on playing the harmonica and teasing the dog. Occasionally he would say things like:

"Why don't you come up the mountain and visit us sometime? It's a bachelor's home up there, so we couldn't lay on anything special, but I'm sure we could manage a cup of tea or something."

The neighboring room had for some days been occupied by a refined but emaciated man in his mid-thirties, with neatly trimmed whiskers. He looked ill and would cough painfully, sometimes spitting phlegm into the ashtray. He seemed envious of the group of soldiers passing by or the other guests chatting happily to each other and exchanging the occasional bit of gossip as if very familiar with each other, just as though he himself wanted to act in this unreserved manner. Sometimes he would wander out alone to the rocks and stand there looking forlorn, while at other times he would sit quietly in his room, not even reading or smoking. He looked thoroughly run down.

Anyone else would have found it easy to take advantage of some slight opportunity or other to talk and joke with the other guests and get to know them, but for him this seemed impossible. He just couldn't get close to people, even when they went out of their way to be friendly to him.

The newspapers came every morning around ten. A young man wearing an old hat, and looking rather like a student, brought an assortment of them out from the town in a bamboo box. When they heard his bell people would hurry to buy a paper, anxious for news of the war. Soon rumors would spring up, and for a time there would be laughter and discussion everywhere.

Around that time an elderly commissioned officer of about fifty and in a major's uniform would pass in front of the verandah along the seafront, his sword rattling, a smile on his face, and greeting the occasional acquaintance.

"The major's setting off late, isn't he?"

"Where's he staying, anyway? He comes from over that direction every morning, but from where exactly?"

"He's staying over in that annex—he's renting it."

"Is he on his own?"

"So they say," the commander's wife laughed, and added:

"They say he's very good-natured, and that he's always telling jokes. . . . I wonder if he's up here on reserve with the Sakura Regiment?"

"You mean by 'reserve' that he's not normally an army man?"

"That's right; I've heard that he's some sort of businessman in Tokyo."

The refined gentleman in the next room listened in on their conversation as he sat leaning against his balcony window, reading a newspaper. Somehow, what with the commander's wife coming to the resort all alone, with the soldiers constantly and wearily watching the sea, and with the elderly major being called up on reserve, he had come to feel an anxiety in the air, anxiety about possible attack by the enemy's main fleet.

"Heard anything from your husband?" the fat private went on to ask.

"No, nothing," she replied. "He's probably busy," she added as something of an afterthought.

"It would be enough just to hear that he was safe."

"Well, letter writing was never in his nature anyway."

"Where exactly is he at the moment?"

"Where is he? Well, I can get letters delivered to him if I send them out with the Fuji-Sasebo boat, but I have no real idea where he actually is."

With this the conversation came to an end. She returned to her room.

At that moment a brown and white dog of foreign breed poked its head in at her neighbor's window and started to whine. He looked up from his newspaper and gave it a cake that was lying nearby. At this, the dog started barking loudly.

It was with this dog that he had made his first friendship. He had started to throw it leftovers, and now, at mealtimes, it invariably poked its head in at the window. Whenever he went for a walk along the shore it would bound out from a nearby fence and frolic happily along beside him.

"Before making friends with anyone, I have made friends with a dog with cute yellow eyes," he had added as a postscript to a letter to his wife in Tokyo.

But that had been during the first few days. Now, he had gradually managed to get to know his fellow guests. He had even talked with the commander's wife. The fat private had also extended his invitation to him: "You really must come up. The view's tremendous."

Out beyond the pines behind the inn and across the fields lay Mount Atago. On its summit was a triangulation-platform for surveying, and the military observation post had been set up alongside. To get there you turned left from the Gyōkeikan through the pines, across the fields of green barley and yellow mustard flowers, across the dusty white road with the occasional vats of manure, and eventually came to the mountain. Actually, although it was called a mountain it was only some 120 meters high and not particularly hard to climb either. The soldiers could even manage the climb carrying buckets of water.

As you climbed up through the pines on the mountainside you came unexpectedly to a level stretch. Here the trees had been cleared and a little hut put up as quarters for the soldiers. Surrounded as it was by pines, from below you couldn't tell it was there.

It was a hastily and crudely erected hut, made simply of boards. Inside, it was divided into two parts and contained a table and chairs and a telephone. Some documents lay on the table. Swords, khaki uniforms, canteens, some new boots, and other such paraphernalia had been hung on the crossbeams. There was also a large heap of dirty bedding.

This was where the soldiers lived out their monotonous existence. Their only duty was to stand in the observation post in hourly shifts. After that, there was nothing else for them to do. It was a question of eating, sleeping, going down to the village to chat or play the harmonica, or just doing nothing.

Out of boredom one of the soldiers had stuck some paper on

a board, ruled some lines, and bought some clay counters down in the town. Then they'd played *go*. But they'd eventually got bored with that too, and nowadays the board was usually left lying in a corner.

One day the guests in the resort came as a group to the hut. The commander's wife had worn herself out coming up the mountain, and the moment she entered the hut she gasped for a glass of cold water. Her neighbor had carried his heavy Kodak on his shoulder and now was repeatedly wiping the sweat from his forehead with his handkerchief. The well-to-do young man from the merchant family had been helping the consumptive girl and had almost had to carry her up.

The drab hut brimmed over with color.

The fat harmonica-playing private had a grin on his face. His sergeant-major spread a white blanket over the dirty floor—about the size of a typical living room—and ushered in the guests. Two other soldiers, who had in fact been playing *go* at the time, stopped halfway through their game and, looking very pleased, also welcomed the guests.

The water from the bucket wasn't exactly cold, but the commander's wife had a second glass anyway.

"I'm sorry it's so warm, but please try to put up with it. We have to bring it up from down below, you see," said the fat private as he handed her the second glass.

"It's a nice place you have here," she said presently, looking around her.

"Yes, it must be really interesting, living away from it all like this," laughed her neighbor.

The girl with the consumptive chest had picked some vetch along the way. She'd arranged them into a bouquet, and was holding them wrapped in a handkerchief. Her deathly white face and gaudy splash-pattern silk kimono stood out vividly against the surroundings.

With great generosity the sergeant-major tipped a large tin of crackers—kept in reserve for just such an occasion—onto a tray. One of the soldiers went off to the kitchen section to wash the cups and teapot, while another went to fetch a handful of charcoal from the sack outside. He put the charcoal into the stove, placed the kettle on top, and noisily started fanning the flames. A private second-class stared in blank amazement at the

Kodak. "Can you really take photographs with it?" he asked.

The group spent a pleasant hour or so with the soldiers. Going up to the observation post, they could see all around in a vast panorama: there was the Tone River pouring into the sea, there were the houses of Chōshi, and the shrine at Kawaguchi. Over there was Kurō, and across over there Ashikajima, Cape Nagazaki. They could see from Tokawa to Inuwaka, make out Byōbugaura and even far-off Cape Iioka. They were all amazed at the view.

Finally the gentleman with the Kodak assembled them in front of a little stone shrine on the summit and took a photograph —in commemoration of the occasion, he said. The five soldiers all stood in a row behind the guests. The elderly major, who had also come along, was persuaded to stand in the middle of the group. They also got in the dog, which had come tagging along.

(July 1909)

The Sound of Wheels

IT was already cold by the end of September. The mornings and evenings were frosty. The sorghum had started rattling in the wind.

A flock of small, white-bellied migratory birds had arrived earlier than in previous years, perhaps sensing some unseasonal pickings left from the fighting, and landed near a sparse group of houses belonging to the Chinese natives. They searched around for food and then flew off again, with a noisy flapping, towards the plain and the setting sun. Their cries were utterly cheerless.

The willow leaves had turned yellow and had started to fall. A single reddish road of hardened mud stretched across the vast plain, five miles or so between villages. It was broken by the traces of an occasional stream. One of the streams was quite wide and still had water in it. The Russian troops, which had been in the area until a month ago, had spanned it with a wooden bridge, which the gun-carriages of the advancing Japanese army had rolled valiantly across. On that day of the battle, ten days ago, it had been just as though the area was displaying some grand panorama: the nearby village with the willows had been totally enshrouded in the white smoke of exploding artillery shells, while on a neighboring hillock a group of officers of the Japanese Supreme Command had stretched flat on the ground, watching the progress of the fighting through telescopes that never left their eyes for a moment. The scene as the army tried to move from the plain into the village had been one of dreadful chaos— gun-carriages trying to plow forward through a sea of mud, infantrymen trying to weave ahead between them, officers with drawn swords barking commands, a mounted orderly dashing about at top speed.

In a sorghum field just a short distance from the village the mortar corps had finally—after arriving late—set up position and had for some time since been filling the heavens with a terrible noise. An officer had climbed onto a command platform and could plainly be heard yelling the range. A broad, shallow stream flowed right through the village, but the troops had all pressed on valiantly across it. Shells were exploding everywhere, sending up white smoke, but no one had paid any attention to such matters. Across the stream was a postal relay-station, its row of large inns closed up. Beyond, directly across the vast plain, could clearly be made out a deep purplish range of low hills occupied by the Russian troops, and there, too, had been a concentration of ash-colored shell smoke. The artillery positions had been clearly visible in various spots among the sorghum fields, and so too had been the infantrymen marching ahead at the double along the perfectly straight road. There could be heard the sharp reports of small-arms, the sounds of deathly struggle, the cries of death . . .

The artillery fire had continued for four days.

Now it was quiet. The road, the village, and the plain had returned to normal. From the houses around the relay-station Chinese in pale yellow clothing were nonchalantly watching passers-by. A number of families who had fled the immediate area came back on mule-carts. Some of the women were carried across the stream by their husbands. The Chinese had already set up stalls on the bank and were displaying sorghum buns. Some Japanese troops, lagging behind their units, pulled money from the pockets of their khaki uniforms and, in faltering Chinese phrases, bought some of the buns. The evening sun lit up their bayonets and rifles and sunburned faces.

In the village at the foot of the hill from which the Supreme Command had supervised the fighting, in a spot where the willow leaves had started to turn red, a small flag with a red cross fluttered in the wind. All the houses in the vicinity had been used as casualty wards during the recent fighting. This one was just like the others, set back from the road among fields of sorghum, leek, and garlic, and surrounded by pagoda trees and apricot trees and by a thick, roughly built earthen wall. At the doorway, over the customary Chinese seasonal inscriptions, a *katakana* notice had been stuck up to indicate the number of the division and regiment for which it served as hospital ward. Inside the door was an earthen-floored section with a cooking stove. The flat lid of the boiler had been put down and a utensil of sorts, made from a gourd and looking something in between a bucket and a ladle, had been put on top of it. The rooms to the right and left were full of wounded soldiers.

In each room there was at least one seriously wounded soldier. Being so soon after the fighting there had still not been time, in any of the field hospitals, to separate the seriously wounded from those with minor wounds. Irrespective of regiment, the medics would simply bring the casualties straight from the battlefield to the nearest house. It was also no easy matter to deal with those serious casualties who died shortly afterwards.

The sun came into the rooms. Everywhere was bright. Spreading blankets on the warmed floor, three of the casualties were at least managing to sleep. Another was sprawled on some sorghum husks spread over the earthen-floored section. Blood-stained bandages covered arms and heads and legs, and the whole place was filled with an unpleasant, moldy smell.

The headquarters of the hospital was a large house where the willows were particularly thick. At the height of the fighting the Supreme Command had been stationed there and horse-soldiers, servants, and so forth had been hurrying about outside wearing their white armbands, but now it was uniformed figures, with green stripes of rank, that were coming and going.

In the evenings smoke would inevitably rise up from the little hillock behind the hospital. When there was no breeze it would lie thick and heavy over the village, but usually it could be seen drifting lightly on the hillside. It was the smoke from the daily cremations. A large pit had been dug crossways on the hillside, and the pale, stiff corpses, brought out on a blood-stained stretcher, were placed in it, still in their uniforms. Sorghum husks and firewood were placed over them, petrol sprinkled on, and then lit. The soldiers assigned this duty would light their cigarettes from the flames, and laugh and talk quite nonchalantly.

In one of the houses along the roadside there were, in just the same way, half a dozen or so casualties, including a sergeant-major who had been pierced through the chest and was close to death. A willow tree stood outside the house, and its rather sparse leaves, filtering the evening sunlight that spread across the plain, filled the house with dappled shadows.

The plain had already started to turn cold in the evening.

A soldier was attending the seriously wounded sergeant-major, who had been groaning since the previous day. The others knew he was now beyond help. Indeed, the army surgeon had said the same thing and had gone away again. Among the other casualties there was none who was particularly seriously wounded, so everyone felt very sorry for the sergeant-major, but there was really nothing they could do. And his groaning was naturally unpleasant and made the rest feel depressed.

The sergeant-major had been born in Akita Prefecture. He had attended the Toyama Military School for a considerable time, but just before the war he had been attached to a regiment of the Third Division and then sent out to the front. His original family home in Akita Prefecture was some seven or eight miles deep in the hills beyond the town of Kakunodate, which was itself far into hill country. His mother and younger sister lived in that remote home. His common-law wife lived in his present home in Ushigome in Tokyo. She was young and pretty.

His far-off family home was just too removed for people to show concern about it, but they were all much moved with pity at the thought of his young common-law wife. She was called Okinu.

He had for some time now been resigned to dying and would frequently make the same request to them: "When you all get safely back to Japan, please go and visit my wife, and tell her how I ended my days here in your care." With an unsteady hand he pencilled the details of his address on paper from his note-book, tearing it out and handing it to them.

When he lost consciousness and started rambling deliriously, her name came frequently to his lips: "Okinu! Okinu!" It sounded as if he could actually see her. His eyes were moist, his face pale, and he looked more dead than alive.

It was that same evening.

"Hey! Hey!" It was the voice of the officer in the next bed to the seriously wounded sergeant-major. He himself was wounded in the legs, and couldn't stand.

The soldier in attendance was busy with something and was slow in coming.

"Hey! Something's wrong! Come and see!" the officer yelled again.

When he went to look, the attendant found that the sergeant-major had stopped breathing. He tried his pulse, but there was nothing. The officer spoke from his bed, "Just now I heard him groaning strangely, and when I took a look he had his hands up by his chest, acting as if he was trying to brush something away. Just as I was wondering if something was wrong he moved his chin and made this sort of sobbing sound a couple of times —he was blocked up with phlegm."

Naturally everyone was upset. But no one felt any need to rush off for the doctor.

The plain outside the window was quiet. Just as before, the lower half of the white blanket over the dead man, and his feet sticking out from beneath it, were lit by the rays of the evening sun. A couple of flies, which grew too torpid to move in the morning and night, were still buzzing about by the bright, warm windows.

The soldier in attendance went out, thinking he should at least report the matter to headquarters. Just at that moment some carts could be heard coming along the road—a train of mule-carts, laden with people and baggage, coming from the direction of the front. The pigtailed drivers were urging on their mules with long cracking whips and shouts of "Giddup!" The carts drew nearer, lurching along the bumpy road. On board were some half-dozen war correspondents, the name of their companies printed in white on their red armbands. There were some photographers too. Each had his own equipment and photographic plates in his baggage. They were now setting off on the road for home.

The soldier in attendance and the casualties watched the carts pass by, watched them rattle noisily away across the quiet evening plain.

(November 1908)

One Cold Morning

"MUM, is the mouse still there?" asked the children the moment they got up.

Their mother was busy in the kitchen. White steam coiled up from the rice cauldron, and green turnip leaves, chopped up for the breakfast soup, lay ready in the colander on top of the pot-lid.

The younger boy, still in his nightclothes, stood there shivering with the cold. His elder brother was peeping into a wire-netted mousetrap that had fallen under the footstool.

"Yes! It's still here! Look—it's all quiet and trembling!"

"What?! Let me see!"

The younger boy had a look too.

"Gosh! It's ever so small, isn't it? I thought it'd be bigger than that. It definitely looked bigger last night!"

"That's true."

His brother sounded pensive, as if he too was remembering what had happened in the night. They had put left-over fried bean curd in the trap and placed it on the cupboard. In the middle of the night the trap had fallen to the ground with a terrible clatter, waking everyone up. "We've caught a mouse!" their mother had said, and with a general cry of "A mouse! A mouse!" they'd all gone off to look, even the little six-year-old girl. "Will it live till tomorrow, Mum? Will it?" the younger boy had asked.

"It was up to mischief, that's why it got caught," the little girl had remarked as they'd all trooped back to bed. By now the light had been on for quite some time, and the children seemed to find it difficult to get to sleep again as they lay in their bedding. Before going back to her own bed their mother had asked, "Doesn't anybody want to go to the toilet?" "Me —I'll go!" the elder, seven-year-old girl had answered, getting out of bed again. She left the door leading out to the toilet open, and a cold breeze came blowing in.

When she came back it was the two boys' turn. "Me too— I'll go!" "And me!" They'd both jumped out of bed and raced noisily off to the toilet. It was quite bright there inside the toilet. The moon cast a clear, frozen light onto the window.

Even after the bedroom light was switched off it was some time before the children could get to sleep again. A sort of clattering kept coming from the kitchen. "Mum, it sounds like the mouse is trying to get out, doesn't it?" the younger boy had remarked, anxiously.

The clattering could be heard all night, penetrating the darkness.

"Aren't you cold, standing there like that? Go and get dressed!" The younger boy did as his mother told him and went off back to the bedroom, where the bedding was still to be cleared away. He was sniffling with the beginnings of a cold.

By the time the youngest girl had been dressed by her eldest sister and come into the kitchen, the trap had been moved down onto the earthen floor at the edge of the kitchen.

"Ah, Sei-chan, you've got up! And without your Mummy too—aren't you a clever girl! And what's that then? It's a squeaky little mouse, isn't it!"

As she spoke she took down the cauldron and transferred the rice into a pot. The white steam rose up suddenly, in clouds.

The little girl crouched down into a ball, staring in wonder at the mouse. It had stopped moving. Having spent the entire night poking its nose through the wire netting in an attempt to escape, it now seemed to have given this up as a waste of effort, and was simply hunched up, trembling, in the center of the cage.

"Well, what is it then, Sei-chan? A squeaky little mouse, that's what it is!" Coming to look for herself, her mother added, "Our little squeaker got caught because it was up to mischief, that's why."

Father came into the room, having just got up.

"What's all this, then? It's a bit small, isn't it? Why, it's still a baby!" He went off, toothpick in hand.

His wife suddenly noticed a piece of the bean curd left on a corner of the cupboard. "Well, it's going to die, so let's give it a last feast," she thought to herself, and dropped the morsel into the trap. She watched expectantly, without even moving her hand away. However, the mouse made no attempt to eat.

It was breakfast time. "Ah well, it doesn't look as if this one's going to eat anything, anyway," she laughed.

Her husband snapped back at her. "That's typical of you women! Don't you think it's a bit sick to get so friendly with something you're just about to kill? It only makes it harder to kill it, doesn't it? It's always the same with mice. On a cold morning like this it should be killed within the hour. If you like it enough to give it bean curd, then you might just as well try keeping it as a pet. You can't bring yourself to kill any creature, no matter how small, unless you feel bad towards it."

"You're right, but I just wanted to see if it would eat or not," she laughed.

"Mum, do you think it's the same mouse as before?" the elder boy suddenly cut in.

"It could well be. After all, that was only small too, wasn't it? It was so mischievous its luck just had to run out sometime. When it got away that time it seemed as if it had a charmed life, but it turned out to be a brief salvation after all, and it won't be getting up to any more mischief."

"Yes, that time was really annoying. But you did things wrong, Mum. You were supposed to have blocked up the hole, but you didn't do it properly. When I chased it out from behind the chest of drawers you got all panicky and started hitting in the wrong place!—And then it got clean away through that hole!"

"Yes, that really was annoying, wasn't it!" laughed his mother. "But anyway, things should be a bit quieter from now on. I honestly don't think there's anything quite as mischievous as a house mouse. They gnaw the cupboards, they make holes in the walls, and there's nothing you can do about it! I do wish we'd caught a bigger one, though—there're bigger ones about, you know."

"And so, that's why I say it would be a good idea to keep a cat as a pet," cut in the third girl, the eldest child of the family, as she drank some hot water to wash down her rice. "Mother, shall I bring one home? They've just had a nice little tortoise-shell born over at my music teacher's house. Its color isn't the prettiest, and it's female, but . . . Well, anyway, can we have it? That way we'd get rid of all the mice—at least, there aren't any mice in my music teacher's house."

"If you're going to have a pet, then a dog's better than a cat. Wouldn't you say so, Mii-chan?" suggested the elder boy, turning to his brother for support. "After all, a dog could keep watch for burglars."

"I can't stand dogs!" retorted the eldest girl.

"And as for me, I just can't get on with animals at all. Even cats and dogs—I get the shivers when they come near me," added their mother, more to herself than to anyone in particular.

Father was sitting in front of the brazier, smoking a cigarette. Mother cleared away the breakfast things to the kitchen and then came and sat next to him. She took a spoonful of tea from a large tin and put it into the tea-roaster, which she placed on the fire to heat up. A fragrant smell filled the room.

"It's cold this morning, isn't it!" her husband commented.

"It's the coldest we've had recently, that's for sure," she replied. "The well-rope's frozen, you know. And the frost's really white."

"Oh, is it frosty?" He pulled back the sliding-door a few inches and looked out. "Yes, it really is white. And it'll get even colder from now on, I suppose."

The elder boy came back in, ready for school. His mother spoke to him:

"Saki-chan, *you* do it please, before you go to school."

"Okay," he muttered, and then called his brother, "Mii-chan, come on! I'm going to kill the mouse!"

"You're going to kill the mouse?!" came the reply, as the younger boy rushed up. He'd been putting on his *hakama* trousers ready for school.

"Sei-chan, Chiyo-chan—you two come as well!" added the elder boy. He went out of the room, only to return a few moments later.

"The bucket's no good, Mum."

She went out to look, and found, there among the various vessels in the sink, the bucket full of water with the mousetrap floating upside-down in it. The mouse, wet through, was flapping and floundering about with its nose out of the water.

"Goodness me! What are you doing it here for? You know this is where I wash food! Do it outside, at the well!" she scolded. She put on her outdoor sandals and took a large washtub out to the well.

The elder boy took hold of the frozen well-rope and tried with great effort to draw water. However, the well was situated on a hill and was therefore quite deep, and it was no easy job to raise the bucket. And the well was almost dry. The first bucket was barely half full. The second time, he made sure he lowered the bucket right down to the bottom, and the water poured from the bucket to the tub like a little waterfall.

After three bucketfuls the tub was more or less full. The younger boy took the mousetrap out of the first bucket and went to put it into the tub.

"Hey! That's not the way to put it in!" His brother took the trap from him and placed it in the deepest part of the tub, which was resting at an angle.

The little girls stood looking on in wonder.

The mouse moved about in the water, rising and sinking. Its struggle for life had begun. It thrashed frantically about, trying to get its nose out through the wire netting, its pale little hands and feet making waves as it struggled. The children looked on in complete silence.

But it didn't last long. Half a dozen bubbles floated up to the surface of the agitated water, and the mouse's movements grew gradually weaker. Slowly it raised the tip of its nose once more towards the wire netting above. And then it was all over. Rolling over onto its back, it made as if to clasp its little hands together. Then the corpse floated gently onto its side.

"It's dead now!" said the elder boy. "Come on—let's go!"

"Okay, let's go!"

Picking up their school satchels, the two boys marched triumphantly off out through the garden gate.

The two little girls stood for some time in bewilderment. The younger one's red muslin apron looked dazzling in the crisp morning air.

"It's dead now."

"Yes, it's dead, isn't it?"

Presently the girls went back though the kitchen door and into the living room to their parents.

"Mummy, the mouse is dead . . . You should have seen its pale little hands!" said the younger one, clinging to her mother's side.

(January 1914)